SOMETHING

for

Warmest good
wishes

Lynden Hill Clinic
August 2003

ALAN DAVIDSON

SOMETHING QUITE BIG

PROSPECT BOOKS
1993

First published in Great Britain in 1993
by Prospect Books
Allaleigh House, Blackawton, Totnes, Devon TQ9 7LD

A CIP catalogue record for this book
is available from the British Library

ISBN 0 907 325 51 3

Typeset in 12/15 Perpetua
by Serif Typesetting Ltd, Leeds

Printed by Short Run Press, Exeter

AUTHOR'S NOTE IN THE ORIGINAL EDITION, CLANDESTINELY PRINTED IN BANGKOK IN 1972.

This is Number One in a series of attempts by the author to create artificially, for the eventual enrichment of his (or her?) grandchildren, what are known as collectors' items.

Care has been taken to ensure that the number of copies printed will never be known; but it is Something Quite Small.

Preface

This book is presented as an entertainment. Yet it deals with an organisation which really exists, which is in some ways the most powerful organisation which the world has ever seen and which is generally recognised as having a most serious character. I mean the North Atlantic Treaty Organisation, NATO to English-speakers and OTAN to the French.

Because it is such a serious institution, and because most of its work and documents are classified (CONFIDENTIAL, SECRET, and even TOP SECRET), it has not emerged in the public mind as a familiar entity; still less as a source of entertainment.

It follows that to present something very surprising happening to NATO, as this book does, is an enterprise hampered by the circumstance that most readers, even if they know what NATO is, will have little idea of what it does.

Fortunately a small injection of knowledge will suffice to remove this difficulty. The facts which need to be known are few.

In 1949 ten European states, the USA and Canada signed the North Atlantic Treaty. Their objective was collective defence against the Soviet Union. To this end they established a permanent organisation (the 'O' in 'NATO'), created the necessary arrangements for joint military planning and command, welcomed several new members, including Germany, and generally kept their powder dry.

NATO headquarters began life in Belgrave Square in London, but soon moved to Paris. The military headquarters was lodged nearby. But in 1966 President de Gaulle withdrew France from the military arrangements of the alliance, whereupon both headquarters moved next door into Belgium.

The political headquarters of NATO is on the outskirts of Brussels, in a suburb called Evère near the airport. The military headquarters, known as SHAPE (Supreme Headquarters Allied Powers Europe) is situated near Mons, in the south of Belgium. There sits SACEUR (Supreme Allied Commander Europe) and his multinational military staff, constantly perfecting their plans for the defence of Western Europe and always ready, in an emergency, to assume direction of NATO forces in Europe. 'Be prepared' might be their watchword.

But 'be prepared' would not be a sufficient watchword for NATO itself.

The organisation has long since grown into a complex mechanism for doing a wide range of current business among the allies, not all of it connected directly with defence. Like a growing tree, NATO has periodically sprouted new branches of activity. Early in the '50s it developed the practice of regular political consultation. In the mid-'50s, impressed by the Russian sputnik, it gave itself a scientific arm; later an economic arm; and more recently an additional limb for dealing with environmental problems. This last is known as the CCMS (Committee on the Challenges of Modern Society).

All NATO business is done in committee. Except for those which deal exclusively with defence matters (on which France does not sit), they follow the same pattern – one representative of each of the fifteen allies and one chairman drawn from the permanent International Staff of NATO. The top committee is the North Atlantic Council. Its chairman is the Secretary-General who personifies the collective interests of the alliance. He is the servant of the fifteen governments, but he can and does push them around to some extent.

The most important subordinate committee is the Senior Political Committee. The North Atlantic Council itself usually consists of the 'Ambassadors' (properly styled the 'Permanent Representatives' [PermReps] of the fifteen governments). The Senior Political Committee (or SPC) consists of their number 2s, who are normally of the diplomatic rank of Minister and described at NATO as 'Deputy Permanent Representative'.

In each committee there is, inevitably, one member who has been there longer than the others. He is the 'Dean' (Doyen, the French would say) of that committee and is consequently saddled with various small formal tasks and duties.

The Ambassadors are 'Excellencies'. In British usage an Ambassador is referred to by his staff as 'HE' (pronounced aitch-ee, short for His Excellency).

Prologue

The only windows in the tower were archers' slits. Anna looked through one. Morning mist seeped up from the pines on the opposite slope. Nothing else moved.

Her eyes lost focus, becoming very big, as she thought of what was going to happen. She was glad that the plan did not require her to issue an order or to press a button. Her resolution has been expressed in six months' careful planning; she would not have wished to express it now in a momentary act.

But none was needed. The central room, where she stood, was ready. Above, at the top of the circular iron staircase, was the trap door leading into her own rooms, which occupied the top of the tower and communicated openly with the rest of the château. Below were the old storage rooms built into the face of the cliff, long disused but recently made ready for their new purpose. Her team had needed the whole of their summer vacation for this. But the result was as faultless as the set of secret drawers in her oriental escritoire.

She turned back from the window and addressed those of her team who were present, in manner giving but in reality seeking reassurance. 'It is like waiting for a match of rugby football.'

'No,' said James, who was English (and who had to be James Minor because there was another James, distinguished as James Major), 'that's fifteen a side. This is sixteen a side. Don't forget the Chairman.'

'True. And we're sixteen too, if you count me. An even greater contest.'

Anna's ancestors had held the château for nearly seven centuries. Many of them had engaged in contests, in the surrounding valleys and far afield. But no previous Clairvault had taken on, alone, the great military powers of the day.

Anna looked serenely at the ancient stone walls. Aloud she said, 'They should be arriving at their offices about now. Does anyone have a spare set of the photographs? The Icelander is so important this morning that I'd like to look at him again.'

Alexander, known by the others as Alexander the Great, produced a white folder labelled 'The Hostages' and handed it to Anna. There were sixteen pieces of cardboard inside it, each with a photograph and biographical data written underneath. Anna found the Icelander and looked thoughtfully at the photograph. Before she handed the folder back she riffled through the remaining cards, and paused casually to read one. 'Lund, Hans, Danish, Chairman of the Senior Political Committee since eighteen months ago. Age 47 . . .' The face above these details was youthful but slightly lined.

'Thank you, Alexander.'

'Would you like to see "The Adversaries" too?'

The folder of Adversaries also contained sixteen cards. It began with the Prime Minister of Belgium and ended with the President of the United States.

'No, thanks, they are not on the agenda today. We must take things according to plan.'

Anna had a sudden memory of her old convent school, of how they had crept from the dormitory one night to clamber by a carefully plotted route to the campanile; of the moment when she had taken the bell-rope in her hand. 'What will happen?' the little Swiss girl had asked, 'what will happen when you start ringing?' Anna had said, 'You'll see!' In fact she had not known exactly what would happen, and had had to conceal from the little Swiss girl her surprise at some of the things which did happen.

Anna kept this memory to herself.

Chapter 1

Piet gulped his coffee, appraising in the mirror his ruddy confident face, then switched his gaze to the window. Out in front the fifteen flags of the NATO allies flapped in the damp breeze. Traffic hummed up the boulevard towards Brussels Airport. At this hour only a few cars slid out of the stream into the NATO slip-road. Most of the two thousand men (mostly middle-aged, mostly married) and women (mostly young, mostly single) who worked in the NATO headquarters had already arrived. But there were always stragglers. Behind his glass, Piet made as if to speak to one of them, a black Peugeot approaching the gate guards a hundred metres away: 'I am the Deputy Permanent Representative of the Kingdom of the Netherlands,' he stated with easy confidence. 'Now I will be the Netherlands Ambassador in Tunis. Today I will say goodbye to my colleagues here, the other fourteen members of the Senior Political Committee. I will make a fine speech. They will be sorry to see me go – sorry, sorry, sorry.' An uncle in Haarlem had taught him to say things like that, aloud, before any testing occasion.

The Peugeot had crawled past the gate guards and was accelerating into the parking lot. Piet frowned. He could recognise the Frenchman Brasfort, like himself Deputy Permanent Representative and member of the SPC. He did not like Brasfort, who was a bachelor but always looked pleased with himself. And it was late to be arriving. The SPC met at 1030. You had to read your telegrams beforehand, prepare material, perhaps telephone to your capital for final instructions. Piet had already done these things. He was quite ready for the meeting. Brasfort would not be.

David Lute walked very fast along the main corridor of the NATO building. He held a black despatch case, subtly battered, gold-crested. Inside the despatch case was a brown paper bag containing the broken pieces of a light fitting. Lute's eyes scanned the corridor ahead of him, identifying faces and backs in the traffic streams. He gave little quick smiles and amiable grunts over his shoulder, sideways, ahead.

He knew one in thirty. But one in twenty knew him. At 72 metres from the side entrance he shot through the glass doors marked 'You are now entering the Security Zone'. At 90 metres he showed his pass, the best kind of pass, with all possible special access symbols on it. The Belgian guard took a glance, nodded. At 105 metres Lute turned sharp right, bounded up three flights of stairs, darted through a door marked 'UK Delegation', and had a near collision with a blue-smocked Flemish girl wheeling a super-market trolley full of rolls of toilet paper. The guard who was escorting her twitched the trolley aside. Lute headed down the long straight corridor towards his office. But here he knew every-one and everyone knew him. More smiles per minute. A big smile for his secretary as he settled into his chair, right hand reaching out for the sheaf of shadowy xeroxed telegrams, left hand groping in the despatch case. Already half immersed in something from Berlin, he held out the bag of broken bits.

'Mrs Lute wondered if you could get the admin people to do something about these. Some sort of accident. Say it was a dinner guest. I'll be in the SPC all morning, then lunch for the Dutchman. Can you get on with the next dinner, that list's settled now. Nail down Brasfort first, the fellow's like an eel but we must have him this time . . .'

No reply; good, none wanted. Berlin did go on and on, but he must be up to date with the latest trouble on the autobahn, which would certainly be discussed at lunch.

In another part of the building, the tiny suite of offices which housed the Icelandic Delegation was, as usual, in a state of complete calm. The four members of the delegation, between them, had to represent their distant island in scores of different committees. Their wits were fully exercised in arranging their diaries so that the presence of Iceland would be manifest in at least the most important of these; to have gone further, and sought instructions from Reykjavik on all the matters under discussion, would have been beyond their powers. It was therefore their practice to say little at meetings; and in this way they did more to further the work of the alliance than many of their colleagues in other delegations who, by zealously compelling their governments to instruct them on every detail, and by zealously following these instructions, could create quite intense debates on matters about which nobody, themselves included, really cared a fig.

The Icelandic Permanent Representative had gone to Antwerp for the morning. The two junior Secretaries had departed to attend each a round of meetings, leaving Asgardsson, the Minister and Deputy, in sole command. By virtue of his long stay at NATO, he had become the Dean among the members of the SPC. He thus enjoyed certain privileges and exercised certain ceremonial functions on the Committee.

Although he was not hungry, he was thinking about the lunch arranged that day to bid farewell to the Dutchman, off to Tunis, when the telephone rang. The secretary whom he shared with the absent Permanent Representative answered it briskly.

'Yes, who is this, please? From SHAPE? The Colonel Waterfield? Yes, a moment, if you please, and I pass you to Mr Asgardsson.'

'Asgardsson here. This is Colonel Waterfield? How do you do, good morning . . . Yes, the lunch is today . . . What? A bus? . . . You mean it is SACEUR's bus? . . . Yes, yes, this is very kind of you . . . But of course, 1300 precisely. You know, I must inform my colleagues, but I am sure they will be pleased.'

'Where's Felix? Find him. Search the Delegation. I've got to go down in five minutes'

Lute also had to go to the lavatory in the next five minutes. He did not mention this, naturally. But his secretary knew.

'I think he's in with HE. Shall I try and get him out ?'

'Have him here in two minutes. I'll be back.'

'Yes, I'm off on leave this evening,' Felix Blayne was saying. My God, he thought, does no one ever read leave applications? Why do they always look so stunned when you go off, like you said you would, like they said you could, what's the matter with them, huh?

'Going over to the UK?' HE was recalling the leave application vaguely, making an effort to seem benign to the newest and therefore least familiar of his six First Secretaries; least familiar, but in some ways least dispensable. 'Will you look into the Department?'

'Well, no, Sir, I thought I'd go bicycling in the Ardennes'.

Sir Ambrose Lavenham grunted. It did not sound to him like a good way of spending leave. He searched for a suitable comment, found none, and was relieved to be saved by his secretary, whose Scottish voice pealed clearly across the olive room.

'Excuse me, Sir Ambrose, but the Minister is just going down to the SPC and wants to see Mr Blayne first if you can spare him.'

A further grunt, delivered with a permissive twitch of the nose, was enough to release Blayne. Sir Ambrose turned back to his Defence Policy Committee papers. He began to absorb their complexities happily. His lack of appetite for humdrum socialising and the trivial contacts of daily life was matched by a sharp intellectual hunger which had to be constantly assuaged by new problems. He had been a natural choice for the post, the only grade I Ambassador in the Service who really seemed right for it. He looked and was rather old-fashioned. But he had an intricate and rapid intelligence; and he was in a milieu where this mattered more than anything else.

Blayne and Lute, lesser intelligences, surveyed each other.

'Look, Felix, I'll be late back from lunch, but we simply must have a session this afternoon about how to play next week . . .'

Oh God, thought Felix, he's forgotten too.

'Fine, I'll be here this afternoon; but I'm going on leave, you know, tonight.'

'Really? What an inconvenient time. But I do remember now. Yes, yes. Well . . . Let's forget next week. I'll have to get George to deal with all those sea-bed chaps. Have a good leave. I must fly, where are my papers for the SPC?'

Hans Lund, the Danish Chairman of the SPC (a member of NATO's International Staff, unconnected with his country's Delegation), was talking to a Canadian colleague. They sat at a coffee table in the Chairman's room, which measured 8 metres by 4. The Canadian liked being in there. His own room, like the great majority of rooms at NATO, measured 4 by 4; a single module as the architects put it, a small box in lay terms. The Chairman, however, was an Assistant Secretary-General and rated two modules. Moreover, he waged, with assistance from his secretary, a discreet and largely successful campaign against the austerity of the offices. A vase of freesias stood on the table. Through the half-open door the secretary could be seen pouring very strong coffee from a thermos into delicate white cups. Three cups. Another member of the International Staff was to join them for a last minute run over the morning meeting. He arrived with the coffee, and the three men began to talk; a Dane, a Canadian and a Belgian. They spoke quietly, sipping the coffee. The Chairman sipped more gracefully than the other two, and he asked the questions. The Canadian wanted to smoke a cigarette, but the smell of the freesias and the absence of an ashtray deterred him. He and the Belgian mapped out for the Chairman the course of the meeting.

'Will my countryman give us trouble over this too?'

'I'm afraid so. With all respect to Copenhagen, they do send impossible instructions on this subject.'

'Hmmm . . . By the way, you are welcome to respect Copenhagen, but please not on my account. We in the

International Staff serve only the Secretary-General, a fact which often affords me pleasure, and you too, no doubt. But what about the Norwegian?'

'He'll follow suit. But in one sentence. He wastes no words. The trouble will come from France. Brasfort can't see the Danish statements as pieces of ritual, which is all they are, and instead attacks their logic. Of course they have no logic. But Brasfort will spend twenty minutes demonstrating this, and provoking the Dane to reply. And so it goes on.'

'Ah, well, I have my chess problem hidden in the folder, and I am sure that you will listen to every word.'

The Chairman picked up his black folder, on which his secretary had placed neat Dymotape strips: 'Confidential. SPC folder. ASG for Political Affairs: NATO/OTAN. 1000 Bruxelles. Confidential.' Between the black leaves were the agenda, the papers for discussion, papers for reference and the chess problem. There was also the current journal of one of the great ornithological societies, in which a letter from the Chairman had been published.

'Are you coming to lunch?' he asked his junior.

'No, I wish I was. I liked old Piet – and the Dean seems to have chosen a better restaurant this time. But I couldn't make it.' The Canadian thought to himself, not at 400 francs a head, I couldn't, not on my pay.

'Well, we must try to finish by a quarter to one. I want a few minutes to polish my notes. I have two jokes and one splendid quotation, but I still need to work on the sentence about Piet's great contribution to the Committee's work – quite difficult because he will take it so seriously.'

The Chairman left. The others followed him, holding their less smart folders.

◇◇◇

At one end of the long wide lobby between the twin rows of conference rooms was a board with a schedule of the day's meetings. It appeared to visitors to be in code.

'1030 AC 119 niv. el. 1'

'AC 119' meant the Political Committee. 'niv. el' meant the senior one. '1' referred to Room 1, the Council Chamber. When the North Atlantic Council was not meeting the Political Committee had first call on their room, a priority which they regarded as their due, being convinced that the political work of the alliance was its prime function. The members enjoyed sitting in their masters' seats. They had pleasant day-dreams in them.

1030 did not mean 1030. It meant 1040. All Political Committee meetings began 10 minutes late. So it was with this one. At 1030 the Council Chamber was empty. At 1035 it contained four members of the Committee, who had all come down to catch a colleague before the meeting, bent on the transaction of some minor piece of business. None of the four was the colleague sought by any of the others. So they greeted each other with no special enthusiasm and chatted with an eye on the door.

At 1038 there were thirteen members of the Committee present. Ten had sat down in their places on the rim of the doughnut-shaped table. Two were talking to the Chairman and Secretary. One was walking round in a very small circle in a corner of the room with his attendant Second Secretary.

At 1039 the Italian and the Greek came in, together but apart, rather like two boys who had been fighting in the playground at break and who were seeking unsuccessfully to dissemble. Since the seating round the table followed the alphabetical order of the countries they sat near to each other, with only the small bushy-haired Icelander in between. At 1040 the Chairman lightly tapped his gavel on the block.

The fifteen other seats round the table were now occupied. Nine grey suits, two black, three blue and two brown, including himself. But his was the only bow tie; an amber one of silk from Thailand. He straightened it and opened the meeting.

'Good morning, gentlemen, I think that we have a short agenda today, and I am sure that the prospect of the lunch which awaits us in the countryside will help us to get through it in good time. Now, before we go on to Item 1, I will give the floor to the representative of Iceland, who has a statement to make as Doyen, a statement not unconnected with this same lunch which he has so kindly organised.'

The Icelander adjusted his spectacles and beamed round the table.

'Thank you, Mr Chairman. It is a piece of news which I think will give pleasure to the Committee. I have heard earlier this morning from SHAPE that they have a new bus, a vehicle which I understand is intended for use in certain circumstances by SACEUR himself, and which has been sent over to Brussels for familiarisation trials. The Colonel who is controlling the trials has kindly suggested that it might take us all to lunch and bring us back again. There are twenty seats, so we will all fit in. May I ask my colleagues, if they wish to take advantage of this offer, to be at the front door at exactly 1300?'

The Dutchman Piet raised his pencil. 'Mr Chairman, I believe that I can detect an unspoken consensus that this is an excellent scheme, and certainly of the greatest benefit to me, since I always lose the way on these occasions and would be embarrassed to be late for a lunch in my honour. But may I ask whether we can be sure that the Military Budget Committee will not object?'

Several members of the Committee smiled. They enjoyed this kind of joke. Lute agitated his pencil.

'Mr Chairman, I'm sure we needn't worry. From my knowledge of the MBC I feel quite confident that they can't have authorised a new bus for SACEUR, and therefore have no locus standi. I expect that we'll find that the bus is a piece of mobile infrastructure, or an out-moded toy with which our friends in the Security Committee have been playing and which they are now incorporating in the arsenal of the alliance.'

More laughter. The American leaned over to Lute. 'You're sure right about the MBC. I just know they haven't authorised any new bus. The civil budget boys complain all the time about SHAPE's transport fleet.'

The Chairman pulled the meeting together. 'Well, gentlemen, I think that we can pass on to our business, noting this kind offer and evidently resolved to avail ourselves of it, despite the doubt which surrounds the financial authority for the purchase of the bus in which we are to ride.' His eyes swept round the table, confirming the unanimity . 'So, Item 1. Statements on Political Subjects. I understand that our Turkish colleague has a communication to make, and give the floor to him.'

One hundred and forty kilometres away Anna turned to the Turkish member of her own team. 'Kemalettin, pass me the list of duties again. I keep thinking that we've overlooked something.'

Kemalettin had been to the Harvard Business School, and spoke with an American accent. But he looked every centimetre a Turk, exuding an aura of Anatolian toughness which Anna found reassuring. She was not very strong herself.

'Sure, here it is.' It was nice of him not to tell her that she was fussing. She read the list carefully although she knew it off by heart.

KEMALETTIN, JACOPO, GIOVANNI – security, diary, programme

JAMES MAJOR, JAMES MINOR –transport, supplies

TIM, PETE – communications, the press

Except for Kemalettin, these had all left an hour ago. The two Italians were rather stolid, as befitted security men; but there should be no need for them to do anything except follow their simple instructions. The others were clever enough to improvise if something went wrong. Pete and Tim, both American, were especially quick-witted. And they were wholly devoted to the task in hand. Anna recalled her insistence on choosing students who were free of distracting political obsessions. So many of the bright and resourceful had other irons in the fire.

ALEXANDER THE GREAT – psychological studies, family welfare

INGRID – physical culture, wig and wardrobe mistress

FRANCOISE and ELIZABETH – diet and cuisine

SISTER AGNES – health (with Tim), special measures

SECUNDA and TERTIA – service in the confinement area and supervision of cleaning

Secunda and Tertia were two who had chosen not to use their real names. Alexander the Great had wanted to give them Greek pseudonyms, but had settled for Latin. There was to have been a Prima too, but for all her demure appearance she had turned out to be an anarchist and had not been recruited. It was much better to have girls who were doing it for fun, or to exercise their special talents. Ingrid, for example, would go back to Norway, where she was training to teach drama, with useful new experiences; and both Françoise and Elizabeth were supremely happy in their big kitchen. If they were rather vague about the purpose of their work, this hardly mattered. The main thing was loyalty. It was Franz who had perceived from the very beginning that it was only among students that they could hope to find a completely loyal team. Older people would not do at all.

FRANZ – deputy director, mystification measures

ANNA – director of the enterprise

Franz was on his way from Algiers to Paris, and should arrive in the evening. Anna was eager for his return. Since that first encounter, when he had offered her not his seat, for he was squashed on a bench and the place would have vanished if he had risen even for a second, but a perch on his knee at a rally in Rotterdam on Rhine water pollution, he had been her principal ally, perfecting her plans with her and impressing on them the stamp of his own ambivalent personality, in which a Bosch-like love of the fantastic was welded to a remarkable facility for dealing with the practical problems of the real world. It was Franz, while he ran a student hostel in Amsterdam, who had recruited most of the team, picking out from his transient charges over a period of months the tiny proportion who had the right qualities. He had made no mistakes.

Sister Agnes, towards whom Anna now directed an appraising look, might sometimes seem too quirkish to be wholly reliable; but she was Tim's find and Tim, who had been nursed by her for several weeks in a London hospital, insisted that she was entirely dependable.

As if prompted by Anna's glance, Sister Agnes gave voice to matters which were on her mind. She wore a faded green track suit, and toyed unenthusiastically with a luxurious auburn wig of shoulder length curls.

'Listen, I'm willing to be special measures, of course, but I don't want to be stuck with it if any of the trouble-makers aren't my type, I mean if I'm not their type. I mean supposing we have trouble with someone who has his eye on Tertia all the time. I'd much rather we set her on to him rather than waste time with me just because I'm down for it.'

Anna agreed. 'Of course. We shall be quite flexible. But we do need a plan in the first place, in case special measures have to be applied to one or two of them. And Alexander has worked it out very carefully.'

Alexander leaned forward, magisterial in his appearance but appealing in his enthusiasm.

'Yes, the ages of the group are known, and from this I calculate a mean puberty date of around 1937. We should look there, or a little earlier, for an idea of the first, and strongest, sexual images. Of course there are variations from country to country, but by that time the American film was international currency and the strongest formative influence in this field. So I've spent a few days studying contemporary magazines and identifying the main features of feminine glamour as portrayed in the cinema – you know, Ginger Rogers, Myrna Loy, Deanna Durbin and so on. Sister Agnes here can be adapted very easily into a sort of composite of these. She has all the right basic features and it's a probability – not a certainty but a good probability – that she could deal most effectively with anyone who starts being awkward. Of course this is all on the premise that we use persuasion rather than punishment. But quite apart from Anna's well-known views on the question I feel sure that this is right.'

Alexander looked anxiously at Sister Agnes. He was keen to have his theory well tested. He even hoped some day to publish both theory and experiment in a learned article, although at present he could not see how to do this without risk of inadvertently unmasking Anna and her group.

Sister Agnes shrugged. She knew that she was attractive, but she was nervous, and afraid of possible humiliation. Her relations with men had been reaching an interesting stage when they were suddenly stunted by an ugly encounter at Hexham, just as she was approaching her seventeenth birthday. She had not often been alone with a man since then, although the passage of five years had transmuted fear into something not much more than awkwardness. 'Oh, I'll do my part if necessary,' she said in a flat North Shields way, 'I just think the whole idea is a bit daft, that's all.'

Alexander raised his bushy eyebrows. 'But surely you realise that the strongest driving force in any normal male . . .'

He tailed off as the phone rang close to his left ear, took it, and carefully said 'Yes?'. A few seconds later he put it down again and nodded to Anna.

'Stage One accomplished. The bus is now moving towards Brussels, ETA still 1255.'

Chapter 2

The Committee thought that they had finished at twenty to one. They had dealt with all three items on the agenda. They had agreed to meet again next Thursday morning. The Chairman's gavel was poised, and they were gathering up their papers when the pencil of the Italian representative Portentoso flickered up and the Chairman with a wry frown gave him the floor.

Portentoso recalled gravely that at a meeting in the previous month there had been some discussion of Soviet naval visits to NATO ports. He reminded his colleagues that the discussion had been left open in case any further information might become available. He revealed that his government had sent him such further information, which concerned the reasons why a projected visit to Palermo by a Soviet fishery protection vessel had been cancelled. He thought that the Committee should know about this, even though the cancellation had taken place eighteen months ago, since otherwise they might be left with the impression that the fishery protection vessel had in fact visited Palermo.

As usual, Portentoso became emotional under the influence of his own prose. The thought of Italy's allies harbouring such a misconception, expressed in his sonorous French, filled him with horror and indignation. He waved his arms around, banishing the misconception in a flow of rhetoric. The facts were quite otherwise. The truth could be stated quite simply and without prevarication. The fishery protection vessel had not visited Palermo. It had not entered the port, it had not dropped anchor there, it had not even been sighted by the coastguards. To put it another way, the visit had quite indisputedly not taken place. If any references to it survived in the archives of the nations of the alliance it was only just that they should be expunged completely. Portentoso thanked the Chairman for giving him the opportunity to make this clarification. He thanked his fidgeting colleagues for listening with such close attention to his communication. He stated that he had made the communication on instructions, pausing to permit his hearers to visualise the Italian Foreign Minister suavely dictating from his desk in the Palazzo Chigi a telegram which began 'Portentoso should take the earliest opportunity to place the true facts before the members of the Alliance.' He expressed the belief that his colleagues would agree with him that despite the lateness of the hour this matter would have brooked no delay. He stopped.

The gavel descended and the Committee streamed out of the door. It was nearly five to one. Four members of the Committee who came from large Delegations and had Second Secretaries in attendance were able to shed their papers at once and go for a wash on the way to the main door. The others had to make journeys of up to 125 metres to their Delegations and back. They did this crossly, resenting the unnecessary hurry which Portentoso had imposed on them. Some of them reflected that it was just as well that they were going to the lunch in a bus; otherwise they might be late. They normally drove themselves singly to these lunches and two or three would usually lose the way. They had often discussed the imperfections of the system but had never seen a solution; let alone been offered one.

The bus cruised slowly along the slip road, and paused at

the main gate. It was a small Chevrolet, fairly smart in matt olive green paint with a black legend on each side: 'SUPREME ALLIED HEADQUARTERS ALLIED POWERS EUROPE'. The driver wore American uniform. Up at the front, beside him, sat a youthful American colonel and a sergeant. The gate guards nodded, and the bus went slowly past them and up to the main entrance. The Secretary-General's Rolls was standing at the door, with a couple of ambassadorial cars just behind. So the bus came to a halt on the off-side of the Rolls, and the driver kept the engine running in case he had to let one of the cars out. Perhaps because they observed that the bus was in the fairway the members of the SPC came out briskly. The colonel greeted them each with 'Good morning, sir,' and the sergeant counted them under his breath. Lute came last, chancing to walk through the doorway with the Secretary-General, who remarked the troop boarding the bus and asked where all the Deputy Permanent Representatives were going. 'To a farewell lunch which will take us miles away and last for ages,' replied Lute, who tended to think of time away from his desk as time lost.

'Well, be sure and come back some time,' said the Secretary-General, 'we can't do without you gentlemen for long, can we?'

As Lute boarded the bus the sergeant said quietly to the driver, 'Sixteen, that's the lot – get moving, gently now.' The bus had slipped off on its way towards the gate as the Rolls edged out behind it.

Predictably, the Committee members, sitting two by two, spent the first five minutes of the journey talking about the meeting which they had just finished. They did not look out of the windows as the bus ran along the cobbled road beside the cemetery which adjoined NATO. They were all very familiar with this road and the outside of the cemetery. Only Portentoso knew the inside of the cemetery. He had heard that the Secretary-General took a walk there in the lunch hour, alone. So he had adopted the practice himself, foreseeing a chance meeting among the tombstones, the SG baring his secret worries, Portentoso giving him counsel, and the subsequent telegram to the Palazzo Chigi: 'Portentoso had the opportunity to discuss with the Secretary-General for two hours today the general direction of the policy of the alliance. No-one else was present . . .' But he had never seen the SG, and had wearied of walking up and down between the graves.

The colonel filled in the first few minutes by talking to the sergeant and fiddling with some communications equipment fastened to the roof of the bus. He had headphones on and was holding a small microphone when he turned round to address the passengers.

'Well, gentlemen, welcome aboard what we call the Special Mobility Unit. My name is Ken Twigg, colonel in the US Army, currently serving at SHAPE, and it is my privilege to brief you on the way to your lunch about the tasks to be assigned to this unit, and how you are helping us at SHAPE by consenting to ride in our bus today.

'Incidentally, let me confirm to you our ETA at the Auberge. This is 1325, repeat 1325. I mention the point, gentlemen, because as part of our proving run we will be taking a route off the main road. I just want you to know that this will not affect the time of arrival at your destination. Right, Sergeant?'

The Sergeant nodded, and continued the patter. 'Yes, Sir. ETA remains 1325, elapsed time of journey twenty four repeat twenty four minutes. During the journey we will traverse part of the Forêt de Soignes and rendezvous with two other vehicles of the Special Mobility Unit at a spot which has to be arranged as we go. The colonel here has a very nifty communications system on which he will speak to our auxiliary units. This is a free-play exercise, gentlemen, to be executed in the framework of a pre-planned mission, and we are grateful for your co-operation in riding with us today.'

Lute whispered to his companion, Luke Grannery, the American: 'Honestly, the games these soldiers play. I can't believe that this wretched little bus could play a role if the balloon was going up. What on earth could SACEUR do in it?'

Grannery had once been attached by the State Department to a liaison group in the Pentagon. He was therefore proud of his knowledge of military matters, and unwilling to admit that military behaviour was incomprehensible or misguided.

'I can see you're surprised. But you've got to realise that there are situations where you need simple equipment like – well, like a bus. Frankly I can imagine what it's for, but I don't think we ought to talk about it. It's pretty obvious that this colonel doesn't plan to go into any details.'

By now the bus had threaded its way through the suburb of Kraainem, where bourgeois villas with heavily treed gardens stood in asymmetrical rows, and had taken the main road to Waterloo, cutting straight through the forest. A faint drizzle was falling and the light was poor. A few of the cars shooting past in the opposite direction had their side lights on.

The bus took up position to filter left, stopped, crossed, and headed down a side road into the trees. Almost at once it turned off the side road on to a track. The colonel had been talking rapidly into his apparatus, apparently giving a series of map co-ordinates. After a kilometre of slow progress the bus halted smoothly in a small clearing, where two forest tracks met. Piles of sawn logs stood at the side, moisture glistening on the bark. The driver cut his engine.

'This is the rendezvous, gentlemen, and here are the other units taking up position.'

Two small, anonymous-looking Peugeot camionettes were nosing down the other track. They took up position alongside the bus, and their drivers gave the thumbs-up sign through the windows.

'Well done, C5 and C6. Please fall in behind and escort us to the Auberge. We have five kilometres to cover. Maintain radio contact throughout. Over and out.'

The bus driver flicked his ignition switch. A splutter. He flicked it again. No splutter. He jumped out, raised the bonnet from one side and peered in the engine. The colonel joined him and they conferred together. The committee members at the front of the bus could not hear what they were saying but they saw the colonel's face cloud over with anxiety. They imparted this observation to the colleagues behind them. There was some laughter, but also some sucking and tapping of teeth. They all remembered that there were still five kilometres to go, and they could all see the drizzle falling. By the time the colonel had finished his pantomime and come back into the bus they had worked out what he was going to say. The Chairman stood up, a slight but authoritative figures, and good-humouredly cut short his speech.

'Well, this sort of thing is bound to happen sometimes. Let's just hope it doesn't happen when the bus is being used in a real life situation. Now, you want us to get into the vans. That's fine if we can all squeeze in – and if we move quickly we won't be more than a few minutes late.'

They moved quickly, eight into each van. The vans had doors at the back and benches along the wide with elaborate safety belts fitted. The colonel at one door and the sergeant at the other briskly explained that these had to be worn, especially as the track was a bit rough, and the committee members resignedly allowed themselves to be strapped into place.

As the doors clicked home and were bolted into place the colonel and the sergeant looked at each other with unmilitary expressions of glee on their faces, then raced round to the front of the vans, climbed aboard, waved to the bus driver and were off, jolting down the track between the tall beeches.

The bus driver watched them leave, looked carefully round the clearing, and then set to work, swiftly peeling the adhesive olive green strips off the sides, roof and bonnet of the bus. There were twenty strips. It would take him seven minutes to remove them, roll them up and stow them inside the bus, which was now sky blue and bore the address of a tourist company in Maastricht. The driver changed the plates, stowed them in a carton with the rolled strips, added the bogus radio equipment, taped the carton, and set off back for the main road and the Dutch frontier. Beside him was a map which showed where he was to deliver the carton en route, the telephone kiosk from which he was to make a call at twenty minutes to four, just before crossing the frontier, and the package of débris, suggestive of a group of school-children, which he was to litter round the bus before handing it back at Maastricht. They called him James Major, but he was Flemish. He was a very methodical young man. He foresaw no trouble at all.

Tim just had time to catch the 1345 for Namur after making his telephone call. It was a nuisance having to make it from Brussels. The cell at the University could probably have handled it. But it was important to do it exactly right, and it had to be done by someone who could improvise if the Auberge asked awkward questions. They had, too. They had wanted to know all the details about how they would be paid. They had wanted to explain at length how it had never happened before that a lunch for sixteen people had been cancelled at half an hour's notice. Tim had hit all the right notes. He said that it was quite disgraceful, that the perspective of these people at NATO, many of them foreigners, was grossly distorted, that the Secretary-General did not show a serious attitude in having an important gastronomic event cancelled in order to permit a meeting on some so-called emergency, that Mr Asgardsson was disposed to take the matter further, and that in the meantime he insisted that the bill for the lunch, including the aperitifs which the guests would certainly have consumed and a suitable amount of cognac, should be forwarded to him without delay, for immediate payment. The Auberge had been mollified. They had promised not to delay in sending the bill. They had a good impression of Mr Asgardsson's colleague.

The advertisement on the platform showed an electric train travelling at such speed that it seemed to be leaving the track. It said 'Bruxelles–Namur 36 minutes'. Tim checked his watch, and as the train drew out began to sort the medical equipment in his Gladstone bag. Since he was a medical student, and since the bag and equipment were his, he was quite at his ease although there were two other people in the compartment. His only worry was for Sister Agnes. She was only a nurse, after all. She might not know what to do if she ran into something unexpected. Still, she would be inspecting her patients by five past two; she would have more time for remedial action.

The two vans came out of the forest on different tracks at about the same time. The colonel and the sergeant had already cocked the canisters connected to the ventilation shafts and depressed the plungers. There had been no noise from behind. If one or two of the passengers had realised, in the thirty seconds available to them, what was happening and tried to undo their safety belts they must have been delayed successfully by the non-opening release mechanisms. None of them could possibly be conscious now.

The sergeant's van, with Jacopo at the wheel, turned on to the motorway for Namur at 1338 and increased speed to a steady 90 kilometres an hour. Although the road was less good after Wavre, Jacopo kept up a good speed. It was lunch time and the traffic was light. The brothel-bars had switched on their lights, pink and mauve and plum, and a few cars were parked by each. Jacopo noticed that the Rêve de l'Orient was doing the best business. He reckoned that he would be cruising round the Place Léopold, one block from Namur station, at 1430.

The colonel's van, driven by Giovanni, left the motorway at Wavre and took the road for Huy, then branched off to the left, down through the sleepy village of Bonlez, round the back of the local château and on to a cross-country track.

Giovanni drew up in a disused quarry just off the track. A Naples yellow Mini stood nearby. Giovanni went into the bushes, and was lost to sight for a couple of minutes, which he spent enjoyably in studying the gentle contours of the landscape, not unlike certain Umbrian vistas which he knew from childhood. When he came out he went to the Mini, and drove off in it.

Sister Agnes sauntered out of the bushes and crossed to the camionette. She spoke to the colonel and accepted a small package from him, and a black Gladstone bag.

Inside, she let down a folding table for her kit, fiddled with the gas mask for a moment until it sat on her chin more comfortably, and set to work on the figures lolling in their harnesses. She did not hurry. First, the pulse. Next, the eyes. Tongue not bitten. Harness not twisted. As soon as she had checked each man she took his left trouser leg, slit it neatly along the seam with a razor-sharp sewing implement, reached inside and pulled the leg of the underpants up. One blonde man (the Norwegian) had long woollen underpants. They had to be slit too. Then she dabbed each exposed thigh with surgical spirit, and administered an intra-muscular injection, using a disposable syringe, charged in the Mini only minutes ago with a pheno-barbitol solution.

It was all routine. The pulses were all in the normal range. No tongues were bitten. Only one man stirred as thought he still had a fingerhold on consciousness. Sister Agnes did not know which he was. But she knew what to do. Lifting the head slightly, and observing with distaste the wiry brown hair sprouting in his ear, she intoned softly at close range: 'We are now crossing the Alps at an altitude of 30,000 feet. We expect to arrive at our secret destination at 1900 hours. The stewardess will now serve orange juice.'

The man had already had his injection. No doubt he was back in the colourless depths by now. All the same he was given a drop from the orange juice bottle, just enough to leave a taste.

Sister Agnes looked at him. Unlively, unlovely. She pursed her lips in the Tyneside way, slipped off her mask, sniffed cautiously, tilted his head in the other direction and with neat, nacreous incisors nipped the lobe of his left ear. 'Promise that you will never leave me, my sweet,' she whispered, enunciating the words carefully and without expression, 'nothing matters except us. We can only live if we live together.'

She attended to the two remaining patients, relocked the door and joined the colonel. The whole operation had taken nine minutes. The camionette purred into life and jogged along the track in second gear towards the road for Huy.

Elizabeth served tea early. She had brought a large supply of Robert Jackson's Earl Grey to the château with her, and matching quantities of Abernethy biscuits. The simple refreshment calmed the company, and they discussed plans without excitement. The Girard-Perregaux chronometer on the battered rent table which Anna used as a desk showed 1535. The blackboard on the wall opposite the window outlined the programme:

1425	*? confirmatory call from Pete at Namur*
1505	*? ditto from Sister A. near Huy*
1540	*James Major reports about to cross frontier on way to return the bus (call via Brussels cell)*
1545	*Giovanni returns*
1600	*Stand by to receive first group*

1610	*First group arrive*
	Reception routine
	Cubicles A–E
1630	*Stand by to receive second group*
1640	*Second group arrive*
	Reception routine
	Cubicles F–J
1725	*Report from Brussels cell*
1730	*Anna's meeting to review operation*
1800	*Anna joins hunting party for high tea*
1900	*Franz due in from Paris*
1915	*On costumes*
1930	*Wake guests. First briefing (Anna)*
2000	*Dinner (Italian menu). James Major returns*
2100	*Second briefing (Anna and Franz)*
2130	*Sleeping tablets*
2200	*Lights out*

Anna answered the telephone, then nodded to Tertia, who ticked off the 1540 item.

The sound of a Mini in third gear could be heard briefly through the window.

'Is he going round to the front?' asked Secunda, a nice girl from Jutland, so outstandingly nice that few people noticed how pretty she was, or that she was rather slow-witted.

'Yes, of course,' said Kemalettin benevolently, 'the Mini's been official ever since it arrived, and Giovanni mixes with the hunting party.'

'Well, I must admit that can't remember who's supposed to be known to them, I wonder how they can.'

'They can't. All they know is that some students have been hired to run the château, and that they come and go, like students do. They're quite prepared to see fresh faces every day, and with a bit of changing around they can never be sure how many there are. Not that they'd want to know. They really don't seem to be interested in anything except hunting and eating.'

Giovanni came in. 'So, all is well. I left Sister Agnes to do her job. No sign of trouble. And here I found no one except that huntsman who hurt his leg who sits in the hall all the time. Tea, please.'

Anna reflected. 'It is rather convenient that the Count hurt his leg. If any visitors come they'll find him there, and he'll answer their questions.'

'I wonder,' said Alexander. 'He is completely genuine. That may arouse suspicions.'

'Oh, do not be so complicated, Alexander. Anyway, everyone for a long way around knows about the hunting, and approves, and the guns keep going off, and altogether I think that these rich gentlemen are providing us with a perfect cover. Besides paying me a lot of money.'

'Enough to pay our expenses?'

'Almost. But no one will ever know, I hope, that our activities were financed by business men from Antwerp and Brussels.'

Kemalettin stood up. 'Let's go down,' he said. 'The first lot may be on time. I'll wait in the hangar and help Jacopo and James Minor get them into the lift. Françoise and Elizabeth will do the search as soon as they come out of the lift. Remember, every single thing from every single pocket, plus watch, and do use those plastic bags and labels. Secunda, you and Tertia will have to get them into the pyjamas. Tim may be able to come up and help you with the last two or three, but you'll have to manage on your own with most of them.'

'It is not too difficult. I have taken clothes off men before,' said Tertia annoyingly.

'Thank goodness you have,' said Secunda. 'I'd really be lost trying to do it by myself.'

Tim had joined his camionette at Namur, and had switched from front to back, and treated his patients, in a lay-by near the bridge over the Meuse. He stayed with his patients for the rest of the journey, and spent a bit of time working out which was which and studying their faces. He liked the Chairman, of whom he had seen a photograph. A serious, intelligent face, but with humorous lines. He looked fit. So did Lute, the Englishman; but his moustache was displeasing. The American was a little on the podgy side. Ingrid would have to work on him with her callisthenic fitness programme. The Dane was disconcertingly powerful and looked quite fierce even with his face in repose. The Portuguese was the best dressed, the German older than the others and studious in appearance; the other two he could not place. When he felt the van swerve on to the bridge at Dinant he lifted a flap for a second and enjoyed a glimpse of the onion-shaped spire on La Collégiale. Then he settled down to read some lecture notes. After Beauraing he made his rounds again, then embedded himself comfortably on top of a tarpaulin in readiness for the minor roads.

At 1602 the van went round a hairpin bend and started to descend into a valley. Then came the jolt which marked the turn on to the private road leading to the château. Tim peered through the flap again and saw the familiar silhouette against the wet slate-coloured sky. The body of the château lay snugly along the top of the cliff. The single octagonal tower branched out and up at the end. He could see Anna's windows, one of them lit, at the top, and the tiny dark slits below which marked the control post. It would be blacked out now. The incurving base of the tower rested on a massive buttress of local stone which ran down the whole length of the cliff face, concealing in its upper part the ventilation shafts for the storage chambers. A horizontal band of masonry, heavily rusticated, ran along the side of the cliff from the buttress. The chambers lay behind this band.

The view disappeared as the van bumped along in first gear, closer and closer to the foot of the cliff. It turned left into and through the old stabling, inched into position in what had once been the tobacco hangar and stopped between two stacks of sawn logs. As Tim opened the door at the back he saw Kemalettin smiling in. Jacopo and James Minor hurried round, and they set to work with the two stretchers.

In the days when tobacco as well as timber was grown on the estate Anna's great-grandfather had built a lift on the south-west cliff. It was meant for two kinds of traffic. It brought logs up to the wood-store, by the furnace room. And it took great-grandfather and his friends up and down from the stables to the main floor of the château forty metres above. The lift was cased in, like the tobacco hangar, with slats of pine which had weathered to a dull grey.

Anna's grandfather had used the lift, but her father had not. Anna had arranged for it to be overhauled and oiled in the previous year. A man had come from Liège. He had told her that this was the only surviving example of its kind, and had wanted to dismantle it and take it away to some museum. But in the end he had consented to leave it in working order – smooth, entirely silent, and capable of carrying four persons so long as there were two others to turn the huge brass wheel.

Jacopo and James Minor turned the wheel and consigned their human cargo, two by two, to the ready hands of Tertia and Secunda, far above.

Chapter 3

Felix Blayne was organising his departure. Every day he spent at least ten minutes tearing up his copies of telegrams and NATO documents – a ritual which had to be carried out before they were put into sacks and taken away to be incinerated. The incinerators at NATO were the only items of capital equipment in the whole building which were used with proper intensity. So, anyway, had opined a team of efficiency experts two years previously. It was a pity that the material could not be recycled, so that the production and destruction of documents could have become a process quite independent of the outside world. As it was, the headquarters depended on external supplies of paper, without which it would have come at once to a standstill; and produced a great deal of ash.

Felix' wrists were stronger, after a few months at NATO, than they had ever been: for many of the documents were thick. Normally he kept some of them for a few days or even weeks. But now, about to go on leave, he was sparing nothing. His wrists worked methodically, and he steadily tossed the débris across his twilit desk into the paper sack which he had borrowed for the purpose.

When the desk was bare and the sack full Felix tugged the grubby string which hung from the ceiling and bathed his cubicle in light. There were some files to be dealt with too, and he would have to write on these; with care, since he had been sitting on them for a week.

He looked out of the window. In the cubicle directly

opposite his in the next wing a Norwegian girl stood pensive and outward-gazing. He wondered whether she was looking at him or just looking. In the box to her right a lanky figure stirred at his desk, got up and disappeared through the door. Five sectons later he appeared in the girl's room. Felix had often wondered whether if he watched the windows opposite for long enough he would eventually observe a scene of violence or romance. But the Norwegians were very sedate. The man spoke to the girl. The girl picked up a pile of papers and followed him out of the room, Felix was watching for them to reappear in another box when the telephone rang.

'Mr Blayne, sir, a call from a restaurant, the Rally at Hoolart, they say Mr Lute was delayed but not to worry sir, he's on his way into Brussels.'

'Did they say why? Or why he's going into Brussels?'

'No, just not to worry. It sounded as though Mr Lute had left a message to ring us so you'd know he wasn't coming directly back. The secretary isn't there, so I told you.'

Felix wondered casually what mischief had engaged the SPC and whether he should ring David Lute's wife, Beta. He thought not, pulled the three sat-upon files towards him and considered how to handle the first. It had a Secret label on it, and was called 'Hungary, Volume B'. Felix riffled through the pages of the top document, noticed some economic statistics embedded in it, and minuted: 'This is an important despatch from HM Ambassador in Budapest. I have been considering whether to use part of it in the Economic Committee, but hesitated to do so while Mr Lomax was away, since some of the figures need checking against the Committee's last survey. Would Mr Lomax care to attend to this now? The Committee could be given a note next week, although unfortunately I shall be away myself.'

Right, Lomax, he thought. Pick that one up and start running.

The phone rang. Felix lifted the handset. 'Hallo darling. I'm just getting ready to pack up . . . What? . . . A piece of the Maison du Peuple? . . . But I thought you said it was all in little parcels out at Tervuren? . . . Oh, I see. Well if you've got it and it's genuine, that's marvellous, very exciting . . . Yes, I'm excited too . . . Yes, in about an hour.'

Felix regretted his light lunch in the cafeteria. Mushrooms on toast and yoghourt were not enough to keep him going until nine. But Marie had recently become aflame with admiration for the architecture of Baron Horta, and Marie had found a new Horta relic, so bang went their early dinner. She was too excited. That spelled sex, early sex, sex before not after dinner, dinner late in the evening.

Felix pulled up the next file. 'Reached me today,' he wrote, adding an illegible date, 'but I should like to see with the papers on the Franco/Romanian talks before minuting.' He would put this file in a special place in the Registry where mislaid files often reappeared. No one would know how long ago he had written his minute.

Thus by simple destruction or ingenious diversions did Felix clear his desk. He rang Beta Lute from the security desk as he left, suddenly remembering the message from David. 'No, no, the message was quite vague. Sounded as though the lunch had gone on for hours and they'd all been ashamed to come back late, so they'd headed off somewhere else . . . Well, I expect he'll reappear soon. Yes, I'll enjoy myself. Do the same. Bye.'

Beta's voice had been composed. Beta was a calm, neat, small person. Marie, in contrast, was tempestuous, untidy and looked six feet tall as she charged across the hall towards

is at 9 Ty-Groes Drive, Margam, Port-Talbot
West-Glamorgan SA13 2AG. Tel: 01639 77226
Open by appointmen

tral Africa and displays many colour ions. It can be planted out in summer.

atiens keilii 11 is an epiphytic species wild, found growing in leaf litter in otches of tree branches. A smaller plant . *niamniamensis* 10, it carries dozens of orange-red and yellow flowers and well to pot culture.

utiful *I. auricoma* is a bright yellow-ed species from the Comoro Islands in dian Ocean. It can be grown outside ltered places but is better suited to a rvatory or glasshouse. A bushy plant ng to more than 1m (39in) high, with usion of yellow cupped flowers, it can 1 for most of the year.

essful hybrids

ens auricoma has been used in breeding mmes for many years in the hope of cing the elusive yellow busy Lizzie.

GROWING AND BUYING *IMPATIENS*

Cultivation

Grown in the garden, most hardy perennial species of *Impatiens* perform best in a semi-shaded position that does not dry out, enjoying a well-drained soil enriched with organic matter. Perennial species of borderline hardiness such as *I. tinctoria* are best given a thick mulch to protect roots over winter. Thin annual species heavily to prevent them becoming a menace, and remove most of their seedheads quickly after flowering.

Suppliers

B&HM Baker, Essex, tel: 01787 476369 (no mail order); **Cally Gardens**, Kirkcudbrightshire, tel: 01557 815029; **Cotswold Garden Flowers**, Worcs, tel: 01386 422829; **Crûg Farm Plants**, Gwynedd, tel: 01248 670232 (no mail order); **Fir Tree Farm Nursery**, Cornwall, tel: 01326 340593; **Sue Hartfree**, Kent, tel: 01795 842426.

THE GLASSHOUSE

r glasshouse cultivation. Popular s grows epiphytically. A variegated *keilii* 11. A smaller species, it is a prolific *erdoniae* is among the most spectacular nber. The blooms are up to 5cm (2in) 25cm (10in) high. Similar-sized

e mounted with a little moss on cork pt in a light position under glass.

Some success has been achieved by crossing it with *I. walleriana*, resulting in the *I.* Sea Shell Series hybrids offered a few years ago.

The range of colours included 'Sea Shell Papaya' (red) 7, 'Sea Shell Tangerine', 'Sea Shell Yellow' 8 and 'Sea Shell Apricot', which were something of a revolution. However they did not perform well in British weather conditions and the yellow cultivar often faded badly, although all fared better under glass.

Other *I. auricoma* crosses with different species have produced various *I.* 'African Orchids' hybrids which have a wider range of colours including many bicoloured. Conveniently, these may be grown from seed.

For those gardeners looking for something new and different, long-flowering *Impatiens* offer months of summer colour, and the plan him, holding an ochre painted piece of metal work. 'Look,' she cried, emotion dilating her grey eyes and expanding the amber tiger-flecks in them. He looked, he enthused, he embraced her and said, 'Yes, yes, let's not eat until afterwards.' She was so happy as she bounded backwards into the bedroom. He began to feel happy too. NATO man, already half dissolved on the journey home, melted quite away and l'homme des Marolles stood in his place. The Marolles was where they lived, Felix and Marie, tenant and landlady, in flats which had been fashioned out of two old houses in the Rue de l'Epée, flats which interlocked differently on every floor, reaching into each other at surprising angles and levels, apartments with a double kitchen in common, a double bicycle garage, two double bedrooms and a quadruple studio on top. The lines of demarcation were drawn where Marie's tidal wave of architectural débris met Felix' overspilling books. The areas had one thing in common, that nothing new was to be seen. Everything was old, not necessarily very old, but old enough to be used, scarred, faded, worn.

Marie Smulders was a child of the Marolles, the tiny unreformed relic of old Brussels which runs like a leg from east to west between the flea market and the mammoth Palais de Justice which Poulaert reared on the cliff above in 1886 and which is too heavy for even the Bruxellois, those unhesitating and remorseless demolishers, to pull down. Marie's great-grandfather had been arrested for demonstrating against the construction of the Palais de Justice, which robbed the Marolliens of a piece of their territory, as important to them as, say, Alsace-Lorraine is to France. The memory of that rape has lingered on in the quaint Marollien use of 'architecte' as a prime term of abuse.

'You architecte, you,' cried Marie in mock anger, pushing Felix off the lofty farmers' bed, 'you exhaust me, you are too much, are we never to eat?'

Felix relaxed gratefully on the floor. He was ready for a rest and ready for some food.

'Chez Vincent?'

'Yes, moules, and you'd better ring up so that we can sit in the prow.'

Chez Vincent was only three kilometres away, far beyond the boundaries of the Marolles. Before opening the bicycle garage they went for a beer in their own neighbourhood, choosing from the numerous possibilities a Mort Subite at the Au Baride, which they liked because of the Société Colombophile which gathered there. Marie visited the boulangerie and arrange for a ketje to come round in the morning with four pistolets. Felix paused outside the Old People's Home and slipped some coins into a slot which said 'Dieu Bénisse la main qui donne son obole ici'. He had taken some trouble to work out what the Little Sisters meant by an obol; at current rates of exchange, about seven francs.

Felix was not quite so hungry when they dismounted at the end of the Rue des Dominicains and wheeled their machines along to the secret bicycle park used by the waiters at Chez Vincent. But the beer had made Marie ravenous, and her eyes were incandescent under the Medusa head of hair.

'The usual,' said Felix to the captain of the Vincent team. They all knew him, down to the good lady who presided over her plate of five franc pieces in the cour, and all knew that he and Marie shared their love of the pre-1914 tiled walls and the fantasy of the original Vincent who had set sections of a boat down the room, so that one sat in the prow or stern or on the cross-benches amidships, a nautical ambiance which affected the waiters, causing them to sway and glide with the panache of ocean stewards.

Marie contemplated the tile painting opposite her with fierce affection. It showed a coastal scene, with fishing boats in the middle distance and a brown beach, on which precisely one hundred and thirty shells and small marine creatures were depicted with trompe l'oeil precision, in the foreground. One sou'westered fisherman, astride a giant cart-horse, appeared to be regaining the shore. Another, blue-jacketed and wearing on his craggy yet noble face a look of apprehension, was guiding his steed into the turbulent waters.

'One day, you know, some fiend, some architecte, will pull all this down and replace it with something totally banal. Do you realise the danger, do you know how I tremble on every visit for fear that it could be the last? What have you to say about this at NATO? What plans have you made? You say that you protect the free world. Well, this is part of it, and a precious part. But if you hear that it is being destroyed what forces will you muster for its defence? Haa. Your face betrays the answer. How then do you hope to make me a supporter of NATO, when it is not the Russians I fear but the demolition gangs of my own city, the same gangs whom my great-grandfather defied?'

Felix began to eat his forty mussels.

'Marie, you are absolutely right. There is no NATO plan for defending this room, not with guns anyway. But remember, we have glimpsed the logic of what you say. Think of the CCMS, our Committee on the Environment. All right, snort. It may not have done much so far. But admit that it exists, that its members have the right idea. They need encouragement, not . . .'

‘Oh, those pennelekkers, what they need is a kick in the pants. What has this CCMS done, tell me? It has talked. It has written papers. It has held meetings. It has . . .’

‘Hush, you have had too much babbelwoeter, let me think. You have reminded me of something. The CCMS meets next week, and I forgot to send the agenda in tonight’s bag. Crumbs, and more crumbs. What shall I do?’

Felix looked at his watch. The Queen’s Messenger would already have settled down in the night sleeper to London, surrounded in his compartment by twenty white bags of NATO documents, two or three hundredweight of them, but not including the one which was actually awaited in Whitehall on the morrow.

‘Wait a minute, it’s unclassified, so there’s a copy in the cupboard in my room. I could still get it off in tomorrow morning’s air bag, and maybe no-one would notice . . .’ Felix thought hard.

Marie finished her last mussel and her last piece of bread and turned to the coffee.

‘Listen, why don’t we bicycle out to NATO and do this thing together? We’ll go to Daskalides first to buy the chocolates; then to NATO. On the way I will show you some things – they do not require a détour, I promise you – and when we are there you will show me your office.’

Felix liked the idea. The reactions to the NATO building of someone who was fanatical about art nouveau should be worth having; especially when the someone was as outspoken as Marie. But on the whole it seemed preferable that she should see it when it was empty except for the guards. A visit by day would expose his colleagues to an unsettling presence, perhaps even to verbal onslaughts. Supposing for example that she met HE?

'Right, we're off. I'll just pay. Do you want to visit the pissenwaif?'

'No.' Marie shook back her tousled mane of twisting hair and carelessly stuffed the curling ends under the collar of her pea-jacket. It did not occur to her to think of her appearance. She was busy planning the route.

Daskalides was still open, and the doyenne of their advisers was in her usual serene posture behind the square trays of chocolates. Unhurriedly they conspired with her to build up a 1 kilo box, in eight layers, so that on each day of the holiday they would have a suitable assortment. Each layer contained two praline-filled huîtres for Felix and six dark Mexican galettes for Marie. Only the top two layers were judged suitable for the concoctions with fresh cream. The longer-lasting marzipan centres were grouped lower down. While the box of delicious and nourishing morsels was being wrapped the three of them went through the usual ritual conversation about the weather. Felix liked these conversations. They were untaxing and predictable, little pools of tranquillity in a turbulent world. He sighed as they left (bonne fin de soirée, bonne nuit, bonnes vacances) and stepped into the hubbub of Avenue Adolphe Max, sighed again as they rode out into the bad-tempered traffic and started their spasmodic progress south, cycling from one traffic light to the next, through brightly lit Place Brouckère and the tourist-thronged Grande Place.

'The most distinguished parking lot in the world,' called Marie, gesturing across the car roofs to the floodlit guild houses in the south-west corner. 'Some day a Burgomaster will take courage and sweep these beetles out.'

They rounded l'Eglise de la Chapelle, passing Aux 10,000 Casseroles and dismounting in Place Emile Vandervelde.

Felix could see that something was wrong with it. Three quarters of the oval were congruent in height and compatible in style. The remaining quarter was usurped by a modern office block, which towered high aloft, making a toy of the nearby church. From its raw concrete haunches sprouted suggestively ugly street lamps.

Marie gripped his hand. 'Exhibit One. This terrible building, this home of the evil CODEP, stands where Horta built his masterpiece, the Maison du Peuple. Constructed in 1896, destroyed in 1964 – to make way for this.'

'And that is what you got a bit of today?'

'That is what I got a bit of today. A fragment of the ironwork which was as important in the construction as in the decoration.' She fished a file out of her battered Florentine saddlebag. 'See, this is the facade. That circle marks the spot where my fragment must have been. Look how beautifully all the functions of the buildings were combined. This is where the socialists went in for their meetings and their doses of culture. And there are the little shops at street level. Imagine to yourself how exciting it all was in those days, when Brussels was the artistic capital of Europe and Horta was making these buildings such as no one had ever seen before.'

Marie remounted and set off to the north-east. Felix managed to stay no more than half a length behind. He was becoming curious about Horta, and not only because he liked always to share Marie's latest enthusiasm.

'What do you mean, buildings such as had never been seen before? Surely Horta belonged to some school, or something?'

Marie slithered skilfully over cobbles and tramlines. 'No, no. He began again, he created things which were truly new.

It is not too much to say that he founded the modern style, call it art nouveau or what you will. He gave Belgium, little forty-year old Belgium, something to be so proud of, and look what we do with it. Pull it down. But not everything, not yet. Wait a moment and you will see something that survives.'

The something had to survive another eighteen minutes until they reached it. It was a pair of houses in Avenue Palmerston. Felix was glad to find that they were on the way to NATO. This helped him to like the houses; but they were in fact very handsome. No 2 in particular provided a subtle solution to the problem of an obtuse-angled corner site, and had a front door with organic curves which appealed to him. He said so, and was rewarded with a hug.

'And look up at the first floor, that is the library behind that big window; it has a whole set of bookshelves designed by Horta, and a Horta desk all curved and beautiful and made of yew. See now how the house next door fits in – it is occupied by the Electrogaz Company but they take great care of it. And now, surprise for you, turn around and look across the road and what do you see? Another one. Do you know that this is the only place in the world where you can see three of Horta's houses at the same time?'

'But how extraordinary. That is the NADGE office.'

'NADGE? What is NADGE?'

'Well, it's a part of NATO. Let me see, how can I explain? It is the office where they work on the system of radar which tells us if a Russian aeroplane flies towards us even up in the Arctic and other remote places.'

'And they have chosen a house by Horta for this purpose? Truly this NATO is an organisation with some aesthetic principles. I can wait no longer to see their main building. Lead me to it quickly.'

'Dear pimpelmies, I love you. But do not raise your hopes so high. It is not typical of NATO to occupy architectural masterpieces, still less to build them. Remember, when NATO had to move out of France in a hurry it was necessary to build a new headquarters here in six months. The design is rather plain . . .'

Felix expected to find NATO, at half past ten, in its usual night-time state. As he and Marie pedalled up to the gate-guards' small office he was disagreeably surprised to see quite a few lights on in the main building and ten or more of the big black ambassadorial cars drawn up at the main entrance. As he showed his pass to the guard, who was unused to night-time bicyclists and insisted on a good look, he was wondering whether it could be some new incident in Berlin. But the Permanent Representatives themselves were hardly likely to turn out after dinner unless something quite extraordinary had happened. The North Atlantic Council could meet at any time, as visitors were always told; but in practice it scarcely ever met outside working hours. A crisis was more apt to bring the members of the SPC or the Military Committee flocking in.

They rode round to the press entrance, passing under the lee of Block A. Lights were on in HE's room. Felix thought, without conviction, that the guard might be doing his rounds.

'Why did we leave our bicycles outside?' demanded Marie, surveying the long central corridor. 'This would be marvellous for practising sprints.'

'Not really. It's usually full of people, and there's a check-point half way down. Come on and take a look round before we go up to the Delegation. Have a kijk at these glass cases.'

The glass cases were on a wall by the cafeteria. The first contained a cigarette lighter and a plastic notebook with the NATO symbol on them, and two dark blue ties similarly adorned; also a key ring with the inscription 'Club Philatélique OTAN'. A placard said in French and English that such articles could be bought at the main reception desk. All the articles and the placard were covered with a thin film of dust. The second case contained a silver cup, currently in the possession of the NATO football team, surmounted by a midget bronze footballer who was about to stub his toe by kicking a bronze football which was visibly welded into place, and various smaller trophies representing minuscule triumphs in the past by NATO ballroom dancers and table tennis players. All were tarnished. There was also a row of flags of the NATO countries, fastened to little wooden flagpoles.

'For esprit de corps. The pulse quickens, does it not?'

'Yes, but not very much. Is it not your chapel where the real esprit of the organisation is enshrined?'

'We don't have a chapel. SHAPE do. I suppose that soldiers are more religious than civil servants.'

Felix turned Marie around. 'But we do have a shopping centre. See. Travel agency, barber, bookshop, bank, post office. All the essentials are provided. We can eat, groom ourselves, communicate with next of kin, lay plans for escaping and manipulate our finances, all in the lunch hour.'

They walked on down the corridor and Felix filled in a visitor's pass for Marie at the security desk. The guard was English and he was listening to the BBC on a transistor radio. Behind him was a large green poster, dating from the Second World War or drawn more recently with deliberate archaism. It showed a gardener, grey-green in hue, bespectacled and behatted, kneeling to insert a carnation cutting in the soil. The inscription said: 'Plant Security Consciousness in Your Own Mind – Cultivate Security Consciousness in the Mind of Others – Reap the Satisfaction of Doing Your Part in Protecting the National Security.' Marie asked whether she could have a copy. The guard, pleased to be passing the time, speculated about what procedures should be followed and what authorities consulted in order to achieve this; but said that in his opinion the posters in the cafeteria were brighter, the ones which said: 'Discretion while Socialising'. Marie liked the word 'socialising'. She said that she had not met it before in her English studies. 'No,' said the guard, 'you wouldn't have, it's not really English. The Yanks brought all these posters in, they really run the place, they do.'

'It's strange,' said Felix as they climbed the six flights of stairs to Block A, 'how many people go on about the Americans dominating NATO. It's one of the most popular questions for visitors to ask. The truth is just the other way round. NATO is the unique instrument which enables the Europeans to exercise influence, often decisively, on the Americans. Now, we may have to wait a moment before we're let in.'

The UK night guard winked at Felix. 'I wondered whether you'd escaped, going on leave. But it's all hands to the pump tonight. I really got a shock when HE came in. I wonder how much longer he'll be. Should I brew my tea later, or do you think he'd like a cup? I expect your young lady would, anyway.'

Felix found it a disadvantage of being in British Government service that he was constantly entangled in questions about when tea should be consumed, and in decision-making about whether to have some, and second cups and so on. But he had learned not to give offence by untimely rejection, and nodded pleasantly. 'Yes, I'm sure HE will be ready for a cuppa, and so are we. By the way, do you know what he's come in for?'

The guard lowered his voice. 'I'm not supposed to know, sir, but I think it's something to do with Mr Lute.'

An accident? But it passed belief that ten Permanent Representatives should have come in to confer about an accident to one person. David was popular, and he and Beta entertained a lot; even so . . . Felix was still thinking as he guided Marie up the long corridor, past the neat brown doors which bore labels such as 'First Secretary, Infrastructure' and 'Mr Bilston'. The Registry door was open and a voice floated out, '. . . at present no clue whatsoever as the . . . hell I can't read this bit, I wish the Head of Chancery would tell HE about his handwriting instead of lecturing the rest of us . . .' Felix was digesting this fragment when HE appeared at the end of the corridor.

'Hello, Felix, I thought you'd gone on leave. Er, . . .'

'Yes, sir, I just popped back to . . . er . . . do something. May I introduce you to Mejuvrouw Marie Smulders, my landlady? Marie, may I present Sir Ambrose Lavenham, my Ambassador?'

Marie pushed back her dishevelled hair and shook HE's hand. Felix could feel her radiating an animal mixture of friendliness and distrust. She certainly did not look or act like a typical Brussels landlady. HE was looking at her with a distant curiosity. But after minimal pleasantries he indicated firmly that she should retire into Felix' room while he spoke to Felix on a business matter.

Felix rejoined her quite quickly, and was attacked at once.

'This is a terrible room, a plywood box, a cardboard carton. How can you bear it? Demand of your Ambassador a setting more sympathique for your personality. What is this tea-cup? From which pottery have you ordered it? It is so thick, and it is cracked. Is this a catastrophe which has happened today? The conditions of life here are insupportable.'

'Tootoot, I quite agree, but let us speak of other things. There are strange portents in Brussels tonight. Listen, sixteen of the top people in NATO have vanished without trace since lunch-time. Ports and airports and frontiers are swarming with vigilant policemen. My friend David Lute is among the missing. You remember – the one who played the piano that evening. The Ambassador has just gone to see the Secretary-General, who is going to see your Minister of Foreign Affairs at midnight . . .'

'Is it an accident?'

'Quite excluded. The sixteen were last seen in a bus going off together for lunch. They never arrived. The roads yield no trace of an accident. The bus has been discovered to be bogus – I mean it was a real bus, but not an official one. The evidence all points to kidnapping.'

'Someone then has really put the petrol in the soup. For NATO and for all these governments. But not for us, I hope. What of our holiday? Should we not leave tonight?'

Felix was addressing an envelope for the CCMS agenda. It struck him suddenly that he need not bother. No one was going to notice tomorrow whether the agenda had reached Whitehall or not. He tore up the envelope.

'Let's go. Race you to the door.'

Skidding to a halt at the door they met Sir Ambrose returning. Felix noticed that he looked livelier than usual.

'We were just leaving, sir. I don't want to be in the way. But if you think I ought to stay . . .'

'Of course not. We shall manage perfectly well. Even without David. I shall be handling this myself. The Secretary-General believes that he will hear of some clues when he talks to Pierre later on. There is some report from the Reuter's man in Algiers . . . But who knows. I must call London. Have a good holiday.'

Marie grasped the Ambassador's hands. 'Oh, thank you, Sir Lavenham, you are a good man. Felix needs his holiday and I need Felix. But I promise you we shall look for clues while we tour the countryside. One sees more from a bicycle than from a motor car or aeroplane.'

Observing that Felix was troubled, quite unnecessarily, by her speech and gestures, Sir Ambrose responded with a gallantry which was not wholly assumed.

'My dear young lady, this is a charming and shrewd thought. It befits a countrywoman of Hercule Poirot. Knowing Felix' need for a holiday, and acquainted now, to my pleasure, with his charming companion-elect, I despatch you both with my blessing. I shall wait with confidence to hear that you have had a splendid time and solved the mystery.'

He kissed Marie's hand, and sped off along the corridor, swaying slightly under the unaccustomed load of adrenalin.

Chapter 4

Anna despised the hunting party. They were almost totally ignorant of country ways, and would quickly become lost and helpless in the woods without their retinue of guides and beaters from the village. But two of them had managed to shoot a sanglier each during the day, and this was useful for housekeeping. She returned from her high tea in a good mood and got out her script for the first briefing. Franz came in, looking brown and stroking his little blonde goatee beard in a pleased way.

'Clothes bought and clues planted,' he announced. 'And your agent had a very pleasant two days on the beach, not to mention lunch with the Paris cell on the way up. How goes it here?'

'Fine. Alexander has gone off to the library with his bags of stuff from their pockets, and is making notes. Ingrid is busy helping with make-up and costumes. Everything has happened according to plan. But I'm so glad that you're back – I felt uneasy while you were away, and there will be a thousand things to discuss tonight. But first we have to wake our guests and I will speak to them.'

The Committee did not all wake up readily. Some of them seemed to have difficulty in believing that they were awake when they looked up at the towering figures of Jacopo and Giovanni. But eventually they had all been got to their feet and herded through to the hall. There they stood in their scarlet pyjamas, blinking around at the bare windowless walls and muttering to each other. Jacopo and Giovanni, whose faces were those of Piero della Francesca angels, vacuous and heavy, and whose bodies had been developed to a remarkable degree by weight-lifting at Padua University, wore the uniforms of carabinieri (winter-weight) with goggles.

The loudspeaker crackled faintly and Anna's voice, level and assured, sounded in the wide room.

'Good-day, gentlemen, I am the woman who has captured you. I am sorry if the experience was disagreeable. You will learn later why it was necessary.

'You are still sleepy. You don't know where you are, nor who I am, nor what is happening to you. I will speak to you again later. Meanwhile, I have a simple message. I wish you no harm. Indeed I plan to do you all some good. You will probably have to remain here for ten days or more. But you will be well looked after and will have interesting work to do. By exercising your skills you may be able to advance the date of your release. Meanwhile steps will be taken to alleviate the distress caused to your families.

'Do not waste time by trying to escape. You are behind very thick walls. A large number of devoted guards watch you. Not all, but most of them are trained in judo. You will undoubtedly be hurt if you attack them. And it will be useless, since from the control room we are able to release a stupefiant into your quarters which will send you all to sleep very rapidly.

'Now, I wish you bon appétit. Sit where you will at the mess table. The menu is Zuppa alla Pavese, Lasagne al Forno, salad and fresh fruit. One glass of wine for those who wish it. No coffee tonight. I will speak to you again later.'

There was a moment's dead silence. Then the Committee coalesced into little groups and moved over towards the dining table, whispering to each other.

'Have you any idea of the time? My watch has gone.'

'So has mine. Did you notice that the food is Italian?'

'David, would you say that she had an accent? Is she English?'

'Hard to tell. She just might be, but I fancy not.'

'My pyjamas are too big. Could we swop?'

Seated, they began to examine the cutlery and plates. The knives and forks were large and old-fashioned, and were inscribed 'Grand Hôtel des Voyageurs, Toulon'. The plates were stone-coloured pottery; nothing on the bottom. The glasses were English rummers (as Lute was able to tell his neighbours). The fruit bowls were old cut glass, and no one could identify them.

Speculation about the fruit bowls ceased when Secunda and Tertia came in, flaxen-wigged and black-masked and black-aproned, with two steaming tureens of soup. They served the soup demurely and copiously, speaking bad French, then distributed bread.

The bread was French, but Brasfort said that it did not in his view come from France. Portentoso meanwhile announced that the soup was authentic, and that they were certainly being looked after by an Italian chef, even if not in Italy.

The Chairman was at one end of the table, and Piet at the other. The others wanted him to have a place of honour, as he had missed his farewell lunch. Not that they now expected to say farewell to him for some time. Some optimists held that they would be found quite quickly, but the majority were impressed by the degree of organisation which their captors had already displayed. They were unanimously gloomy over the prospect that NATO would ever be able to agree on a ransom, if this was required.

Piet himself was especially pessimistic. He insisted that they had been for a long trip in an aeroplane, and believed that they might be in Yugoslavia or even Albania. He looked very worried and restless. His companions supposed that he was afraid that someone else would be sent to Tunis in his stead. But even this did not seem quite enough to account for his abstracted expression.

Anna and Franz listened in to the conversation for a while, then switched off.

'Well, they certainly are baffled,' said Franz.

'Yes. I hope that this is right. We are depending very heavily on Alexander's theories about human behaviour.'

'Well, he's done two years' post-graduate work at Sussex, and is very impressive. I feel sure that he's right. They must be completely unsettled and mystified before they are set to work. In this strange atmosphere they will reach hungrily for anything familiar like committee work, and will perform brilliantly. You'll see.'

Anna laughed. 'Besides, it is rather funny. I wish I could see them in their red pyjamas reading the name on these knives. My uncle picked them up in the flea market and put them in a box for children's picnics. We often took them with us when we went off into the woods for the day.'

Franz wondered how long ago that had been. Anna could be any age from twenty five to thirty five. Franz also wondered, not for the first time, about men. For all the time he had spent with Anna during the last fifteen months, he had learned very little about her past, or indeed about her present except for their work together.

The cap of black hair slid forward as Anna tucked her legs under her and bent over the next script, reading it with a kind of wondering intensity . . . Franz decided to go down and see how it went over. He found James Minor in the changing room and they both put on the uniforms of sergeants in the Finnish Army, with shoulder flashes which betokened membership of the United Nations Force in Cyprus. Ingrid made them up lightly, and they went down to the double-locked communicating chamber, checked through security and slipped into the back of the hall.

Secunda and Tertia were carrying in the Hindeloopen milkmaids' stools and setting them in rows against the wall opposite the loudspeaker. Their French had become even worse than at dinner, but the Committee understood the smiling invitation to sit down and did so. A few of them glimpsed Franz and James Minor in the shadows and looked startled. Others gazed with apprehension at the stern figures of Jacopo and Giovanni. A few found comfort in following the deft movements of Secunda and Tertia. The Chairman merely looked at the loudspeaker, waiting.

'Good-day once more, gentlemen. I hope that you enjoyed your meal. Now I am going to explain to you why you are here.

'You will find it easier to understand if I begin by dismissing some ideas which may have occurred to you.

'I am not seeking money for myself, nor for any organisation. I am not going to require your governments to release prisoners or to eliminate blemishes in their political systems or to take one side or the other in any of the notorious conflicts which have in the past prompted crude kidnappings. I am not an Arab, an Israeli, a Basque, a Latin American revolutionary, a Rhodesian, a Cuban, an Algerian. I am not a relic of the ban-the-bomb movement. I have no intention of insisting that NATO disarm herself.

'I am not an habitual criminal nor an associate of

criminals. I am not what is sometimes called a crackpot.

'I am not an agent of the Soviet Union, nor of China. I have little inclination towards communist views.

'I am not a liberator of my sex, nor an activist in the world student movement, nor one of those good people who battle against the oppression of minorities.'

Anna paused. No one spoke.

'Gentlemen, I am what you would call a young woman. But in my perspective much of my life has elapsed already, and I am impatient. My impatience is about the quality of the life which I – and you – enjoy, but enjoy imperfectly.

'When I was a child the problems of our environment were unrecognised. Today they are familiar to all, perhaps too familiar. All the talk about them gives people the idea that they are being dealt with, by governments and international organisations.'

Anna's voice became less formal.

'The trouble is that they aren't doing nearly enough, and what they do is done too slowly. My . . . someone in my family was in a tragedy which . . . No, it is enough to say that I know this from my own experience.'

Before she continued there was a faint crackling of paper over the loudspeaker.

'Of course I have a vote, in my country, and I have used it in support of my beliefs. I have done other things too, all of them quite proper and legal. The results, naturally, have been negligible. That is why I am impatient and why you are here.

'Like you, I know that the fifteen countries of NATO, which you represent, command the greatest resources and power in the world today. This is the power which I have chosen to harness to my good purposes, by making you my hostages.

'The price of your release, gentlemen, will be the application of that power, in a way in which it has never been applied before, to preserve and improve our environment.'

Anna paused again. Franz slipped out of the back of the hall. Little whispers arose from the Committee. The Canadian said to Brasfort, 'Sounds as though she doesn't know about the CCMS. D'you suppose we can get out of this by offering to set it up all over again?' Brasfort shrugged. 'It sounds to me as though she is perfectly aware of the CCMS. A study of its work so far is no doubt what has provoked her to extreme measures.' The Canadian frowned. He was one of those at NATO who supported the CCMS.

Anna turned over the last page but one of her script.

'Exactly what steps will be sufficient to secure your release is an open question. You yourselves, if you are willing, can help to find the best answer. I will talk of that tomorrow, in the morning. Tonight I will finish by explaining one point which may puzzle you – why have I made you my prisoners rather than your Ambassadors? It is not, of course, because I would have had difficulty in capturing them. And it must be admitted that their disappearance would cause even more excitement than yours. But they are older men, less resilient physically, less open to new ideas, ill prepared to function in unforeseen situations, and handicapped by their Ambassadorial dignity. You, on the other hand, are in the prime of life, and at that point in your careers when the sum of intellectual capacity and experience is at the maximum. Moreover you are quite sufficiently elevated in rank to cause a great stir by disappearing all together. You are precisely the kind of men I wanted – and now have.

'By the way, you may refer to me as Anna. I hope that you sleep well. I will ask one of my colleagues to make routine announcements in a few minutes, before you retire.'

At the end of Anna's speech many members of the Committee had been nodding their agreement. She had struck a popular note when she explained why they had been chosen in preference to the Permanent Representatives. They were, of course, consistently aware of the validity of the contrast which she had drawn. It was no secret to them that their Permanent Representatives were in a sense figureheads, men past their prime and lacking the capacity for daring thought and swift decision. But it was uncommon to find an outsider who grasped the point so clearly.

Several of them tried to imagine their Permanent Representatives sitting on the milking stools in scarlet pyjamas and yet preserving their sang froid and showing ability to adapt to strange circumstances. The effort of imagination was too great.

Franz came on the air. Where Anna had been deliberate in speech, investing her clear, low voice with a certain solemnity and earnestness, he spoke fast and lightly.

'Good-day, gentlemen, here are some announcements.

'First, I know that most of you have found the toilets. Over there in the corner, where the archway is. You'll find all the facilities inside in duplicate, one set to the left, one to the right. Please go in one at a time only on each side. Soap and towels are provided, but no razors. You'll all be growing beards, and they should look very handsome too.

'Next, clothes. Yours are in safe keeping. Don't worry. And you'll find something to wear here beside your beds when you wake up.

'Now a medical announcement. This applies to today

only. In the recent past, as you obviously know, you have been drugged. There could be rather unpleasant after-effects for some of you. But these can be neutralised by a harmless tablet if you take it within the next half hour. Get it? Swallow the tablet, nothing happens. Don't swallow the tablet and you may be in trouble. Sister Agnes will bring the tablets round to you in your cubicles when you've sorted yourselves into them. Two in each of seven cubicles and one each in the eighth and ninth. I suggest the Chairman has a single, but I don't really mind.

'Finally, welfare arrangements. We can guess that some of you may have little problems which you don't want to spell out to everyone. So each of you will see the Welfare Officer every twenty four hours, whether or not you have a problem. That way, no one will know you do have one, except the Welfare Officers of course. Sister Agnes and Ingrid. Nice girls, very sympathetic. Don't go taking up their time with questions about where you are or anything. They won't tell you. But married men can ask about their families. Some news may come through about them. And I can answer one question now, which the five of you who smoke must be planning to ask. The answer is no. A great opportunity to shake off a bad habit for good and all. Now, off to your cubicles, and Sister Agnes will be on her rounds in five minutes. Sleep well. We'll turn the lights out for you.'

Jacopo and Giovanni impassively watched the reactions. The first thought for some was to choose an agreeable cubicle companion. The Greek and the Turk went off at once, presumably to choose the best cubicle. There seemed to be no doors within the confinement area, only archways; but one was plainly marked 'Cubicles'. The Benelux trio talked unhappily together, the Belgian and Luxemburger in subdued tones and Piet in his usual bow-wow fashion. They seemed bothered by the fact that they could not all be in the same cubicle. Piet was taking it for granted that he would not be the odd man out. But Portentoso bore down on the group and asked Piet to share. The Belgian and Luxemburger smiled in polite acquiescence, reflecting that it would be well to have the two loudest speakers in the group in one cubicle, and planning not to be in an adjacent one. France and Portugal left together, Giovanni wondered why; he was unaware that the French Government were cultivating Portugal at present. The Icelander and the Norwegian paired off. So did the Dane and the Canadian, who were used to sitting side by side in committee. That left the American, the Englishman, the German and the Danish Chairman, who sat hunched together on their stools, speaking in very low voices. Neither Jacopo nor Giovanni could make out what they were saying; but they would find out when they went upstairs later.

Lute said slowly, with an upward flick of his eyebrows, 'We must discuss the situation when we can do so freely.'

The American said, 'It's a pity that we can't go to the bathroom together. I often have good ideas when the shower's on full.'

The German nodded. 'Noise assists me also. Even the clatter of cutlery can stimulate conversation. Incidentally, shall we sit together at breakfast?'

The others nodded. But the Chairman did not say anything. He went off to occupy the ninth cubicle. The German, as the oldest, took the eighth. Lute and Grannery departed together to have an additional, unnecessary wash. Jacopo followed them and watched from the archway as they separated, one to the right, one to the left. Water ran. Splashing took place. Lute looked out. Jacopo was still there.

Lute went back in. Then they both came out, with an off-hand air, and were hailed by Sister Agnes.

'Come along, you two. You'll miss your tablets if you don't hurry.'

Sister Agnes had put her wig on, with the abundant curls pinned on top of her head. She wore a white nurse's uniform. It has been issued to her aunt by the Northumberland Hospitals Board in 1938, and was a tight fit, but it was still dazzlingly white. Her eyebrows were thin and arched, her eyes bright and her lips a full cherry red. Lute and Grannery looked at her, jolted by a madeleine de Proust effect. She smiled pertly and held up her bottle of tablets. 'Come on, lads, nurse is waiting,' she said, and followed them to the seventh cubicle. Jacopo and Giovanni walked along behind, and watched closely as the sixteen pink sleeping tablets went down. There was no real trouble. Portentoso wanted to know why he was given one and a half, but accepted the explanation that he was half as big again as the others. The Norwegian refused at first, but changed his mind when Sister Agnes shrugged and made to leave, saying only, 'All right, strong man, but don't go calling for me later on – I'll be off duty.'

Jacopo stayed behind in the hall with Sister Agnes until 2200.

'It's funny,' he said, 'they don't know whether it's today or tomorrow. And when they see the clock at breakfast time they won't know how long they've slept. I suppose they'll be all right, just being left like that?'

'Oh, yes, each tablet only had a hundred milligrams of Sonorol. That won't hurt them. They'll sleep like logs and wake up feeling fine. Hungry, too. I wonder if Françoise got enough of those brioche things?'

Jacopo thought of the brioches and found that he was looking fixedly at the white linen straining over Sister Agnes' breasts. He looked down. That didn't help. He simulated a yawn, stretching his arms out and gazing up at the ceiling. The old store rooms of the château were built of stone throughout – floor, walls, ceiling. Above where he stood the stone was stained pink. Perhaps this had been where they kept the wine, and a bottle had exploded.

'You seemed to make quite a hit with them.'

'Did I? That's nice. Alexander will be terribly disappointed if I can't twist them round my little finger.' She help up her left little finger, crooked it and stroked it with her right thumb. 'It's a minute to ten. Why don't you put the lights out? I'd love to see the hall with only the night light on.'

'But all the light switches are in the control room. And Kemalettin's waiting to let us out.'

'Golly, how forgetful I am. Of course he is. Let's go and report to Anna.'

There was some competition for reporting to Anna. Jacopo got in first and said that all was well below. Kemalettin announced that the security doors were closed, night lights on, monitoring equipment switched off for the night and air conditioning units functioning correctly. Tim said that there was nothing on the 10 o'clock news. Alexander the Great started to report on the contents of the committee's pockets, some of which had been of exceptional interest, but was persuaded by Anna to go away and type out a summary of his findings. Elizabeth shyly circulated the list of menus for the first week. There was some discussion of this.

'Is it safe to give them sanglier on the third day? It might make them think of Belgium, and I shouldn't be surprised if some of them suspect that they haven't crossed a frontier.'

'No, I think it's all right. The Dutchman is spreading his tale of being in an aeroplane. They've had an Italian meal, and will have a Tunisian one tomorrow. That should be enough to put them on the wrong track. And after all you find sangliers elsewhere, even in North Africa.'

'Yes, what I wonder is whether we've overlooked something else that would tell them where they are. Let's see, they have no windows, they can't hear any noise from the road or the village – we tested that – they have a mish-mash of objects from all over the world, we're a mixture of nationalities and the food is too. I think it's safe. I hope it is for Anna's sake.'

Anna said, 'It really is rather important for me. But I do believe that we've thought of everything. I agree about the sanglier. Apart from anything else we must be careful not to use up the frozen specialities too fast, otherwise they won't last a fortnight. We'd always counted on serving some local produce. Now let's tidy up any loose ends and get to bed ourselves. Who's doing tomorrow's programme, and who's on early telephone duty? I'm upset about the wives. It's lucky that so many single men are sent to NATO. But there are seven wives who must be worrying dreadfully. I hope we can pass some messages before breakfast tomorrow.'

Jacopo said, 'I'm doing the programme.' He wondered whether he dare ask Sister Agnes to help him. Cosily settled in a big leather armchair, she had partly unbuttoned her tight uniform and let her hair down. She was pensively stroking her chin with one of the smaller curls. Jacopo doubted whether she was thinking of him. He decided not to risk a rebuff, and went over by himself to the table with the typewriter.

Kemalettin, with easy strength, scooped Sister Agnes out of her chair. 'Come on, lass,' he said, showing an unexpected talent for mimicry. 'There's work to be done. You can help me with the journal.'

'Since it's you who ask . . .' Sister Agnes slithered slowly down Kemalettin's side and put an arm round him. 'Let's go.'

Anna smiled with the others, but her smile was qualified. She looked round for Alexander. But Alexander had gone to write his conclusions on the contents of the pockets. He had probably not yet noticed the change in Sister Agnes' demeanour.

Chapter 5

The Secretary-General had arrived home late from his interview with the Belgian Minister of Foreign Affairs, who had brought in the Minister of the Interior too. It was already after 1a.m. when he sought his bed. But first he had drunk a large mug of Ovaltine and had given numerous instructions to the Duty Officer in the NATO Situation Centre. One was that he should telephone all the Permanent Representatives at seven o'clock and summon them to a Council meeting at eight. The Secretary-General often reached his office at about that time himself, but he had never called a meeting before nine thirty. Now he had no hesitation. It was clear that the press had got wind of the kidnapping. The AP man had been at a cocktail party at which Beta Lute, ever conscientious, had turned up by herself the previous evening. Beta had been perfectly calm, but had told quite a lot of people that she could not imagine where David was. No one at the party had known about the other fifteen, but the AP man must have done some checking afterwards because the first story was on the ticker just before midnight. The NATO spokesman was holding everyone at bay for the moment, but an early statement was obviously needed. A breakfast statement, not a lunchtime one.

They began in the SG's private conference room, where the windows were always open, even in winter, and the yellow curtains flapped silently. The summons had been for 'one plus one', but not all the Permanent Representatives had managed to muster an aide. Indeed not all were present themselves. One was sick, and one on leave. But all fifteen seats round the table were occupied by two minutes past eight, two of them by First Secretaries.

The SG outlined the facts, so far as they had been established. The Belgian Sûreté had been working through the night. So had their colleagues in neighbouring countries. Frontier posts had been alerted by 10.15 p.m. on the previous evening. Sailings from all Dutch, Belgian and French North Sea ports had been checked. A great deal more had been done or started, including a survey of non-scheduled flights from airports within 300 kilometres of Brussels during the afternoon and evening. The results of all this work were being collected in the Situation Centre, where the Council could have a briefing shortly. For the moment he only wanted to say that there was no clear indication of what had happened, and to express his sympathy and that of his colleagues with the families of the missing men. He added that it seemed important to discourage speculation that Warsaw Pact agents had spirited the Committee away. They would discuss what to say to the press as soon as they had their briefing. But he would like them to have this point in mind already, since there were strong reasons for taking care not to upset East/West relations at this particular time.

The Council had nothing to add. They streamed downstairs and along the vast amber-carpeted conference lobby to the SITCEN corridor. For some reason the corridor was decorated with photographs of the Council. It was noticeable that most of the Permanent Representatives looked older and less handsome in the flesh than in the photographs. All the same, they seemed quite alert and impressive when they sat at the horse-shoe-shaped table in the briefing room, facing the three screens. The lights dimmed, a figure stepped on to the rostrum, and a plan of the western half of Greater Brussels appeared on the left-hand screen.

'Gentlemen, Colonel Margaux will tell us what is known about the . . . I suppose we must say kidnapping, although we still hope not . . . of our colleagues in the Senior Political Committee.'

Colonel Margaux did not have much to say, and had the sense to say it quickly. As he spoke wands flickered across the screen, demonstrating the route taken by the bus as far as the Forêt de Soignes, and indicating the Auberge. What he did make clear was that only vague descriptions were available of the three men who were in the bus when it arrived at NATO. He was succeeded by Major Pittakos, who had a map of Belgium on the centre screen and who took ten minutes to explain where road blocks had been set up on the previous evening and to draw attention, unnecessarily, to the roads and airports. The Permanent Representatives may not have known their way round Belgium, but they certainly knew their way in and out of the country.

The exhibit on the third screen was a map of Europe and the Mediterranean, on which a number of crosses had been marked. Colonel Scott explained their significance.

'Gentlemen, there is an unconfirmed press report from Algiers that an unknown person attempted, in suspicious circumstances, to charter a plane for 20 persons to fly to a destination in Central Africa. This was yesterday evening. Algiers is three to five hours' flying time from Brussels. No direct scheduled flights left Brussels for Algiers yesterday. There were three such flights from Paris, but Air France report normal passenger lists.

'Moving further north we have a report from Rome, Italy, that an unidentified aircraft flew over Sardinia, from north to south, without lights, at about 2100 local time yesterday. Air traffic control centres have no trace of this aircraft.

'During the night a Chevrolet tourist bus hit a tree on the Route National No. 83, just south of Roanne. The bus was travelling to the South. The accident happened at approximately 0430 local time today. An investigation is still being made, but it seems that the bus was empty except for the driver, who was killed.

'The black cross in the North Sea represents the present estimated position of the Soviet freighter *Rimsky-Korsakov* which put out of the port of Antwerp at 1930 local time yesterday evening. The *Rimsky-Korsakov* is a vessel of 10,000 tons, built at Leningrad last year and capable of a speed of 18 knots. She is bound for Leningrad with a cargo of machinery. Her visit to Antwerp was scheduled two months ago, and no unusual circumstances were noticed by the port authorities.

'Various reports from Belgian frontier ports are under study. These include a report from Liège that between 1600 and 1615 local time yesterday four new Mercedes Benz ambulances, of which at least one had Lübeck number plates, crossed the frontier from Belgium to the Federal Republic of Germany at West Tor, south of Aachen. In each ambulance were two men described as being of powerful build and wearing some items of dark blue uniform. The rear sections of the ambulances were not inspected on either side of the frontier. Enquiries are being made of all hospitals in Belgium and Germany in order to establish whether genuine ambulances are known to have made such a journey for official purposes, or found to be missing. A report from Lübeck is expected immediately but is not yet available. Thank you, gentlemen, that concludes my briefing.'

The lights went up.

The American Permanent Representative turned to Sir Ambrose. 'What strikes me is that the gang who did this could pretty well count on four hours before any alarm was given. In fact they had longer. But even four hours, at 70 kilometres an hour, gives nearly 300 kilometres. And if you start from Brussels and travel in any direction you can't go much more than 200 without crossing a frontier. Most ways you hit the frontier long before that. I reckon they could be just about anywhere by now, maybe split up into two or three groups. Sixteen is a lot of people to move around or hide together, unless of course they've been taken behind the Curtain.'

The Secretary-General allowed the hum of talk to die down.

'Gentlemen, I should be interested to have your comments, and any suggestions on action which we should take. It is possible that some members of the Council will already have received instructions from their capitals. Their intervention will be of especial interest.'

He paused briefly. He never lost the opportunity to convey the thought that a member of the Council speaking on instructions was worth ten speaking without them. This did not prevent several members of the Council from regularly making long speeches which began, 'Speaking on a personal basis . . .'

'I suggest for my own part that we should take two immediate decisions. First, there is a procedural matter. We should decide how to continue dealing with the developing situation. I mean, precisely, which committee of the Council should be entrusted with the necessary work. Secondly, we should authorise the NATO spokesman to issue a statement to the press. The draft of such a statement has been prepared to facilitate your discussion. It is being passed round at this moment. It is of course no more than a suggestion which the International Staff have prepared and which is not meant in any way to prejudge your conclusions on this important point.'

The Permanent Representatives gratefully read the draft.

Sixteen senior officials working at NATO headquarters are missing after leaving together for a lunch at 1330 on 7 November. The party consisted of the Assistant Secretary-General for Political Affairs and the fifteen members of the Senior Political Committee (list attached). They did not reach the restaurant where they were to have lunch, but the fact of their disappearance only came to light during the evening of 7 November. There is some evidence to suggest that they have been kidnapped. Members of the North Atlantic Council conferred informally with the Secretary-General during the night, and a special meeting of the Council was held at 0800 on 8 November to review the situation and to expedite measures to trace the missing diplomats. The Council expressed gratitude for the prompt co-operation of the Belgian Government. The Council agreed to keep developments under constant review.

Sir Ambrose's yellow pencil was the first to be raised.

'Mr Chairman, this seems to me an excellent draft, but I should like to raise a point of order. You suggested that we should first consider a procedural question and then issue a statement. I believe that the procedural question may need rather careful discussion. But I expect our spokesman is under pressure to make a statement at once. I wonder whether we would not do well to authorise the statement first. It so happens that I have the text of the unofficial guidance which my authorities are using with the press in London. This goes slightly further than your statement. But the two are consistent. I suggest that in the interests of speed we take your draft as it stands, unless any of our colleagues have strong objection, and that you arrange for your statement to be issued immediately.'

The Secretary-General and the NATO spokesman smiled their approval. There was a brief silence while various members of the Council wrestled with their desire to tinker with the draft. Each had his own ideas about how to improve it. But each thought it possible that all the others would be willing to take it as it stood, and hesitated to be solely responsible for starting a discussion.

The Secretary-General was skilled in the nice handling of such situations. After seven seconds he said smoothly, 'Well, gentlemen, do you agree with the proposal of Sir Ambrose? I think myself that it is a good one . . .' He gave them four more seconds. 'If that is agreed, then, the statement will be issued at once. And it may be useful if the text is telegraphed on the NATO-wide system to all the capitals. Thank you.' The spokesman was already on his way out.

The Council turned with relish to the procedural question. They loved procedural questions. They were all on an equal footing in handling them; there was no need for specialised knowledge or the mastering of long briefs.

The Secretary-General gave them no lead. He knew that the discussion would be long, and was saving up his own ideas for a later stage. But his sharp, lightly-bronzed face registered keen attention as the various possibilities were canvassed. In the normal way such a task would have been assigned to the Senior Political Committee. But this was ruled out a priori. The regular Political Committee was evidently regarded as rather lightweight for the occasion, although no one said this directly; many of its members were sitting in attendance behind their masters. It was agreed that since they would have to take over much of the political work of the SPC, notably preparing for the next Ministerial meeting three and a half weeks hence, they could not be expected to deal with the kidnapping.

The French Permanent Representative suggested that since a ransom would almost certainly have to be negotiated the Civil Budget Committee might usefully assume a central role from the beginning; but this was unpopular. The Turk believed that that whole affair should be put on a military basis. The International Military Staff were already sifting and reporting on the available intelligence. The Military Committee were used to meeting early in the day. It seemed to him that they were the obvious choice. But again there was opposition. The Dane in particular feared that if it became known that the Military Committee was involved the idea would gain ground that the whole affair was some sort of confrontation with the Warsaw Pact. He praised the wisdom of the Secretary-General in having already pointed to this danger.

For a time it looked as though agreement could be reached on an American suggestion that the Security Committee should be the selected organ. But someone remembered their terms of reference and when these were read out they seemed unsuitable. The Italian suggested delicately that the Economic Committee, whose valuable work was normally of a non-urgent character, might switch their considerable resources to this new problem; but everybody else winced and he did not pursue the idea. The only major committee which was not mentioned by anyone was the CCMS.

The Secretary-General summed up. Various organs of the alliance would have an important part to play in the work before them. None seemed quite suitable to take the leading and coordinating role. He suggested that in the circumstances the Council itself should shoulder the work as well as the responsibility. They would have to meet far more often than usual, and at inconvenient hours. But public opinion would expect this. It was of course for the Council to decide, but he must express his strong personal view that their duty was clear and that no subordinate body could approach this unprecedented problem with the necessary combination of authority and experience and a broad perspective.

The Council bought the suggestion, and agreed to meet again at noon.

As they trooped out through the SITCEN corridor the Canadian said to Sir Ambrose, 'I wonder how long this will go on. We can hardly go away ourselves until the SPC are back. I'd been planning to take off right after the Ministerial.'

Sir Ambrose incorporated the faintest rebuke in his reply. 'Hard to tell. I'm sure that you're right to fear a long haul. But I must confess I hadn't begun to think of leave problems yet.' He walked on through the lobby, thinking hard about his own Christmas holiday plans, which he now realised to be imperilled. Georgina would see the danger quickly enough. He wondered how to handle her. It might be best to belittle the danger. She would certainly exaggerate it. Then if the holiday plans were wrecked her wrath would be tempered by satisfaction at being proved right.

The telephone had rung just after nine in the little house in Imperial Road, Fulham. Outside, some employees of the North Thames Gas Board were hurrying past, late for work. A light rain was falling, but a group of West Indian children were playing football in the road, or rather in that half of it which was not occupied by the queue of incongruously sleek cars taking the short cut from Wandsworth Bridge to Chelsea.

The man who answered the telephone was big. He almost filled the tiny hallway. His name was Paddy and as he picked up the receiver he pushed a crate of empty Guinness bottles aside with one boot.

'Hallo.'

'Hallo yourself. Could we have a communication?'

'If you like. What sort would you be thinking of?'

'Registered post would be best. To my temporary address. Could you catch the nine thirty mail?'

The burly man glanced at his watch. 'Just about,' he said. Then he hurried upstairs to put on a tie and jacket. Registered post meant the Regent Palace, much the best place from which to make an unmonitored telephone call, but the commissionaire did expect people to look respectable.

Paddy left the house very fast. There were plenty of cabs on their way into town for the morning trade, but he was careful to walk three blocks before hailing one. And he asked for the top of Lower Regent Street, not for the Regent Palace Hotel. Top speed was indicated, but with at least minimum precautions.

While the taxi wound its way along the back streets between the King's Road and the Fulham Road, avoiding the heavy traffic, Paddy wondered what Kevin would be up to now. He was a great boy for ideas, was Kevin, and some of them were good. But he had a habit of acting impulsively, and this sometimes produced awkward results. The right hand didn't always know what the left hand was doing. Paddy glanced at his hands and, with the commissionaire and the switchboard operator in mind, used a discarded match-stick to clean his nails.

Beta Lute arrived at NATO headquarters at a quarter past ten, parked the dark green Mini in her husband's empty parking space and walked round to the reception desk. There were a number of press photographers hanging about, but none knew who she was. She was taken straight up to the Secretary-General, who was looking out of his window, and eyed her with momentary surprise.

'Oh, it's Mrs Lute, isn't it?' He kissed her hand. 'I was expecting you, of course. But my personal secretary, the one who looks after my appointments, has gone on leave – hardly a good time to choose in view of what has happened – and my office is a little disorganised. But please; make yourself comfortable. Let us sit over here.'

The light blue eyes looked at her keenly, but sympathetically. Cambridge blue, she thought idiotically, Cambridge was where she and David had met. She swallowed and took a minute to arrange her handbag on the low table beside the Swedish reindeer skin armchair. She noticed scuff marks on the bag, and wondered whether the tear marks were quite gone from her face. She had wept suddenly and copiously after breakfast, after reassuring Millicent and seeing her off to school.

The Secretary-General thought that she looked remarkably composed. He said, 'My dear Mrs Lute, first let me give you my heartfelt sympathy. If I talk in a business-like way it is not because I do not feel for you. But we must be practical if we are to have the best chance of finding your husband and his companions. Now, I have already spoken to Sir

Ambrose about your visit, and he understands perfectly. He will be glad to see you himself when we have finished, but if you wish to return home he will arrange to visit you there later in the day. Meanwhile you will speak to me in confidence with his approval. Now, tell me about this message which you received and what you have been doing.'

The effort of ordering her thoughts was good for Beta. She remembered David's views on the grasshopper style of narrative which he condemned as a feminine failing, and took care to start at the beginning.

'At six o'clock this morning the phone rang. I must have been asleep though I had the impression of lying awake all night. I answered and a man's voice, speaking in Spanish, asked me if I was Madame Lute. I would say that his Spanish was about as good as mine. That's to say, fairly correct but not a very good accent. I said I was Mrs Lute, and he said good, because he wanted to give me a message about my husband, that he was quite well and not to worry. Of course I started to ask questions, but he cut me short – quite politely – and said that he couldn't tell me anything at present. But if I wanted to send my love to David I could. So I did, and asked whether he could give the message to David himself. He said no, but thanks to the miracles of modern technology – or some phrase like that – the message could reach him quite quickly. He sounded sort of ironic, but quite friendly. I must say I liked the sound of him. I'd guess he's quite young. Then he said that he wouldn't be ringing up again, but that there might be ways of passing messages and that it would help if I had all the other wives round this morning. I thought for a minute and said yes, I'd call them. He laughed again and said I needn't bother, they would turn up at nine o'clock. Well there are seven wives, including me. Perhaps you didn't know. I had to look some of them up in the NATO directory to be sure that I knew the number. Anyway, it's seven, less than half. I went round to the pâtisserie when it opened and got some croissants and little cakes, and made lots of coffee, and then at nine on the dot the other six all drove up. They'd all had telephone calls too, just saying to come and see me, not in Spanish, all in French, three from a man and three from a girl. They hadn't all noticed the exact time, but it sounded as though all the calls were between seven thirty and seven forty five.

'Well, you can imagine the sort of talk we had. There was nothing in it I need tell you, except that I'm really worried about Maddalena Portentoso, she's just so upset and I know she hasn't any help at present. Still, she did eat some of the cakes. Anyway, at half past nine the bell rang and a boy delivered some flowers. Seven bunches, and really beautiful. Not those formal bouquets that the Belgians like, but a lovely mixture of freesias and greenery. The boy said there was no message, he worked at de Backer's and had just been told to bring the flowers before ten. So we took one bunch each. Mrs Asgardsson said that she was sure that they'd been chosen by a woman. But I don't know that you can tell really. Perhaps the detectives will want to look at them. Well, where was I? Oh, yes, quite soon after the flowers had come the others said that I seemed to have been picked out as a sort of contact point and asked me to be their . . . well, their representative. They said it would be best if I came straight to you and said what had happened. I said that I really ought to go to see Sir Ambrose, but they said no, not if I was representing them all, I ought to see you. That's all; except thank you very much for being sympathetic, and what do you think has happened? Are there any clues yet? Above all, what can we do?'

The Secretary-General thought to himself that someone connected with the kidnappers must know Beta Lute. They had certainly picked the right one. He wondered how many friends and acquaintances she had. Hundreds in Brussels alone, he supposed. Aloud he said, 'Thank you. That was very clear. I hope you do not mind, but I had it recorded. I thought that you would speak more naturally if you did not know. But now I am telling you, and if you wish we will rub out the recording. No? Good. But I will switch off the machine. There is no need to record our private talk.'

The Secretary-General crossed to his desk and flicked a switch. This gave him a minute in which to reflect on what he should say. As he reflected, he began to realise what an enormous convenience it would be for him to deal with a spokeswoman of the wives instead of the whole lot, whether separately or together. Beta Lute might have a very important part in this drama, a part which would for example be much more important than that of her Sir Ambrose, whom she seemed so anxious not to offend. He came back and relapsed into his chair.

'What can you do? . . . For the moment, nothing. It is hard to be inactive, but you and the others must just go on as best you can with your daily lives. If there is any further message, telephone me at once. I will probably hear about it from, hmm, other sources, but nothing else could be as quick as a direct call from you to me. By the way, you must say nothing to the press, nothing at all, except that you are not at liberty to make any comment. Of course you will be pleasant to them. It is their job to ask questions. But you will be quite firm, and so will the others. If there is trouble, if anyone is too persistent, let me know.

'Next, information. Obviously you must share all that we

have. You cannot attend meetings of the Council but I see no reason why you should not be present when the Council is briefed. I will put this to them at noon, and if they agree we will arrange a special pass for you and will let you know whenever there is to be a briefing. I will also try to have a car and driver placed at your disposal. I expect that you have a lot to do, and this will save you time. I do not promise the car. There are some administrative difficulties which even a Secretary-General cannot resolve. But I fancy that if I have trouble I will be able to get one from SACEUR, with a good driver. He is always asking me to use one of his helicopters, so he ought to be able to oblige with a car.'

The Secretary-General smiled, and so did Beta. She had only talked to him once before, at a dinner which the Lavenhams had given, the famous one when the central heating broke down just beforehand. Now that she was getting to know him she liked him. She was happy that he was in charge of finding David. She could tell Millicent that the chief detective was a clever and handsome man with a pleasant smile.

'One thing more. I look forward to working with you. I fear that our collaboration may last for some time. Since I happen to know that your unusual and agreeable first name is Beta I propose to use it with your permission . . . thank you. May I ask, by the way, whether you have an elder sister called Alpha?'

'No, the truth is that I was christened Beatrice, but I've always been Beta since school days when I once got a beta mark for my essays nineteen times in a row. I hope you're not disappointed.'

Beta turned as she went through the door. 'Still, we do have a Felix in the Delegation, and his brother and sister were christened Felicior and Felicissima.'

She hastened to Sir Ambrose's office.

Beta's haste was less than that of the man who passed her in the corridor outside the SG's suite. This man was really running. He held a piece of white paper in his hand and his face was white. He careered into the outer office, rolled his eyes towards the SG's door, acknowledged the secretary's quick nod, and passed in at barely abated speed.

The secretary heard him say: 'This changes everything. We think we know who's got them …' Then the door closed.

Chapter 6

Marcel came up from the village each day with his mother. He was waiting on the terrace, looking up the valley towards the Fief de Bourdain, where the old pines made a band of darker colour between the plantations of Christmas trees. It was not raining, but the landscape was as wet as a sponge. On one side of the terrace could be heard, far below, the gurgling of the Ruisseau des Deux Ponts, starting its journey to the Semois. On the other side was the steady splash of the little nameless waterfall which fell into the gorge from the north.

Anna came out with one of the huntsmen, a plump shipping man from Antwerp. His hunting clothes fitted him, and were timeless. His cranberry complexion could have been by Rubens. He did not spoil the view when he stood still and kept silent. But his movements were clumsy and his voice too loud, not with the slow sonorous twang of the Ardennais but quick and harsh.

He pointed. 'Is that where we go today?'

Anna inclined her silky black head. 'Yes, Marcel will take you again, and the beaters should be over there already. Let me see, there are ten of your this week, that is not too many. Look for the yellow spots on the tree-trunks and you will know that you are in the right place. I hope it doesn't rain, but it will certainly be very wet underfoot.'

The soft damp morning air suited her complexion. The huntsman noted its velvety texture and the almost imperceptible freckles. His small hard eyes locked on to her large ones.

'Countess, this is the most marvellous place you have. And the food is superb. Such variety. But I hope that we're going to eat some of the game. And won't you come with us one of these days? I'm sure you must be a good shot.'

'That would give me pleasure, although I should not join you in the shooting. But I have many things to do, and today for example I shall retire to my tower, which I assure you is not made of ivory but contains quite a busy office. There is a great deal of organisation for one who looks after a château of this size.'

Françoise was doing some of the organising in the scullery. 'And will you peel the canados?' she said to Marcel's mother, having learned the local name for potatoes. 'Seven or eight kilos, I think.'

Marcel's mother was shaped like a sack of potatoes, but her arms were strong and her eyes bright. 'So many?' she asked, not unwilling but curious.

'Yes, some of the students are here for lunch, and everyone seems to be tremendously hungry in the evenings. It is unimaginable how much these people eat.' She smiled, and Marcel's mother set to work.

Françoise was already back in the control room when Anna returned. So were most of the others, including Sister Agnes, who had just finished her morning clinic and was telling Alexander about it. Jacopo and James Minor and Kemalettin and Pete had also gathered round her.

'Half of them had nothing to say except good morning. They all seemed very friendly, I must say. A couple of them asked whether I would be doing the clinic again tomorrow and said they looked forward to seeing me again. Rather touching really, I mean they seem to have a special feeling about me. I wonder if I ought to take over the clinic altogether, Ingrid is so busy with all the costumes and things and she has all those gymnastics to organise. Anyway, there were some problems. The Greek said that the Turk snored like a foghorn, and kept him awake half the night. Actually, with the sleeping pill, it can only have been for an hour or so this morning. But I gave him a pair of ear plugs and he was quite embarrassingly grateful. They're in a little pill carton, so that the Turk won't notice. Then the American complained about the camp bed, but I told him that he would get used to it. There's a spare one in the clinic and I got on to it and wriggled about to show him how to find the comfiest position, and he really paid attention to this and said that he thought he would be all right tonight. The little man from Luxemburg – he's a lawyer, isn't he? – said that he was worried because he is winding up his father's estate and there are some things he simply must sign this month. We had quite a cosy little chat about how sad it is when parents die, and I said I'd ask about the documents, but that it wouldn't be easy. I told him that the best thing would be to work hard for the whole Committee to be released, and he said they were all dying to know what it was they were supposed to do.

'Now, what else? Oh, the Englishman was all blushes and asked whether we had any toothpicks or dental floss. He says a toothbrush isn't enough for his teeth, they're too close together or something. I took hold of his head and asked him to open wide and had a good peer in, and he certainly does seem to have funny teeth. I'll look around for something that might help. The Canadian was the only one who fussed about wearing a djebbah. The others were all quite pleased with them, but he said it was undignified for a white man, which I thought was a bit off, and not comfy. Turned out he had those funny underpants on back to front, so we soon fixed that and he brightened up a bit. He's the only one who was a heavy smoker, so he's a bit edgy. I'm giving him mild sedation for a day or two, I hope that will get him through the worst withdrawal pangs. He did say he'd wanted to stop for a long time, so perhaps he'll manage.

'That leaves the big Italian. He said he had fever, so I took his temperature. Normal. All the same I gave him an examination, just to humour him, and popped an aspirin in his mouth. Then he sort of broke down a little and said really he was worried about his wife and could I please get some messages to her. I wrote them all down and said we'd try, and gave him a little hug, and he seemed all right again though I don't know whether he'll be very good at concentrating on his work today.'

The men reflected on this narrative, with various expressions on their faces. Alexander was still scribbling notes and murmuring, '. . . most useful, most useful'.

Anna told Sister Agnes that she had done well. Ingrid said that she would not mind at all if Sister Agnes did all the clinics. 'Oh, goody,' said Sister Agnes, and gave Ingrid a hug. Jacopo watched disapprovingly. James Minor said, 'Break it up girls, it's almost time to rig up the committee table. I want them all back in their cubicles while we get things ready.'

In fact most of the Committee were in their cubicles, sitting on their camp beds, in groups of three or four. The Anglo-Saxons, certain that all they said would be monitored, engaged in small talk about the djebbahs. The others told Lute that he looked very well in his, just like a Roman senator. Lute had always been proud of his aquiline nose, and was pleased. But memories of Beta's obsession about the amount of laundry at home prompted him to question the choice of white. The others said that white was very smart, and that there didn't seem to be any dirt anyway. 'Yes, but what if we spill at meal-times?' asked Lute, and then immediately felt that this was a silly question. Why should he worry about the laundry arrangements, when there were so many more important things to worry about? If only they could talk freely; if only they had writing materials or knew deaf and dumb language. Could he possibly remember the Morse code from his days in the Navy? And if so would the others know it? He must bring the conversation round to the war and work in some anecdote about signalling and see whether he got a reaction.

In the Turkish/Greek cubicle the discussion was less inhibited.

'I sense that we are not in Italy,' said Portentoso. 'I would always know it if I was there. Do you not agree, my dear Brasfort, that for everyone there is a feeling which is evoked by standing on his native soil?'

'But what is one's native soil? The departments of France are very different from each other. I come from Brittany. If we are in Provence, am I to sense this? No, logic compels me to answer your question in the negative. But which of us is a student of architecture? Is it not possible to make inferences from the construction of these rooms? What do you think, Andrea?'

'I know little of architecture, although I helped to plan my villa on Spetsai. But I will be surprised if this building is in Greece. The colour of the stone is not familiar. I do not think that we can be sure of anything except that it is a big building and an old one, and probably in Europe. Perhaps it will be more useful to study our guards. We do not know what the weather is, but if we see them when they have come in from outside we may know whether it is hot or cold or wet.'

Upstairs Franz made a note. 'Remind everyone to change before entering the confinement area. Check on how to make a little snow.'

He moved a lead from one hole to another in a box like a telephone switchboard and listened for a moment. Silence. The Chairman must be out, or alone. Then came the unmistakable voice of the German.

'You have been very silent, my dear Hans. But perhaps we can talk for a moment. It is oppressive to me, being alone in my cubicle. The outside world is quite shut off . . .'

Franz moved the lead again, and began to monitor the talk in another cubicle. He thus missed the rest of what the German was saying:

'. . . from view, and the only noises I hear are faint and sad, like the wind in a chimney. I am really glad to come out of my den and see a familiar face. Tell me, can you think what work we are to do here? I worry that I may be made to do something of which my government would disapprove.'

The Chairman was unexpectedly genial. 'I know how you feel. But do not worry, we shall all be in the same boat. And I will come and visit you in your cubicle for company. Sit with me at lunch and we will make plans to cheer each other up.'

'Come,' said Jacopo, looking down on them from the doorway. They found the others in the hall, looking with surprise at a new arrangement of furniture. Light trestle tables had been set end to end in a ring, and sixteen folding canvas chairs were arranged round them. In front of each chair was a plastic sign, one saying 'Chairman' and fifteen with the names of their countries. It was all a facsimile of the arrangements in their committee rooms at NATO. There was nowhere else to sit down in the hall. The little stools had been taken away. However, no one sat down.

Anna's voice came over the loudspeaker.

'I hope that you all slept well, and that you are comfortable in your new clothes. I am going to tell you today some more about the arrangements which will be necessary to secure your release, and what you can do yourselves.

'You recall, I am sure, that your governments must bind themselves to take some important steps to reduce pollution and improve our environment. The question is – what steps?

'We exclude, of course, things which they are already doing; not that these amount to much. And we will not consider minor measures. Let it be clear that I insist on something quite big.

'You may think that I am unrealistic, that governments cannot be forced to do big things of this sort against their will. Certainly we could not make them do things completely against their will. But most of them acknowledge in words the need for drastic action. Listen, for example, to the words of the Prime Minister of Great Britain.'

The voice of James Minor, flatly and flawlessly English, was heard. 'This government is committed on your behalf to wage on every front, ruthlessly and relentlessly, the battle against pollution, the battle which will restore to us and safeguard for our children England's green and pleasant land . . .'

'Next, the President of the United States.'

Tim could manage the hint of a Southern accent very well. 'This is a struggle for survival. The achievements of the American people will turn to dust in our hands if we fail to conserve our proud soil in health, our water pure and our air clean. It is almost too late. But with God's help and a determination to sweep all obstacles from our path we will reach the goal.'

'You see, gentlemen, they put the position very well. It is not that they are ignorant of the dangers. It is merely that they are not yet putting into practice what they say. They are like men on the edge of a swimming pool, who state their intention of swimming but do not dive in.

'Now, by taking you as hostages, I am giving them a certain push. But what will be decisive, what is always decisive for politicians, is public opinion. If public opinion, which is being focussed on these issues by my act, supports my demands, then your Prime Ministers and Foreign Ministers and all the rest will begin to swim with great vigour.

'Fortunately for us public opinion is already ahead of the politicians. Your fellow-countrymen will be ready to acclaim our proposals, if they are good ones.

'Now you are welcome to sit round the table and discuss these ideas. I assure you that I will value your advice. I frankly need help if I am to complete this venture successfully and let you go soon.

'A member of my team will distribute pencils and paper. Please tell him at any time if you have suggestions to make to me. I wish you success in your work.'

Anna looked at Franz. 'Now we shall see whether it works. It will be very awkward if they do not co-operate.'

'I think they will. Remember Podduyev's question in *Cancer Ward*. "By what does man live?"?'

'And the answer is creative activity. That helps, if it's true. Also there is nowhere for them to sit except at the committee table.'

'Yes but the main thing is that they're conditioned to committee work and drafting and so on. I bet they started salivating when you mentioned pencil and paper. Remember, these are word merchants, plucked suddenly from their office-boxes, with no skill to exercise except drafting. You'll see, by lunchtime they'll be hard at work.'

'By noon?' The Admiral looked at his colleagues in amazement. 'But we hardly *have* any Marines, you know as well as I do what the last round of defence cuts did. And they're mostly in Northern Ireland at present. It simply doesn't make sense to call a full alert there and simultaneously move the Marines out: even if we had anything to move them out *in*.'

The Chiefs of Staff looked at each other gloomily. They were by themselves, so there was no need to assume just yet the craggy and positive expressions which they would be wearing two minutes later, in formal session and with their staff present.

'Well, we've got to do something. Here are the Americans asking *us* for once. And Ireland's our problem. What about those big new helicopters? Isn't there one of them at Belfast?'

'Yes, there is, but it's under repair. The other one's in Germany.'

'Could we offer a couple of destroyers if they flew some of *their* marines out to them? We must have something afloat in the North Sea.'

'Yes, *Witch* is there, exercising with the new hydrofoil missile-carriers. That could be the answer. We don't want to draw attention to them, but the Russkies are flying over them every hour on the hour anyway, so I can't see that it matters. Anyway, the main thing is to step up the aerial surveillance.'

The Air Vice-Marshal nodded. 'I couldn't agree more. And that's being done. The cloud's down to 5000 feet, but even so we'll have good coverage by the end of the day. It's not been easy, but we've fixed that.' The Air Vice-Marshal permitted himself a faint sigh, the sigh of a man who has achieved things which surpass in difficulty any possible imaginings of his audience. 'But the real problem is dealing with this American idea. I can see how the PM feels about it.'

The three of them left for their Conference Room, adjusting their expressions as they went.

The behavior of the SPC, after Anna's speech to them, was very much as she had expected. The atmosphere in the château was such that none of them felt actual alarm, although all were perturbed and uneasy. At the same time a sort of intellectual curiosity was affecting most of them. Some were experiencing a feeling of quasi-gratification at the thought of the commotion which their disappearance must have created. And all were restless, feeling a need to engage in some activity which would preserve them from endless, and probably fruitless, speculation about what would happen to them next.

So the Committee drifted in random fashion round the table, talking in small groups and showing indignation. But they mostly took care not to be too indignant. They wanted to sit down, and they badly wanted to have writing materials. They saw Jacopo wheel in a trolley with paper and pencils. They watched while Giovanni put a small block and gavel by the Chairman's seat, and they saw Tertia distribute eight water carafes and sixteen glasses round the table. It was all very nostalgic, very magnetic.

The German moved first. 'I am going to sit down. Without commitment, of course. My legs are tired.'

The Chairman sat down too. 'Gentlemen, I expect that you will at least wish to discuss what has been said to us. We may as well use the chairs. It is difficult to have an organised discussion standing up.'

Within a couple of minutes the Committee were all seated. One blue djebbah and fifteen white ones. Lute laughed briefly, then stopped himself. But some of the others laughed too. The atmosphere suddenly became lighter, more permissive. Jacopo wheeled his trolley round issuing pencils and large pads of paper, with the pages of each numbered from 1 to 100. Tertia whispered to the Chairman, who raised his eyebrows appreciatively.

'Gentlemen, this young lady has informed me that she is a skilled typist. She will be willing to reproduce for us in typescript anything which we write.'

Silence. It was clear that the Committee were on the brink. But none wanted to be the first to go over.

The Chairman exercised his prerogative of interpretation. 'Gentlemen, we are in a fantastic situation, which makes it difficult for me to give direction to our discussion. It may be easier if we treat the proposal of, er, Anna as being the matter for decision. This is a remarkable proposal, but it is comprehensible and precise. Shall I first ask whether any of you sees strong objection to it?'

This gambit was well received. Now they need only keep silent, and a discussion would be launched for which none of them need take responsibility.

The Luxemburger decided to help the Chairman. 'If I do not object, it is on the understanding that any discussion which we have is entirely without commitment, unofficial and off the record.' The others nodded approvingly.

Lute intervened. 'We may think the idea preposterous. But there's nothing to be gained by refusing to examine it. After all, if we look at the possibilities – completely without commitment, as Edouard has just said – we may be able to show Anna that her praiseworthy ideas . . .' (his eyes flickered towards the ceiling) '. . . are not feasible or at least need to be scaled down.'

There were more signs of approval. Only Piet looked unconvinced. He addressed the Chairman rather formally.

'I do not agree. A criminal act has been perpetrated. The criminal asks us to join her conspiracy, to help her to extort concessions from our governments. Her fair words about the environment should not obscure these basic facts. I believe myself that the problems of the environment are the most important ones facing mankind. They are of especial importance to my own country. But we have Ministries whose task is to approach the problems in a rational way, not being pushed down this road or that by the whims of a criminal. Our duty is clear. We should refuse any form of co-operation. We should not soil our hands. Mr Chairman, if the Committee is to continue this discussion I must ask leave to withdraw.'

Piet moved his chair back several yards away from the table, but continued to sit in it. He surveyed his colleagues for signs that they had been moved by his declaration; but their expressions registered only disappointment.

Up in the control room Anna and Franz looked disappointed too. They switched off for a moment while they considered the situation.

'A clear case for special measures, I think,' said Franz.

'Yes, I suppose so. But he sounds very firm, and the

Dutch are such obstinate people. Did you notice how he kept referring to me as a criminal? I wonder whether Sister Agnes will really be able to bring him to heel. Will you speak to her, or shall I?'

'I'll go and warn her now. She'll need to prepare herself. Will you go on listening?'

When Anna switched on again there was quite an interesting discussion in progress about motor bicycles. The Norwegian was urging that they be abolished, as part of a series of measures to reduce noise pollution. Others thought that it would be sufficient to introduce progressively stricter standards for their noise level. The Norwegian said no, that was not enough, there were supposed to be regulations already in many countries, but they were not observed. Anna wanted something drastic. The only drastic thing that could be done about motor bicycles was to abolish them. He would be very glad to think that within three years there would not be a single motor bicycle left in the NATO countries.

Anna liked this, but winced when she heard Piet's harsh voice intervene. 'Huh. You are wasting your time. This is all nonsense. I am not taking part in the discussion, but since I cannot avoid hearing it I might as well try to introduce a little common sense. Let me ask how many of you have ridden on motor bicycles? Or how many of you have toured my country and seen the long windswept dyke roads — seen them from your big cars, devouring the kilometres without effort? Have you ever paused to imagine what it is like to be earning your living in such an environment, to have to travel to and from work on a bicycle? Do you realise what a difference the motor bicycle has made to millions of Dutchmen? Do you understand that these Dutchmen are voters, and can you suppose for a moment that any government in

The Hague which even mentioned the abolition of motor bicycles would survive for five minutes?'

Piet spoke tensely, with passion. 'I repeat that I am not taking part in the discussion. But I beg you not to insult my ears with such ramblings. If you think that you can deprive men of something useful to them just so that a few fancy people can enjoy the absence of this plebeian noise you are making a big mistake.'

This time his words did make an impression. The Committee looked dispirited. No one answered back. The Chairman said that Piet's remarks could not be taken into account, but that perhaps the Committee would like to turn to some other possibilities. They did, but they had made little progress when Jacopo came round to collect up their writing materials before lunch. He could see that few of them had made any notes; and that what notes there were had all been crossed out.

Despite the disappointing morning the Chairman was in high spirits at lunch. He sat with the German beside him and kept up a steady flow of conversation and jokes. After Tertia had brought round the roast beef and Yorkshire pudding he passed the horseradish cream to his neighbour and remarked that he knew a very amusing story about horseradish, which he then apparently conveyed in a whisper.

But what the German heard had nothing to do with horseradish. He was told that the Chairman would visit his cubicle after lunch, and would please have complete silence therein, and that no one else was to know of this request or to be told that in that one cubicle a noise could be heard which sounded like the wind. The air of surprise on the German's face was attributed by the others to his well-known difficulty in understanding jokes.

Chapter 7

Marie was ready to leave at dawn. She gave the key of the apartments to old Fretche who lived next door, bidding him go in and gut the refrigerator and larders. She knew that old Fretche would take old Fraske in with him and that she would tidy the kitchen whilst despoiling it. That dealt with housekeeping problems.

While Felix got out the bicycles and finished packing his own saddlebag she stood on the cobbles, umber-trousered and cobalt-caped, and perfected the day's route, inscribing it with an orange felt-tipped pen on the convenient piece of white cardboard which came back from the laundry inside each of Felix' shirts. The list of experiences which she had devised for him was long, and two of them were supposed to happen before breakfast; Marie liked to exercise before eating.

She led him first to the suburb of Uccle, where they climbed the winding road to the cemetery and stopped to look at Bloemenwerf. They were alone in the road, except for a few school children lugging their heavy satchels in the direction of the French Lycée. Felix leaned on the gate and gazed up through the leafless bushes at the house. For some reason it looked to him like a vicarage, such as one might find in Devon, built to the fancy of a wealthy alpinist vicar. He studied the discreet, curved gables and tried to work out how many sides the house had.

Marie instructed him. 'Eight sides, if you're trying to count. Van de Velde. 1896. His own house. Anywhere else in the world this would be a shrine. And who knows that it is here? You and I, and oh yes the postman – come here, and let him through the gate. Mmm! Now we shall speed to our second sight, even less well-known. It is a pair of sansevieria – you know, what you call the tongues of the mother-in-law – in the window of a house in Rhode Sint Genesius, the biggest sansevieria in Belgium. And they say there are twenty million of them altogether, two for every living Belgian. Can you believe it? I have a friend who is writing a thesis on the cult. He is making very complicated theories about it, he thinks that it adds a vertical feature to life in the flat parts of the country, that these plants in the window give Belgians a feeling of looking out at the world through the edge of a jungle, just like the Belgae peering at the Romans from their forest – lots of interesting ideas. Anyway, it is he who has found these very big ones for me, exceeding by three centimetres the tallest which I have found. I have made friends with the owners and have measured them myself. Soon they will have to enlarge their windows upwards or buy a new house. Yes, seriously, it would be unthinkable not to display these plants properly. It is necessary to accept one's responsibilities. Have I not heard that English peasants insist on a larger cottage when their Alsatian puppy dogs grow up? It is the same thing, you see.'

They cycled through Verrewinkel, viewed the champion sansevieria in the outskirts of Rhode Saint Genèse and came to rest at a café for breakfast, still eight kilometres short of Waterloo.

Felix went to buy *Le Soir*, to see what was said about the kidnapping. It carried the story on the front page, but rather indecisively under a small headline. The facts were scanty, and all from the agency report. *Le Soir*'s own reporter merely added that 'diplomatic circles close to the highest authority at NATO were emphasising during the night that there was no evidence to suggest that other governments were behind the kidnapping'.

Marie considered this as she ate her croissant. 'How can they be so sure? They must have some clues already. They will probably find them today, probably not far away at all. I will make a big bet that they are still in Belgium, perhaps even in Brussels.'

'Well, I shouldn't be surprised if they are still in Belgium. The kidnappers must have expected a hue and cry quite soon, and they would plan to have the prisoners safely away in their hiding place before the search began. Going long distances and crossing frontiers would be risky from that point of view. But I can't see them going to ground in Brussels. Not with fifteen prisoners. There aren't many buildings where you could keep that number, and there are lots of police. Come to think of it, where could you hide that number of people?'

The Pentagon had been humming since before breakfast, Washington time. In particular, SKYWATCH had been humming. It had started humming, fed by the élite of its programmers, within 20 minutes of the call from Downing Street to the White House.

SKYWATCH was the Pentagon's newest computer. It was so called because it automatically absorbed and stored all the photographic information transmitted from satellites circling the globe. It also discarded it automatically when it was four weeks old. The bank of information which it contained also included the equivalent of two sets of the *Encyclopaedia*

Britannica in the form of information about ships of all sizes from fishing smacks up to ocean liners. This part of the bank was divisible by tonnage, and was currently set to operate only within the range of 100 to 10,000 tons.

The programmers had fed in to the geographical part of the memory bank, which in effect contained large-scale maps of every square mile of land in the world and medium-scale maps of every ten square miles of sea, a number of variable factors, such as cars travelling at 50, 75, 100 and 125 kilometres an hour from Brussels, starting at 1330 on the previous day and going to any one of 97 ports within 800 kilometres of the Belgian capital; together with ships setting out from any of these ports at any of the times calculated to be possible and travelling in any feasible direction at speeds of 10, 15, 20 and 30 knots.

SKYWATCH's diet also included the input, at a speed which equated an hour of real time with a hundredth of a second of computer time, of all recorded ship to shore radio traffic in Western Europe from 1400 Brussels time on the previous day up to the present.

Besides all this, some other information had been fed in. It was brought to the programmers by a lanky young man with corn-coloured hair and enormous rimless spectacles, a real spook. The programmers thought they knew about every category of intelligence. But when they saw this material they realised that there were at least two categories of which they had been ignorant. None of them referred to this revelation. The conversation was on a strictly superficial and technical level.

'We should have thought of it ourselves,' said one. 'Where *could* you hide that number of people, except at sea?'

'Or in the air?'

'No, you couldn't *hide* them in the air. Well, perhaps we could; but it's not Uncle Sam running this op, it's those shamrock-eating Paddies, and they probably haven't even got a small chopper to their name.'

'Well, the Irish say it's them, but it could be an almighty bluff. Me, I wonder. This idea of feeding the Committee to the fishes one by one sounds . . .'

'. . . fishy, huh?'

'You said it, Jim, not me. But seriously, suppose this baby proves that there's nothing afloat which matches the inputs. What then?'

'Look, the answers are starting to come out! Get them through the scanner.'

In fact, SKYWATCH was not producing answers in the plural. The progammers realised that the very special items of intelligence had narrowed the possibilities to a dramatic extent. One and only one answer emerged. The SS *Ballygowan*, four days out of Gdansk, and now en route from Lübeck to Lerwick and Cork. Mixed cargo. Maximum speed 15 knots. Normal speed 12 to 14. Owned by the Irish-Baltic Navigation Company, set up five years ago and in turn owned by Freightspeed, a company with its headquarters in Panama and of uncertain ownership. *Ballygowan* was 23 years old. Her master was Captain McCrory, age 52, native of Cork, nothing known against but wanted by the Aberdeen constabulary in connection with a brawl two years previously. . . . Had been hospitalised in Murmansk for six weeks in 1974 . . . Favourite beverage, Guinness stout . . .

And so on. No other vessel afloat even rated a mention. But there was one other little output. SKYWATCH had compared the text of the Irish message with those of all other previous such messages and announcements for syntax, word-use and phrase-use, and came up with the simple comment: ‘no incompatibility’.

That was when the messages started pouring eastwards across the Atlantic. The President very much wanted swift action by the British. He suggested that Royal Marines be flown out to the nearest available naval vessel, so that if necessary a powerful boarding party, sophisticated in hand-to-hand combat, could be used. The President had great faith in the Royal Marines, and was unaware of their numerical strength, which had changed considerably since his admiration for them had originally been formed.

The President also wished to have the suspect vessel shadowed at close range by a submarine, which would be ready to break water at a moment’s notice and retrieve any SPC member who had been thrown overboard. He was disconcerted to learn that a Soviet submarine was already following the *Ballygowan*, but at a distance of nine nautical miles. Neither he nor his advisers could provide a satisfactory explanation for this.

Marie pondered Felix’ question. Where *could* that number of people be hidden? Suddenly she thought of an answer.

‘You would need a château, or a large farm, what we call a château-farm. Belgium is full of such places.’

‘Indeed it is, but I don’t suppose many of them are empty unless they’re already in ruins.’

‘An empty one would be no good. The local people would notice at once if someone moved in. At least it would be very difficult to do it secretly, with fifteen prisoners and I suppose about ten guards.’

'Yes. But they could have been taken to a château which is already occupied, one big enough to conceal a prison area inside it. Even so, it wouldn't be easy. And I suppose that whoever's done it would have to be the owner of the château. But the owners of big châteaux aren't the sort of people to go in for mass kidnapping, are they? Or are they?'

'No, they are mostly très highlife – you know, counts and barons with names a metre long, or people who have made a fortune in the Congo or run chains of shops. Not criminals. Still, they sometimes let their châteaux in the hunting season, and we're right in the middle of that. Hmm . . . a large château, let to a hunting party, perhaps of foreigners who have brought their own servants with them . . . is this what we look for? It may not be so difficult. We must certainly consult my uncle, the one I told you about who lives near Vresse and fought the Germans during the occupation. He knows the whole Ardennes very well, and all the big estates. Oh, Felix, let me send him a telegram – he enjoys receiving them so much, that is why he will not instal a telephone – and then we can go and stay tomorrow night with him.'

Felix nodded as he paid the bill. 'If my legs hold out. I shall be stiff by this evening.'

'Not at all. I assure you that the distances are small. Imagine that you are Wellington, riding from Brussels to Waterloo. You are almost there now, and you should still be energetic enough to win a great battle. Let us not talk of stiff legs so soon. Besides, you must give thanks that you have both your legs. Soon you will see the tomb of one leg of your gallant countryman, Comte Uxbridge, a romantic structure over which ivy grows. There we will reflect on the good fortune which has preserved all our limbs, which we put to such good use.'

In fact, Felix was in good shape and his stamina as a cyclist would have aroused favourable comment in England. But he did not show up so well in Belgium, which regularly produces world champions such as Eddy Merckx, nor beside Marie, who had exceptionally powerful legs and the better bicycle. Older, but better. In a dealer's shop near the quayside at Ostend she had found an old FN tourer, with its original number plaque dated 1935 still bolted to the frame. As the dealer drily remarked, it fell in the category of 'one lady owner, has rolled very few kilometres', since it must have been in storage since 1936. One of Marie's neighbours and friends, by which term must be understood the whole population of the Marolles, had restored the machine, substituting aluminium replicas for certain of the heavier parts of the frame, and adding a special six-speed gear (hand made from pieces of discarded racing machines), Mafac brakes and special Michelin tyres. The FN now ran light and sweet.

Felix was having a magnificent old Clément Dambreville rehabilitated, but it was not ready yet. Meanwhile he rode a 1938 Raleigh tourer, fitted with horizontal handlebars, a contemporary Pifco dynamo set and the original Sturmey-Archer three speed gear. It was serviceable and gave no trouble but lacked the speed of Marie's machine. When they rode in single file Felix took care to be in front; otherwise he would have had difficulty in keeping station.

Captain Kistyakovsky was in a state of dismay. His trawler was supposed to keep station five nautical miles to the east of *Witch* and the two strange craft which were manoeuvring around her. So far there had been no problem. He had watched the big American helicopters fly out low over the water and had seen each in turn alight on *Witch*'s landing pad. He had counted forty men debarking from each; a hundred and twenty in all. He had reported this. But now *Witch* had altered course northwards and was increasing speed beyond what his manual told him was her maximum. Forty five knots, fifty, fifty five, sixty. The Soviet trawler, for all the mighty engines which occupied most of the space which would have usually been employed for the cold storage of fish, could not manage more than fifty three.

Kistyakovsky's feelings were shared in Moscow. But the men who worked in the long underground room under the east wall of the Kremlin showed no emotion. One of them ordered an enquiry into the circumstances which had led them to underestimate *Witch*'s maximum speed. In doing so he noted that there was a natural presumption that *Witch* was now proceeding at maximum speed, but that the possibility should be noted that she could go even faster. Another controlled the neat illuminated screen which showed what would be the relative positions of *Witch* and the trawlers two hours hence, four hours hence, and at nightfall.

The Chief of the Ops Room, Nekrasov, kept an eye on all this, but his own attention was concentrated on another screen, showing a relatively small area of sea, with the SS *Ballygowan* in the middle of it. One other vessel was within ten miles. Otherwise there was nothing within twenty five miles except for a couple of trawlers from Aberdeen; and they were steaming south, while *Ballygowan* pursued her slow path northwards.

Nekrasov pressed a button and the scale on his screen was diminished by a factor of four. He beckoned to a subordinate and told him to feed in to this new picture the information about *Witch*. It was at once apparent that *Witch*, with her escorts, was proceeding on a course desined to intercept *Ballygowan*, and that, if she kept up her present speed, the interception would occur in mid-afternoon. Nekrasov jotted down some notes and slipped upstairs with these.

The Soviet Chiefs of Staff took but two minutes to agree that the dilemma confronting them could only be resolved by their political masters. Either an existing source of intelligence must be, at least potentially, compromised; or the prospect of acquiring an important new operational capability would be jeopardised and perhaps lost. In concrete terms, *Witch* must not board *Ballygowan*. A means existed of diverting her, but it was not completely sure. An alternative procedure, also unsure and certainly embarrassing, would be to have *Ballygowan* boarded by her Soviet shadow and the two vital crates heaved over the side. But they were not the sort of crates which could be thus disposed of by, say, leaning on them. They were extremely heavy, for all their modest size.

The Chiefs knew precisely what decisions they wanted. But the paper they composed in three minutes flat was admirably dispassionate and well-balanced. Eight minutes later they had the reply which they wanted, and expected. The messages had already been prepared. The mere pressing of two buttons ensured that, doubly encased in one-time cyphers and compressed to a thousandth of a second so that the squeak which they made in the atmosphere was too brief to be recorded by the human ear, they would reach their destinations instantaneously.

The tomb of the leg of Lord Uxbridge was surrounded by nettles, in a private garden near the centre of the village of

Waterloo. Felix was not disposed to spend long looking at it, once he had read the simple inscription; but he remained in meditation for a couple of minutes, aware that Marie expected him to be moved by the sight. He was glad when she tugged gently at his sleeve and whispered, as if hesitating to disturb his reverie, 'Shall we go on?'

'Mm,' he said, 'yes, but thank you for bringing me here. I expect that I will prefer this to the bigger monuments on on the battlefield.'

'Your judgement is good. But now we must make a détour and approach the battlefield from the west, where the wind is. Otherwise we will be over-powered by the smell of frites, which are cooked all day long at the foot of the British monument. The cooking stoves of the friture stalls provide an everlasting flame, but it is not suitable as a means of honouring the dead soldiers. Indeed the entire place is to be deplored. You will have an unpleasant surprise, and you will also receive the impression that it was Napoleon who won the battle. Wait until we make a tour of the souvenir shops.'

Felix did not believe her until he had been round the shops. But in them he found busts of Napoleon, in wood and pottery and bronze and plastic and what appeared to be painted wax, sometimes wearing a laurel wreath on his head and always with the imperious expression of a victor; he saw Napoleonic calendars and ashtrays and cigar-boxes; he gasped at the opulence of a Limoges tea service in the Napoleon pattern and saw that the Faiencerie de Gien had produced a Napoleon cake service (1 plat et 12 assiettes à gâteaux dans un luxueux coffret); and all the time he looked in vain for traces of the Duke of Wellington. In the largest of the emporia he asked about Wellington. Led to a subsidiary rack of cheap, obsolete postcards he was shown a row of three, in black and white – Wellington, Blücher and the Prince d'Orange. That was all.

As they climbed the grassy pyramid of the Butte du Lion Marie comforted Felix. 'You must understand that it is only because most of the tourists who come here are French. We Belgians know very well that Wellington won the battle. Remember, we and the Dutchmen made up one third of his army, very nearly as many as the British. Waterloo was a great battle for us also. Now look round and I will explain to you the tactics of your great Duke.'

Up on top of the Butte the wind blew hard and cold, flapping their clothes and making Marie's explanations difficult to hear until Felix pulled her into the lee of the lion. There he held her close and she delivered her lecture at short range into his left ear, punctuating her vivid prose with nibbles while the long hair blew wildly like golden pennants between his eyes and the grassy slopes on which Napoleon's men had died. It was a good lecture.

By the time they had climbed down the hundred and fourteen steps it was ten o'clock and the gatekeeper's transistor was emitting the news in Flemish. Marie reported that the North Atlantic Council had held an emergency meeting about the missing diplomats and that a communiqué had been issued.

'Are they keeping the situation under continuous review?'

'Yes, how did you know?'

'I just did. Which way do we go?'

'East and then south. Follow me and look out for the frontier – we'll be crossing it soon'

'The frontier? But we're barely out of Brussels. What do you mean, the frontier?'

'Not the national frontier, woelekop, the linguistic frontier, *the* frontier, the line between the Flemings and Walloons. It runs about twenty kilometres south of Brussels, and we come to it in a few minutes. Observe, please, the significance of the fact that Napoleon was halted and turned back on the very line which marked the limit of the French language. Waterloo is a Flemish name. Quatre Bras, on the line of his retreat, is French.'

Marie blew her small melodious horn. 'Goodbye Flanders. Wallonia, here we come.'

'Do not worry, you will not find small battles taking place on the frontier. It has been stable for over a thousand years, after all, and is quite peaceful. Really, the Flemings and the Walloons would get along fine, if it was not for Brussels. You must understand that I am very dispassionate about this, being of the Marolles. I stand above the dispute. Let me explain it to you.'

'OK. As you're standing above it answer this one; why does Belgium hang together at all? If the Flemish part joined the Netherlands and the French-speaking part joined France, then here would be the new Netherlands/French frontier. Why not?'

Marie flung her hands up from the handlebars. 'Oh, such nonsense. Figure it for yourself. Would the Walloons really want to be the fiftieth department of France instead of half of Belgium? Would the Flemings like to be a mere province of the Netherlands, looked down on by those Hollanders? Impossible! Anyway, we are all Belgian, the name means something. Julius Caesar knew what it meant, when he wrote about the Belgae. Hah! they could show him some things, those ancestors of ours. Tell me, have you ever studied a map of the Roman roads in Western Europe?'

'Yes,' said Felix, forbearing to add more for fear of running quite out of breath as they rode speedily up an incline. He was slightly peeved to think that Marie had already forgotten hearing about his own Roman excavations ten years ago, in France.

'Well, have you not seen that in the whole web of roads there is one great gap – as if a bird had flown through the web and removed part of it? That gap is a large part of what is now Belgium. It is where Caesar could not go, because he was afraid of the forests and the fierce men. Think of that and then quickly revise your ideas about what is to be done with Belgium. Giving it to the French, or the Dutch, I do not know which is more absurd. It is inconvenient that we have two languages, but be sure that we have one country with which we are not going to part. Truly you are among the potatoes in thinking that this could happen.'

'Well, I didn't really think so, I just wondered how you would deal with the idea. You have an interesting historical perspective. I like the emphasis on Caesar. But since then . . .'

Felix fell back for a moment while a Citroën overtook them. Perceiving his train of thought, Marie diverted it.

'Of course, you are curious about the Middle Ages. So now we are going to descend through Cerous-Moustry to Villers-la-Ville to visit the ruins of the abbey. They are very romantic, even in winter. We shall embrace each other in the warming chamber, the object of learned remarks by Viollet-le-Duc.'

The Council meeting called for noon actually began at noon, on the dot. Word had spread rapidly that a clue to the identity of the kidnappers had been received, that it had something to do with Ireland and that the UK PermRep was going to make a statement.

However, the SG chose to take things in chronological order. He told the Council that Sir Ambrose had an important statement to make, but that this would best follow an official account of the first supposed sign of activity by the kidnappers, namely the wives' meeting which they, or a person purporting to represent them, had arranged at Mrs Lute's house that morning. Those delegations which had the privilege of being represented on the SPC by married men would no doubt have heard about this already. However, Mrs Lute had been asked by the other wives to represent them and to give to him, the Secretary-General, a full account of how the meeting had been arranged. The Permanent Representative of the UK was fully in agreement with this procedure, and he had no reason to think that anyone else would object.

The SG then gave a slightly condensed account of what Beta had told him.

'This, then, was the first apparent communication from the kidnappers. It contained nothing which would tend to identify them or their motives. On the other hand, it gave a strong impression of . . . perhaps courtesy is the right word. In the circumstances I find this surprising, yet plausible.

'However, there has been a second message, which cannot be declared to be wholly incompatible with the first, but which seems, to judge by its content and its tone, to come from quite a different source. This further message was delivered in London several hours ago. It identified the kidnappers in general terms, explained their motives – although not, perhaps, their choice of victims – and stated very exactly their ransom terms. I now ask our colleague from the United Kingdom to make the statement which you are all anxious to hear.'

Sir Ambrose spoke precisely and methodically.

'First, the facts, which are few. A telephone call was made this morning at approximately 0938, from an unidentified source, to the personal assistant of the Assistant Under-Secretary in the Northern Ireland Office in London who is in charge of administrative matters. I am sorry, that was rather a long sentence. As the Council may be aware, the Northern Ireland Office was set up some years ago to deal with the political and security problems of Northern Ireland. It contains a number of senior officials, mostly concerned with the political aspects of the problem. There is, however, one such official who deals with administration in the normal sense of the word. It was his secretary who received the telephone call.

'The caller spoke with a slight but fully recognisable Irish accent. He said that he had an important message for the Assistant Under-Secretary, and asked the p.a. to take it down in shorthand. She did so, and I can therefore read the message to you verbatim. It ran as follows: "The Senior Political Committee have been taken into custody by a group of Irish patriots. They are now at sea and their safety is assured for the time being. Their return can be assured quickly by the British Government taking the following steps. First, all prisons in Northern Ireland will be opened, cell doors, inner doors, outer doors, the lot. Second, all activity by prison staff, after this has been done, will be suspended for twelve hours. Third, all activity by the British Army and the police will be suspended for the same period. Once this has been done, the Committee will be landed safe and sound within a further period of twelve hours. If this is not done by 8 a.m. local time tomorrow, Friday, the safety of the Committee will no longer be assured. They will be dropped into the sea, one by one at hourly intervals, and will have to look out for themselves when they are in the water. That ends the message. Have you got it all down?"

'The secretary said that she had it all down and the man rang off. Meanwhile no steps had been taken to trace the call. The secretary was, of all the secretaries in the building, the one least likely to be involved in the receipt of such a message, and she simply took it as her duty to take it down. Once the caller had rung off she reported the matter instantly, but by then there was no technical possibility of tracing the call.'

Sir Ambrose paused. 'I should perhaps add that certain installations exist in the Northern Ireland Office which might have proved useful on this occasion. But for reasons which hardly require explanation these installations do not cover the . . . ah . . . less sensitive parts of the department. This information is of course given in strict confidence.

'So much for the facts. I am instructed by my government to add the following comments. First, the message is being treated very seriously. Every possible step is being taken to verify it and to trace the vessel in which the Committee are allegedly imprisoned. A full alert has been called in Northern Ireland. Special security precautions have been re-introduced in Whitehall, at all airports in the U.K. and at all seaports, however small. Aerial reconnaissance on a massive scale is in progress over the North Sea and adjacent waters.

'Secondly, although Her Majesty's Government are taking the matter so seriously, they are inclined on balance to doubt the authenticity of the telephone call. These doubts have nothing to do with the content of the call or the manner in which it was made. Both are fully consistent with previous demands and methods of communication used by the Provisional IRA. But the action of kidnapping a NATO committee is considered to be uncharacteristic, and also beyond their scope. It is an enterprise very different from hurling a bomb through a window.

'My authorities have, naturally, compared this latest development with the earlier summons of the wives to meet at Mrs Lute's house. It is their tentative opinion that there can be no connection between the two communications. We may believe the authenticity of one, or of the other, or of neither; but not of both.'

Sir Ambrose paused again. 'We are in touch with the Government of the Republic of Ireland, and await their views. We shall also be most interested to have the reactions of our allies.

'Meanwhile, although no public statement has been made, we must reckon with the possibility that the kidnappers, if the message is a genuine one, will choose to make their demands public at any moment. We must also, to be realistic, expect that the press will soon receive from one source or another at least a hint of what has happened. Certain movements by units of our armed forces will be attracting attention. It is for consideration whether a public statement should be made forthwith, either by HMG or on behalf of NATO, in order to pre-empt garbled versions of the story.'

The Secretary-General invited comments.

The US PermRep said that his government agreed with the British action, which they were in fact assisting, and with their analysis. No-one dare assume that the Irish message was without foundation. But on balance it seemed likely to be a piece of opportunism by the Provos. So long as the real kidnappers kept their identity and aims concealed, it was open to any group of activists or terrorists to claim credit for the operation and to pose conditions for the release of prisoners they did not hold.

The Frenchman also had a comment. He was particularly struck by the delivery of flowers to the wives. One could not condone kidnapping, but even the baser activities of mankind could be conducted with a certain style, or without it. It was important to consider style, for – as that famous English proviseur, Guillaume de Wykeham, had said – it is the manners which make the man. (Sir Ambrose blinked slightly at this.) Flaubert had expressed the same sentiment, in the narrower domain of literature, when he said *le style c'est l'homme*. It was well-known that the style of those responsible for violence in Northern Ireland did not comprehend, indeed appeared to exclude, acts of gallantry towards the fair sex. To execute a crime with gallantry was still to execute a crime; but the additional element of gallantry helped to define the criminals and could be an important clue.

The Council absorbed these remarks, which had been delivered at high speed. The Secretary-General, sensing that there were no further comments, sought to close the discussion on a lighter note.

'I trust that these remarks will not be interpreted by anyone as pointing the finger of accusation at the countrymen of that ally in which the tradition of gallantry is most firmly established! . . . However, I assume, my dear colleague, that these were your personal reflections on the matter, and on that basis I thank you for them.'

'Oh, no,' said the Frenchman with complete solemnity, 'I should perhaps have said that I was speaking on the instructions of my government.'

This insight into the deliberations of the French Government was received in a bemused silence. The

Secretary-General was the first to return from the brief reverie thus induced, and reminded the Council that the question of press enquiries had still to be settled.

The Council eventually decided against an official statement. Naturally, if the British Government felt compelled to make one, they should do so. But it might be preferable to wait until there were signs of press interest and then deal with it by off-the-record guidance, in which stress would be laid on the absence of any proof that the committee were in Irish hands.

Just before the meeting was adjourned, the NATO spokesman handed a piece of paper to the Secretary-General. The SG read it.

'Our decision was timely, gentlemen. The news has broken. Several representatives of the press are already in the building, waiting to see our spokesman. It is fortunate that he already has his brief.'

Chapter 8

It was Alexander the Great, listening to the BBC, who first heard the Irish story. He hastened to seek out Anna, who was peacefully eating an autumn pear in her room in the tower.

Anna was furious. Alexander had never seen her angry before; still less had he seen her suffused, as now, by total wrath.

'How *dare* they, how *could* they dare to claim what is *our* achievement, *our* prize? They must be exposed at once. Where is our statement? Let's issue it now, I could never understand why it had to wait until tonight.'

Alexander eyed her anxiously. It seemed to him important that she should regain her usual calm.

'We were waiting until tonight so as to heighten the suspense,' he reminded her, 'and there were technical reasons too – you remember, Tim explained them. But I agree, this is a new situation. I don't think we can accelerate the statement. The machinery is already in motion and the timing is very exact. But we could surely do something additional, and quicker. Look, let me get Franz – he's sure to think of something; and Tim or Pete, since it's really a matter for the press. It's they who are spreading the Irish story, and they'll have to kill it.'

Anna paced up and down, brandishing the jewelled knife with which she had been dissecting the pear. 'Very well, fetch them at once. Never mind what they're busy doing, this has priority.'

It was Franz, the master of mystification, who saw at once how the situation must be clarified.

'Don't forget that so far as the governments are concerned, the Irish message was the second. Our message to the wives this morning was the first. They'll be well aware of that. And I don't think that ours could have sounded remotely Irish to anyone. Not that sort of Irish. I mean most Irish are charming, but not the terrorists. My bet is that the governments are taking us seriously, even though they don't know who we are, and that they already suspect the Irish of bluffing. The question is, how do we prove them right. As I see it, some tangible evidence is needed. There are the flowers we sent, but anyone could have arranged that; and apart from them there's really nothing for anyone to go on but telephone calls, is there?'

Anna eyed him warily. 'What do you mean by tangible evidence?'

'Oh, Anna, you almost look as though you expect me to send one of the prisoner's ears or something. Do relax. We've all agreed all along that we're not even going to hint at violence. None of us would agree; and even a hint would ruin our public image. We're the . . . the Velvet Glove Brigade, if you like, the Kindly Kidnappers.'

Anna looked mollified. She had in fact always fancied herself in velvet gloves, and possessed more than one pair.

'That's quite a good name. Perhaps we should even use it. The Velvet Glove one, I mean. But what is this tangible evidence you are thinking of?'

'Well . . . how about some of their clothes? A shoe or a tie or something. That would be unmistakeable. We could get it to Brussels in two hours.'

Alexander the Great looked thoughtful. 'True, but what

do we prove by delivering, shall we say, a shoe belonging to the Englishman to his wife? Why could it not have come from the Irish?'

Franz thought for a moment. 'The Irish say they have them at sea. They couldn't send a shoe ashore, not very easily. Still, I see what you mean, just a shoe coming through the letterbox doesn't really prove anything. There has to be a note with it.'

'And that must be from one of the prisoners, in his own writing, and must show that he is not at sea. I remember looking at their shoes and noticing that one pair was very worn. Let me check, I shan't be more than two minutes.'

While Alexander the Great was away looking at the shoes, Franz took a piece of paper and started to draft:

"Dear [?], My captors have kindly pointed out that these shoes, which I shall not need until I am released, require repair, and this could conveniently be done during my absence. Could you please arrange this? I am sorry that I cannot tell you anything about our captors, except that they are treating us well; nor about where we are, except that we are safe and sound on terra firma. [Signature]"

Alexander returned holding aloft a pair of black shoes.

'I knew it. They belong to the Norwegian and the heels are worn right down. And look at these cuts on the left toe-cap. They really need attention. And the name of the Oslo shop where he got them is still legible. What more could we want?'

Anna was silent, apparently pursuing a further line of thought.

Franz examined the shoes without touching them. 'I like them. But we must take off all fingerprints. And has it occurred to you that microscopic examination of the dust particles adhering to them might reveal something? The stone of which this château is built may be distinctive, and invisible fragments of it may have fallen into the shoes.'

Alexander looked discomforted.

'But don't worry. Let me visit the Mystification Store, and all will be well.'

While Franz was away, Anna said, more to herself than to Alexander, 'It is too slow, we must do something long before the shoes reach Brussels . . .'

Franz bore back with him a glass jar containing layers of coloured sand. A label, designed without taste, declared the contents to be 'A Souvenir of Alum Bay'.

'I picked this up in the Isle of Wight. I also have some sand from the Sahara in stock and some mud from the banks of the Amazon which I got a friend to send me. But this will be best, it is completely distinctive.'

He opened the jar, poured out some sand of various colours into a saucer, added a little water and mixed it into a paste. He dipped the soles and heels of the shoes into the paste, which adhered.

'Now, when it is almost dry, we shall shake the shoes so that only a little sand remains. Then we'll put them in a plastic bag, a strictly unattributable bag, you understand, and arrange a drop in Brussels and a telephone call either to NATO or to *Le Soir*. But first we must explain the affair to the Norwegian and persuade him to write the note. To whom shall we send it? There's no wife, not even a mistress. So to his Permanent Representative, I think. That would be a pleasant touch, to ask his master to have his shoes repaired.'

'All right,' said Anna, 'I see the point. Pete had better take the shoes up.' She paused. 'If he stayed the night he could go to Rob's in the morning and pick up some tins of coeurs de palmier – I forgot them.'

'Yes, of course,' said Franz, 'you can give him a whole shopping list if you like. But first I must find Sister Agnes and have her talk to the Norwegian. It may take a few minutes to explain it all to him. May I?'

Anna nodded and he left. Then Anna turned to Alexander the Great and made a slight moue of discontent.

'What worries me is that if the wives think their husbands are really in the hands of these Irish, they will be in agonies of fear. By the time the shoes have been dropped and picked up and the handwriting identified it will be – it could even be tomorrow morning. That is too long.'

Alexander assented cautiously.

'The husbands will not wish their wives to go through this ordeal. The same applies to the unmarried men and their relations. So any of them would co-operate with us in killing the story.'

'Ye-es.'

'Now, why should there not be a telephone call within the next ten minutes? We would choose one of them who has a very distinctive voice, brief him, give him a statement to record, play it over the telephone to the Paris cell and let them replay it to someone at NATO who would recognise the voice. The statement would say that tangible evidence would follow.'

'Yes, that's technically possible, I think. We'd have to check with Pete. But I don't like the idea of using a telephone to NATO. Since our phone calls this morning they've had half a day to arrange bugging and to plug in call-tracing devices. Still, we could try it, and then we might even manage without sending the shoes. The voice should be enough by itself.

Anna smiled. 'You forget. The Paris cell have the use of the phone in that empty apartment in rue Jacob. It would be perfectly safe, so long as they were in and out in three minutes, which is quite enough time. And I do think that we should send the shoes. Something tangible is needed.'

Alexander wondered to himself whether what were really needed were the coeurs de palmier. But he agreed, and departed to make the further arrangements.

It turned out that Anna's estimate of ten minutes was reasonably accurate. Only thirteen minutes elapsed before the recorded message had been heard by the Norwegian Permanent Representative at NATO. What was more, engineers had already installed a selective recording device in the NATO switchboard. So everyone could listen to a recording of the recording; and all doubts were thus silenced. Two agency reporters towards whom the NATO spokesman felt a transient obligation were allowed to hear it.

Thus was killed the Irish story, at a few minutes before three o'clock. But it did not quite lie down. The arrival of the parcel and its accompanying note, heralded for the evening, was still awaited with a certain curiosity. And the accidental interfacing of the amateur stratagems of the man Kevin and of Anna and her team with the ultra-professional machinery of the Pentagon and the Kremlin continued for a while to produce bizarre results.

By half past twelve Felix and Marie were in the huge romanesque warming chamber. Despite the dim winter light Marie fitted strong sun-glasses over Felix' eyes. 'So that you cannot see the vulgar messages carved on the walls. Imagine now that it is sunrise and the monks are coming in numb with cold from singing lauds – this is what Viollet-le-Duc explains – and here in front of the great fire they become warm again and grease their stiff sandals.'

Felix quickly transferred the sun-glasses from his eyes to hers. 'Let's imagine that two of the monks are still cold.' He warmed them both up. With her eyes masked by the pale green discs, in which he could see nothing but architectural details, Marie had a different look, cooler and strongly Renaissance. The Flemish tilt of her pale lips snapped into focus, tripping some of the few switches in Felix which she had not yet pulled.

She struggled free and ran laughing through the roofless refectory and kitchen to the cloisters. She still had two things to display. One was a notice bidding the visitor protect the bats' nests. The other was a main railway line running on a viaduct through the monks' burial ground.

'Do you begin to think that we Belgians are your rivals in quaintness?' she asked, putting on the sun-glasses again with the intention, which was immediately successful, of provoking him. 'Be careful of the bats' nests,' she added, as she landed on her back on a moss-covered tomb, 'and look, here comes a groupe scolaire.' Felix picked her up again. She smiled at the chattering school children as they passed them on the way out.

The bus which had brought the school children stood at the gate. Felix and Marie eyed it thoughtfully as they remounted and set off to the south-east for Namur and lunch and the afternoon run down the Meuse to Dinant. Traffic was light on the east bank of the river. Well before sunset they were already sweeping through Dinant, only a short distance from Famignoul, their night stop.

The *Ballygowan* was hove to, rolling in a slight swell sixty miles north-east of Aberdeen. The master had been puzzled during the afternoon by the frequency with which military aircraft had swooped down out of the cloud cover and overflown his ship, often at very close range. Some had been Russian, some British and some American. They had made no attempt to signify any wishes to him, but he had felt uneasily that they wanted something. He greatly feared being made to put into Aberdeen.

What caused him to heave to was the submarine. It surfaced on his port bow at 1510, three hundred yards away, travelling on almost the same course. When it had closed the distance to less than a hundred yards a man climbed out of the conning tower and hailed the *Ballygowan* over a loud-hailer.

'Attention, attention. With us is a sick man. We wish to bring him to you. The matter concerns his life. I ask you, stop your engines and we will come.'

While this was happening, the chief mate drew attention to a phenomenon astern. A large vessel, flanked by two squat ones of unusual shape, was closing in on the *Ballygowan* at a speed which seemed incredible. A signal light winked from the bridge of the centre vessel.

'Heave to. We have had a small explosion, with casualties. Sick bay damaged. Grateful for any medical supplies you have on board.'

'Seems like a bloody epidemic,' said the master to the chief mate, after he had stopped the engines. He prayed silently to his favourite saint, Ursula. 'Let it not be a trick, let it not bring us into Aberdeen, in the name of all that is holy let us sail on to Cork.'

A second figure emerged from the conning tower of the

submarine and conferred with the first. The first hesitated, then raised his loud-hailer again.

'One minute, please. It seems that sick man feels himself better. One minute, please, we will tell you.'

Both men disappeared into the conning tower.

The vessel astern had now closed to a couple of miles and slackened speed. She resumed winking.

'Thank you very much. Damage now under control. Reserve medical supplies have been found. Please proceed.'

The vessel and her escorts wheeled to starboard. It was now plain that she was a large destroyer, almost cruiser-size, and that the escorts were hydrofoils. They gathered speed and were hidden in a curtain of spray as they rushed towards the eastern horizon.

The submarine quietly submerged. The foaming bubbles which showed where she had been persisted for only a few seconds. The *Ballygowan* was alone again.

The master waited a couple of minutes, then moved the lever to 'Half Ahead'. He gave thanks to Saint Ursula as the ship gathered way and headed northwards once more.

Marie had a date in Famignoul with the custodian of the Musée du Vélo, whose genial moustache quivered with pleasure when they finally alit at his door. He had managed to find an original 1935 FN pump, the one piece of equipment which her model lacked. While she happily tested it in the courtyard he took Felix round the museum, explaining with an enthusiasm which five thousand repetitions had not dimmed the history of the bicycle, beginning with what were little more than scooters and ending with a modern racing machine on which Eddy Merckx had scored some of his innumerable triumphs.

Felix grasped for the first time that the bicycle and the tricycle had led to the motor-car. All the evidence was there before him. The invention of the bicycle suddenly stood out as one of the fundamental events in the history of mankind, an event strangely uncelebrated.

Felix' interest led the custodian to even loftier flights of eloquence. 'Let us then go back to the second room. Here you see the first true bicycle, the work of Ernest Michaux, a boy, a mere gosse of fourteen years, to whom in 1860 came the revelation of supreme importance, that a wheel could be driven by pedals. From this, from the genius of this gosse, unremarked save in his natal Bar-le-Duc, followed everything – but everything. Did it not lead to the tricycle with an engine which I have showed you? Did this not produce the motor-car? Is not the aeroplane derived from the motor-car? Let us honour then Ernest Michaux, while according equal praise to our compatriot Charles Rousseau, to whom God gave the privilege of inventing three, yes three, essential parts of the bicycle. You ask what they were? But, the chain, the supremely important chain, which he conceived in 1871. And the brake. Hah, if you had braked a bicycle, as men used to do, by holding your gloved hand on the wheel, you would realise the importance of this. And thirdly, the bell, the voice of this magic new machine, without which it would have been for ever silent.'

Felix caught the excitement. 'I must go to Bar-le-Duc and pay honour to Ernest Michaux. But is it in Belgium? And where did Rousseau work? Is there a shrine in his memory?'

'Ah, Monsieur, it must be admitted that from the technical point of view Bar-le-Duc is in France. Our great river, the Meuse, does not lie wholly within our frontiers. Bar-le-Duc stands on the banks of its upper waters which flow down to us and attain their true place in geography as they wind through the countryside of Belgium. Even so the adolescent inspiration of Ernest Michaux found, in Belgium, its ultimate destiny. Now I will tell you how to reach Les Isnes, which is . . .'

Marie interrupted from the doorway, 'But I know it well, I can take Felix there. Now tell me, Felix, are you convinced that Belgium is the cradle of modern transport as well as of modern building?'

'Almost. The importance of the bicycle is clear to me. But I am trying to balance the invention of pedals against chain, brake and bells, to weigh the claims of France against those of Belgium.'

'What? That is not the correct equation. Our patriotic friend had omitted one item. In the scale of Michaux must be added the free wheel, which he thought of later but which is very important. A bicycle without a free wheel is a pénible affair for the rider. Yet it is still a bicycle. Perhaps the free wheel is not fundamental. Nor is the tandem, that other invention of Michaux, so romantic and practical. But that reminds me, we must hurry now to our lodgings. We will complete the analysis as we ride south tomorrow.'

'Yes. I'm hungry.'

'But we shall not eat immediately. I am too excited by my new pump.' Marie clasped the pump to her left breast, and fireworks erupted from her eyes.

It took them only a few minutes to cover the kilometre from the museum to the low stone farmhouse which had a Chambres notice perched beside the sansevieria in the window.

The arrangement was quite clear, although it had only once been used. If Number Ten heard that Zhukov was on the way to them, a secretary would go at once to the back entrance of the Cabinet Office to await him, and the Principal Private Secretary would take the underground passage to the cubicle reserved for their meetings.

There was no way of smuggling Zhukov in. He had to have a pass and an identity as an official of either the Ministry of Defence or the Foreign Office. The MOD had jibbed at the idea, but the FO – or, to be precise, the Foreign Secretary, the PUS and the Head of Security Department, who were the only ones to know – had acquiesced readily. They agreed with Number Ten that that arrangement could in certain circumstances be superior to the 'hot line'. Thus it had come about that a First Secretary of the Soviet Embassy possessed a pass, punctiliously replaced every three months, which showed him to be Mr George Lensky of the Foreign and Commonwealth Office.

Zhukov was having his tête-à-tête with the PPS in the cubicle by two minutes to three.

'You are wondering whether the missing NATO committee is aboard a certain Irish ship, is this not so?'

'Yes.'

'They are not. I am instructed to give you this message for the Prime Minister.'

'Thanks. I'll pass it on. Does it come with any supporting evidence?'

Zhukov allowed himself a faint smile. 'I hoped you would not ask, but since you do, please read this transcript of a telephone conversation which took place at 0932 this morning. I regret I cannot leave the text with you, but you are at liberty to read it several times.'

The PPS read it. It was convincing. As he re-read it, he considered the implications. It seemed unlikely that the Russians would be deliberately discrediting the present channel of communication, which they themselves had suggested. So the information was almost certainly real. But its disclosure provided at least a glimpse of an aspect of Soviet intelligence which Whitehall believed to exist but of which there had been no previous evidence. So it must be very important indeed for the Russians that the Irish message be exposed as a bluff. Why?

He decided to ask Zhukov. 'This is most useful. May I know for what reason you have shown it to me?'

Zhukov nodded. 'Certainly. And I shall answer your question. It is our aim to further good relations between our two countries. On this basis the decision has been taken to share with your authorities a piece of intelligence which happened to fall into our hands.'

The PPS smiled. 'It is good of you to give such a full and frank explanation.'

Zhukov smiled and retrieved the piece of paper.

'One more question. Have your authorities any idea where the missing men are, or who kidnapped them?'

'No,' replied Zhukov. He looked the PPS full in the eyes. 'We have no idea. The information available to us is purely negative. That is a full and frank statement.'

Zhukov was still smiling as he was escorted out. He walked under the archway under the old Treasury building and across the Horse Guards parade. His car was waiting for him near the Athenaeum. Two bishops were emerging therefrom, deep in what was presumably a theological discussion. Elements of this were being emphasised by the stabbing and rotatory motions in the air of the episcopal umbrellas, which their owners neglected to unfurl despite the drizzle now descending.

Zhukov smiled again as he settled back in the rear seat of the car, an inconspicuous Marina which was stabled separately from the official Embassy fleet of Zils and which had never been seen to draw up at the Embassy's door.

The Marina had travelled half a mile and was halted by a traffic light outside the Ritz when Zhukov noticed the placard with which a vendor of the *Evening Standard* was luring customers. 'Irish hoax exposed'. Zhukov made a rapid calculation, knowing that the answer was going to come out wrong. His journey had been unnecessary. The story had already been dead when he reached the Cabinet Office. This was unfortunate. He had carried out his task impeccably, but his superiors would not be pleased. 'Stop for a minute,' he bade the driver. 'Pull up wherever you can.' The lights changed and the driver drew up outside the main door of the Ritz. Knowing him, Zhukov knew that he would not budge from there until his return, however many commissionaires and traffic wardens might assail him.

Zhukov paused to buy an *Evening Standard*, and glanced through it as he entered the Ritz and made for the nearest telephone booth. He dialled the special number and asked for the extension triple zero. The familiar voice of the PPS came on the line.

'Lensky here. I see that the news which I brought you has also reached the newspapers.'

'Yes, I found it in the evening paper when I got back to my room.'

'May I ask you one thing, please?'

'Of course.'

'My authorities attached importance to the message I gave

you. I should like to think that it was decisive in convincing your government.'

The PPS understood perfectly. He also saw an opportunity for himself. The PM had asked him whether he had made a point of telling Zhukov that any further information, whether negative or positive, would be welcome; and he had had to reply that this had not been said explicitly. A small lapse.

'I think I can answer your question. But may I first ask one of you?'

'Of course.'

'Would you kindly tell your authorities that we should welcome any further information, whether negative or positive, but especially if positive? And would you say that this response comes from the highest level?'

'Certainly. Speaking personally, I can say that the request seems entirely reasonable. Speaking officially, I can only say that it will be brought to the attention of my authorities, at the highest level, immediately.'

'Thanks. Now the answer to your question. I think that it would be right to say that your communication was a decisive factor in decisions which have been taken in the last few minutes.'

'Ah, that is good. I notice that you say "a", not "the decisive factor". Is this significant?'

The PPS paused. 'No, I don't think so. The definite and indefinite articles are easily confounded and often interchangeable.'

'Thank you very much for this clarification.'

As Zhukov drove away he was mentally drafting the second paragraph of his report. 'I was able to establish that, although certain press reports on similar lines had appeared at about the same time, your message was QUOTE the decisive factor UNQUOTE in influencing the decision in the British Government. The exact nature of the decision was not revealed to me, but it seems probable that it consisted in the cancellation of all measures in relation to *Ballygowan*.'

Meanwhile, the PPS put his head round the PM's door. 'Oh, by the way, sir, that request that I should have made of our friend. He telephoned just now and I made it, with full emphasis.'

The PM nodded approval. 'Good – and you might let me know when we hear definitely that *Witch* has been called off her wild Irish goose chase.'

Across Whitehall, in the Ministry of Defence, the Chiefs of Staff were conferring with a visitor.

'The whole thing's too bloody strange unless they had some really vital reason for distracting attention from that damned Irish boat. Don't you think?'

'I do. The Soviet sub is still there. And *Ballygowan* has been quite a regular visitor to Gdansk and to a couple of smallish ports in East Germany.'

'It isn't too difficult to think of what she might be taking to Cork.'

'Or to Lerwick. Think of the oil installations.'

'Have we got someone there?'

'Oh yes. And he's being put into the picture.'

The Soviet Chiefs of Staff were also communing with a visitor.

'It will be better to cancel the operation, that is my opinion. *Witch* might easily have boarded her, but for the prompt action of our friend here. And some suspicions may remain.'

'I agree, but let us postpone rather than cancel.'

'Of course, that is understood. But *Ballygowan* must return to Gdansk.'

'Agreed. It will be arranged.'

'Can we be sure? I understand that the captain is only semi-conscious.'

'Less than that. But he does what his owners tell him to do. He will be changing course within an hour or two.'

'Alexander,' said Anna.

'Yes?'

'You don't think that I made too much fuss about that telephone call – I mean doing it so quickly?'

'No.' Alexander the Great's reply was reassuringly thoughtful. 'One never knows when a few minutes, one minute even, may count.'

'Good.' Anna picked up her knife and began to peel a fresh pear.

The SPC had been quite excited after lunch, when the Norwegian was led away by Sister Agnes and later returned with his weird but finally comprehensible tale of Irishmen and shoes being sent for repair. However, he showed some sensitivity over the circumstance that his shoes were the ones chosen as needing repair, and was less communicative about the whole affair than he might have been. The afternoon relapsed into dullness. The Committee did sit down again to do some drafting, but Piet's presence in the background, tart and disapproving, dried their tongues and halted their pencils.

Only the Chairman seemed cheerful and alert, and it was he who had had the idea of forming sub-committees which could sit in various corners of the hall discussing particular kinds of pollution. This tactic diluted the discouragement which Piet now had to radiate in four different directions, and some of the sub-committees finished the afternoon with a feeling of slight accomplishment.

The Chairman was cheerful because he was beginning to have an idea of where he was. Lying in the German's cubicle after lunch, he had managed to strain out the hum of noise from the other cubicles and the hall and to concentrate his whole aural capacity on whatever faint sounds might come down from the ventilation grid in the ceiling. He guessed that this grid must be the nearest to the main ventilation inlet, and thus the only one through which the outside world could be heard. For twenty minutes he heard nothing. Perhaps there was a faint sighing of the wind: more probably his imagination. Then suddenly it came.

'Tcha, tcha, tcha,' faint but unmistakable, 'tcha, tcha, tcha.' It was a collective sound, the product of hundreds of tiny throats. He recognised it at once as the noise of *Turdus pilaris*, the fieldfare or *grive litorne*, which migrates southwards over Belgium during November. The Chairman could visualise the charts and dates in his ornithological handbook. The birds flew down a band of country in the Ardennes as though through a funnel, and then spread out across France on their way to the Mediterranean and Africa. The period of passage through the Ardennes was 20 October to 30 November. So now, on around 8 or 9 November, he could be up to twenty days' flight north or south of the Ardennes on one of the paths of migration. Or of course, right in the Ardennes. The Chairman thought of the next page in his handbook, and of the habits of the redwing, *Turdus iliacus*. Flies by night. Stragglers make a pitiful little whistling noise as they fly in the wake of the main groups. 'Ssih, ssih, ssih'. Through the Ardennes funnel in the second week in November. Known there as the *roussette* or the *grive mauvis*. So, if they could be heard during the night, that would place the prison in the Ardennes beyond any reasonable doubt. Provided that they had not been kept in a drugged state for days, the date had to be more or less right. But the Chairman was fairly sure that it was. And he was fairly sure that if he stayed awake during the night he would hear that 'ssih, ssih, ssih'. Once one thought of the Ardennes, they seemed like the obvious area for Anna, who had no interest in conveying them across political frontiers, to choose.

So the Chairman rejoiced, and wondered what he should do with his knowledge. Somehow it should give him a hold over Anna. But as he thought of Anna he found himself wishing not so much to discomfort as to impress her. He fancied that she would be ready to admire his detective work, that she would provide a more responsive audience than his colleagues; especially if Piet was still souring the atmosphere.

Piet was still souring the atmosphere at dinner. He had been a lonely boy during the first eighteen years of his life, a shy and puzzled young husband for six months in war-time Amsterdam, and a widower ever since. Dedication to his work, buttressed by an ambition which was not entirely natural to him, provided a counterweight to his need for human sympathy; a need which affected him deeply, and which he sometimes acknowledged to himself, but never tried to satisfy. Normally, he sheltered behind a gruff manner, which was acceptable in a single man of his age and even caused his colleagues to regard him with a superficial affection. But now, under the stress of captivity, he found himself under an intermittent compulsion to be actively disagreeable.

It was especially irritating for him that dinner began with erwtensoep, made just the way he liked it, with little slices of sausage swimming among the vegetables. Tertia served him first, and he reluctantly gave her a brief appreciative smile, hoping that like a lighthouse he could flash it in her direction alone and that it would go unnoticed by the others at table.

Tertia found Sister Agnes being made up by Ingrid. 'Ho, ho, you will have to work hard, my North Sea siren,' she proclaimed, 'you cannot imagine how sour this Dutchman is. He looks as though he has come straight out of a jar of pickles. If you can set him on fire you can set wet haystacks on fire.'

Sister Agnes was nervous enough without this. But not nervous like someone who is going to lose a fight; nervous like someone who is impatient to start.

'Go away, Tertia, I'm sure you ought to be washing up or something. And tell Anna not to forget her announcement, and to make it as soon as supper's finished.'

Anna did not need reminding. She and Franz were seriously concerned about Piet. Until he was brought under control they could not hope for any really constructive work from the Committee. And the Committee had to start working effectively soon. They would be indispensable when it came to negotiating and drafting terms. By that time they must be working like a team, and on Anna's side. Franz felt that today's setback was so alarming that they ought to consider postponing their first announcement to the world, planned for the next day; and Anna was half inclined to agree. She reached for the microphone.

'Good evening, gentlemen. I have some announcements to make.

'Our physical exercise programme will start tomorrow. A trained instructress will be in charge of you, and has devised a course which takes account of your age and physical condition. It should be of great benefit to you. The exercises will be performed at 11 each morning until further notice, and should take about twenty minutes. You will be asked to remove your djebbahs while exercising.

'The representatives of Belgium, Iceland, Italy and the United Kingdom will please remain behind in the hall when I have finished so that they can receive messages from a member of the staff about their wives. I will not trespass on the privacy of these gentlemen by broadcasting the messages; but I am sure that the company as a whole will be glad to hear that the four ladies of whom we have news tonight are in good health.

'From tomorrow the library will be open. Some work has to be done in making it ready, and the member of my staff who is working there this evening has asked for one helper from your number. I have selected the representative of the Netherlands to help her, as he has been especially well fortified for this small task by the Dutch dinner which we served this evening. He will be escorted to the library in five minutes' time, and escorted back to his cubicle when the librarian signifies that she has done all that is necessary in preparation for tomorrow.'

Franz winked at Anna, who returned a faint smile.

Downstairs the benign German winked at Piet, who returned a very faint smile.

In the costume room Ingrid winked at Sister Agnes, who responded by practising her innocently mischievous smile. She was good at this. Ingrid had fitted her with a kingfisher blue cocktail dress, mid-calf-length, thought to have first escaped from its peg in the Army and Navy Stores in 1938.

Lute was last in the queue for wife-tidings, of which James Minor was the dispenser.

'Mrs Lute is perfectly well. She says that you are not to worry at all. Millicent is well also, and has become the most important girl in her class because of your disappearance. And your wife says that she is now becoming great friends with the Secretary-General, which may come in useful after your release. The man who was going to come and sweep the leaves didn't come. But two of Millicent's Christmas surprises have arrived from Peter Jones. That's all, except that she sends her love and repeats that you are not to worry.'

'Worry? Why should I worry? I'm only worried that she's worried. But it sounds as though she isn't. Did you speak to her yourself? Is she really quite calm?'

'I'm sorry, Mr Lute, I can't say anything about our methods of communication. But she certainly is calm, I know that for sure. And she certainly is getting along well with the Secretary-General.'

Lute had a little difficulty in picturing Beta in her new role of intimate of the Secretary-General. Of course he was very proud of her, had always been so, and respected her intelligence – within its limits; but he wondered if she could really have just the right touch, without him there to prompt and guide her. He nodded to James Minor and was turning away to go back to his cubicle when he noticed two figures moving swiftly across the back of the hall. One appeared to be female, but was almost completely concealed by an ankle-length raincoat and an unfurled umbrella, glistening with raindrops and displaying one wet autumn leaf like a badge. The other was Jacopo, who overtook his charge, unlocked a door in the far wall and followed her through it.

Lute raised his eyebrows in interrogation. James Minor smiled. 'The librarian going to work. It looks as though she came straight in from the rain. Excuse me now, please, I must find her helper.'

The library had been a kitchen store, and the shelves were more adapted to château-sized pots than to books. But a few hundred books had been ranged along them, with chalk inscriptions to show the categories; and there was a primitive reading table and one chair in the middle of the room. An exercise book lay on the table, and a pencil. When Piet was ushered in Sister Agnes was standing on an upturned box, straightening the books on the top shelf.

'Here he is,' said Jacopo grumpily. 'I'll be in the hall if you want me. Don't take too long.'

'Thank you, Jacopo, I shan't waste any time. Close the door, will you?'

Sister Agnes resumed toying with the books, so that Piet could have a good view of her before she allowed their eyes to meet. Piet stood and looked. She reminded him of someone. If Alexander the Great had been there he could have told Piet which film it was, seen thirty years ago, which stirred his memory. But Alexander could not have known about the other memory, the one room flat in the Prinsegracht on the day when Piet and Marijke moved in, and Marijke standing on the steps in the kitchen to put away their few pieces of good china in the top cupboard.

Sister Agnes picked out a heavy volume of OECD studies on inland water pollution and proffered it to Piet, with a radiant and disarming smile. He moved forward and took the book, and she jumped down from the box, steadying herself momentarily with a hand on his shoulder.

'Thank you. It is very kind of you to come and help. Won't you sit down, and I'll show you what we have to do. It's a pity there's only one chair, even though it's almost big enough for two.' She upped the intensity of her smile by a couple of thousand watts, taking care to allow no trace of guile to enter into it. 'But I'll have to move around anyway, calling out the names.'

Piet sat down. The chair was indeed a big one, high-backed, upholstered in dark green velvet, with low, plumply stuffed arms.

Humming the tune which Alexander had taught her she passed round to the other side of the table and leaned over it towards him, pressing the button marked innocent mischief and letting it flood into her eyes.

'Shall I tell you a secret? Can you keep secrets? I asked Anna specially if I could have you. I hope you're not cross. Perhaps you were planning to have a peaceful evening chatting with the others. But I knew you were the one I wanted. You seem sort of . . . younger than the others, and easily the most handsome in your djebbah. Not many men look right in one, do they? Now I must come round and show you how the catalogue works, let me take half an inch of the arm as my perch. See, here are the first entries, all the stuff about air pollution. Goodness, I wish the writing was bigger, I can hardly make it out.'

She had sat squarely on the arm of the chair, her legs scissored and swinging in front. As she leaned forward she lightly placed her left hand on his left shoulder, permitted her left breast to play touch and go with his right shoulder and took care to shield her face from his with a generous curtain of hair.

'You know, I heard you talking to the committee today. You sounded so masterful. I loved that bit about the problems of the environment being the most important in the world. It's so *true*, but no one else could say it so clearly. You're not cross, are you, because I was listening in? I was really sorry for the others, you made such mincemeat of their silly ideas. Honestly, you were so severe, I could just imagine them blushing and looking foolish.'

She swung round to whisper into his right ear. He shining eyes were evidence enough of the enthusiasm which made it natural that she should not notice that her right breast was now jutting into his shoulder and that her soft curls bobbed in a moving cushion between their cheeks. 'But you must give them help, set them on the right path. It's so important. They could do so much good if they were properly led. We're all counting on you, you know, specially me – this is what matters most in my life, I haven't done anything much with it yet, but now I can help people like you and . . .'

She jerked herself off the arm of the chair and paced round the table looking agitated.

'. . . oh, I express myself so badly. I never could string words together properly. I ought to be getting on with the library instead of babbling in your ear. I'm sorry, I just got carried away. My mother always said I was a proper little pest when I got excited. See, I shan't bother you any more, I'll get back on my box and read out the titles. I must do what Anna said.'

She tossed her hair back and looked up at the ceiling, as if to express penitence to Anna. She was exactly in profile. The arc of chin-throat-breast was of striking perfection. Piet gulped and dug his fingers into the squashy upholstery.

'No. Do not get on your box. I am not bothered by you. I am very interested in what you say. It is very important, what you were whispering. I . . . come back. Please, I want to go on with our talk.'

Sister Agnes thought to herself, right lass he's hooked, the fisher-girl can relax a bit now, can't she? Her smile was full of eagerness, with a nuance of incredulity.

'Honestly, can I? You don't mind me sitting down, it's a bit of a squash.'

She kicked off her shoes, tiptoed round the table and carefully arranged herself on the arm of the chair. This time the pressure of the breast on shoulder was more insistent. Her curls brushed more decisively against his cheek, high up above the stubble line, where they could be felt better. Her right arm crept shyly over his left shoulder.

'Comfy?' she whispered, then remembered that he was not English. 'Are you comfortable?'

'Yes,' said Piet in a hoarse whisper, sitting very still like a man in a park on whose arm a bird has alighted.

Sister Agnes began to talk, embroidering the themes which she had earlier picked out. She spoke of the idealism of Anna and her comrades, of the fantastic opportunity which now existed to heave forward the struggle for a better environment, of the impatience of the inarticulate majority for decisive action, of the superior intellectual powers of Piet, of his noble and youthful appearance. These thoughts winged straight into the very vortex of Piet's mind, where they revolved inextricably with whorls of romantic nostalgia and sexual excitement.

When his arm found its way round her waist, Sister Agnes wriggled closer to him. She said how she loved talking to him, that she had not met a man to whom she could talk for years. This was true. She had not; and she was enjoying herself. But she was nervous now, coming to the end of her brief and uncertain what to do next, uncertain even whether she was still acting her part or stepping off the stage into goodness-knew what real-life predicament. She found herself wishing that Piet would take charge of the situation. Well, she thought, here goes, we can't go through this routine again, let's improvise a bit.

She wriggled right down into his lap and, still wriggling, gave him a long tight hug. Then she leaned her head back and signalled a thousand green lights to him with her eyes, passing the tip of her pink tongue delicately over her lips as if to indicate something which might have been overlooked.

Piet recognised the green lights, and burst in an instant the strait laces which had cribbed his life for two decades. He crushed her to him with a clumsy convulsive movement, and set his lips hard on hers.

Bliss, she thought, what a terrible kiss, he's a beginner, almost like me, but he does hold me tight, he's really strong.

For the next five minutes no word was uttered in the library. Piet and Agnes were wholly absorbed in holding each other as tightly as possible, as if each feared that the other would escape, and in improving their kissing technique, which they did quite rapidly. In the following five minutes they allowed themselves a little conversation, trading fragments of information about their past lives and expressing the results of introspection about their present feelings.

'Just think, my little nurse, when you were a girl in North Shields and looked over the North Sea you were looking to Den Helder, where my father was a pilot.'

'Now isn't that an impossible coincidence? My father was a pilot too, on the Tyne. To think that you were there across the water. The good old North Sea – our sea, our private bit of brine, isn't that right?'

'The Agnespietmeer, yes, you are right.' Piet eyed her devoutly. 'What do you say, shall we make them clean it up a bit? How's that for an anti-pollution idea?'

Sister Agnes muzzled him. 'That's great. I don't want even the tiniest bit of rubbish floating about in our sea, not even one wee drop of oil . . .' The light went out and came on again. 'Oh, that must be Jacopo telling us it's time to stop. Goodness, we haven't done a thing. And how will we meet tomorrow? Quick, we must make a plan. And you have lipstick on your face.'

Piet thought while she dabbed with a kleenex. 'Tell Anna that there's more work than you thought and that it took me a long time to understand what to do. This stupid Dutchman. But say that I am working very well now that I do understand, and that you had better keep me on for tomorrow evening and the next evening . . . I will come and see you in clinic tomorrow morning and you can let me know.'

'Marvellous. That's what we'll do. Now, one more extra special one – it must last me all night – and out we go.'

Jacopo stood well away from the door, arms akimbo and suspicion etched lightly across his massive face, as they came out. Oh dear, she thought, here's Tarzan putting two and two together, but never mind, he can think what he likes but he doesn't know, these North Italians are always one step behind aren't they? She unfurled her umbrella to hide her mussed hair as she hurried by, and the leaf, now dry, fluttered to the floor. 'Sorry we kept you, Jacopo, too much to do, get him off to bed now will you – see you upstairs later.'

Anna and Franz were happy to have Sister Agnes' report, but surprised that it was so short; almost curt. Anna thought that she must have been tired by her performance. Franz wondered whether Piet would be tired. They waited for Jacopo's report, then closed down the control room for the night. The time was just after 11p.m.

At 11.30 a flock of redwing passed low over the chateau, flying south. They were all together. At 12.45 a second flock flew over. At 12.46 a straggler from the second flock passed directly over the tower. 'Ssih, ssih,' it called. Stretched out on the floor in the German's cubicle, listening intently between his colleague's snores, the Chairman heard it. He stole back to his own cubicle, rehearsing in his mind the routes and calendars and recalculating with growing certainty that he was in the Ardennes, and probably not far from the French/Belgian border. He was very pleased with himself, although he regretted the sleep which he had lost. Without his watch he over-estimated the loss. He thought that it must be about 2 a.m.

At 6.15 the Chairman was awakened by a hand shaking his shoulder. He blinked up at Piet. 'What is it? I didn't hear the bell. Is it time to get up?'

'No, no,' said Piet excitedly, 'you can stay in bed, but I have come to talk to you. I want to discuss the day's work. We must make progress today. I have decided to rejoin the Committee. I . . . well, it was necessary, you understand, to take a certain negative attitude yesterday, to criticise the rather absurd ideas which some of our colleagues entertained. But now I . . . have been thinking during the night, and I see how we must work.'

The Chairman was fully awake now. 'But I thought that you were against doing any work. What was that you said about this criminal conspiracy . . .?'

Piet waved his arms. 'A protest, a statement for the record, a device to prepare for the work which we must now do in earnest. Believe me, dear Chairman, I am now full of constructive ideas. I wish to take a leading part in the discussions today. Are you going to continue with the sub-committees? I think that we should have a plenary session first, and then I should like to chair one of the sub-committees. Listen, suppose that I take over the one on noise, how would that be?'

The Chairman made a pleased sound of assent. Then he got up and excused himself and padded through the hall, where only a dim night-light burned, to the lavatory. Glimpsing something on the floor as he went, he stooped and picked up a golden leaf. By the time he had reached the lavatory, which was not lit at all, he had realised that the leaf was something to be kept and discussed with his Belgian colleague. He found the lid of the lavatory cistern, raised it and popped the leaf in.

Chapter 9

The Prime Minister dipped a large Highland horn spoon into the marmalade pot and deposited in the middle of his piece of toast a gently subsiding heap of the golden faintly greenish jelly. Three chunks, good big ones; but he liked five, one for the middle and one for each corner. The next spoonful produced three. He pursed his thin lips and with gentle dabs of the spoon executed a new pattern which preserved symmetry but found room for all six. He raised the heavily charged toast to his mouth and bit. This was his favourite moment of the morning.

The low slanting table beside him held all the morning newspapers. They told him with convincing unanimity that it was Friday, 9 November. And they all headlined the kidnapper's announcement.

Mystery Woman Holds Diplomats

It's a Girl Whodunit

VGB – The Velvet Glove Brigade

16 Caged by Bird?

The PM wrinkled his nose as he ran his eye over the rival versions. The Irish story had been thoroughly squashed. Several papers dismissed it in a sentence. The announcement from Paris, on the other hand, was treated as the real thing. The PM noted with interest that *The Times* was alone in expressing even limited caution about its authenticity. And he was quick to see that almost all the papers were handling what had happened in terms appropriate to sporting contests. This was dangerous. If a British government became engaged in anything remotely like a sporting contest the British public would want it to lose.

When the Foreign Secretary came in the PM had finished his second round of toast and marmalade, another six-chunker, and had downed his fourth large cup of the cheap strong breakfast tea which he bought, by courtesy of the Defence Secretary, from NAAFI. He was reading the story in the *International Herald Tribune*, which as usual packed more information into less space than any of the British papers.

'Good morning, Prime Minister. I called in at the office on my way, but there's still nothing in the telegrams. And the papers are all based on the same agency story, except for the *Herald Trib*, which seems to be on the inside track again. We're trying to find out from Paris whether there's anything in all this stuff they attribute to a source close to the Elysée. The Quai have already told us there isn't. But then you wouldn't expect them to give a positive answer to anything before breakfast, would you?' The Foreign Secretary's eyes strayed, as he spoke, over the remains of the PM's breakfast.

'No.' The PM mused. 'Or immediately after breakfast for that matter. Have you had yours, by the way? . . . Good. Now let me go over what is known. Tell me if I leave anything out. Yesterday we had the Irish story. That was punctured, with remarkable simultaneity, by the Russians in private and the real kidnappers in public. A real flat tire, that one. Then, just before midnight last night a large brown envelope marked "On Her Majesty's Service" and addressed to Le Chef du Bureau was found inside the door of the AFP office in Paris. No one saw it being delivered. It contained a single sheet of paper – White House notepaper with the letterhead crossed out. The sheet bore the message in typescript – text as in *The Times*, and the same in French on the back. The gist is that a woman is holding this NATO committee prisoner and that she won't release them unless the NATO governments take some quote important new measures unquote to reduce pollution of the environment and improve the quality of life. We will be told before long what measures will be acceptable. In the meantime we are invited to suggest some ourselves. If we wish.

'And I suppose that people are going over the envelope and the paper for fingerprints and so on, and won't find any, and that the peculiarities of the typewriter have already been analysed so that an international search can be made for the machine. A doomed project if ever there was one. This is an efficient operation as well as an impudent one. Did I miss anything out?'

'Nothing. I could tell you a bit more about the investigations which are being started . . . there is something odd about the Norwegian's shoes, and we've sent a geologist over to look at them . . . but, no, I don't suppose that you want that sort of thing. Let's just leave it that every enquiry which would occur to a sane person is being made, and quite a few others too, and that you'll have a report later today. The question is, what sort of tone do we use in comment and how should I handle Questions in the House – there's bound to be a Special Notice one and we'll probably have to answer it without knowing much about how the allies are going to react. We've called a meeting of the NATO Council for 9.30, but nothing much will come out of that unless someone gives a lead. Of course Lavenham wants us to – he says that a firm statement about being outraged and setting our faces firmly against negotiations with criminals, etcetera, would go down well and that all the others would rally round. But I wonder. I wonder. I wonder hardest about the White House. Their day starts at our Question time. It wouldn't surprise me at all if the President came out with some very, very cautious reaction. It wouldn't look good if I was thundering outrage in the House at the same time.'

The PM nodded his approval of this analysis. 'Our face is not firmly set against anything at this stage. Of course we're against kidnapping, which is a dastardly crime. But we're enormously . . .' – the PM gestured with his hands, as if juggling giant balloons – '. . . enormously in favour of anti-pollution measures and . . . and what? . . . and urgently consulting our allies. How's that?'

The Foreign Secretary was silent, mentally turning all this into statements to the House, and estimating how they would go down. He could imagine very easily a supplementary inviting him to say that HMG would in no circumstances yield to the demands of the kidnappers. He saw himself replying that in the present unique situation he would not wish to foreclose any course of action which might be in the interests of the nation, the alliance and the sixteen prisoners. He could hear the murmurs of support. 'Yes,' he said, 'yes, that should be all right. I'll get the department to work and tell Lavenham what to say over in Brussels. He'd better say that he isn't speaking on instructions until we know how the wind is blowing. But he can ask for another meeting at 3 to give them our official line. That could be quite convenient, to have the Council meeting during Question time. I mean I could say that they were meeting at that very minute; give a bit of life to that phrase about consulting allies.' He looked pleased.

The PM smiled. 'Well you'd better go across the road and ring up Lavenham. You can tell him, by the way, that our face may very well finish up being set against, etcetera. But I definitely don't want it set that way today.'

Five minutes later the PM had briefed his own press secretary. 'Good morning, John. Here's the line. My personal influence shaping British policy, guarding against premature reactions. Situation needs a lot of thought, experienced hand at the helm. But not just thought. Action too, where action needed. May not be generally known that special orders from Number Ten set in motion during night unprecedented range of enquiries – search for typewriter etcetera, no cancel that, no examples, they sound too silly, but make sure you have the man of action theme. Or even men of action, I don't want to seem to be running things singlehanded. Tribute to the Navy and RAF for prompt action yesterday. A false trail, but it had to be followed and it was British forces who followed it. Right? And add something about a personal message from me to Mrs Whatsername, Lute isn't it, but be sure it gets off before you mention it. No, hold it, I'll telephone her, then it's done right away. Send George in.'

The Private Secretary took his notes in turn. Mrs Lute on the telephone, right away. The Minister for the Environment at noon. A call to the White House at lunch-time.

Beta was washing her hair when the phone rang. It had run many times already that morning. Another mysterious message, very rapid, that David was all right and sent his love. The Secretary-General, wanting her to call the wives together and discuss the revelation that a woman held their husbands prisoner; wanting her also to have lunch with him. Lots of reporters ('I'm sorry, I have no statement to make, nothing at all').

Still twisting a towel round her dripping head, and dabbing with the corner of it at her cheeks, Beta answered the telephone. 'What did you say? Number Ten? The Prime Minister? Yes, of course, I'll hold on.'

'Mrs Lute? I was going to send you a message this morning, but I thought it would be better if I rang up. I want you to know how deeply I and my wife, and of course the whole government and everybody in Britain, feel for you. What a terrible ordeal.' The PM paused. He was wondering whether to say something about God, but he had failed to establish ahead of time whether Mrs Lute was religious. Come to think of it, he had not even checked that she was British. So many diplomats married foreigners. Still, her crisp 'yes' had sounded British . . . The pause was hardly perceptible before the smooth, authoritative voice continued. 'We must all pray that you have courage to endure it and that it will be short. We are doing everything humanly possible to rescue your husband.'

A soapy drop of water was irritating Beta's left eye. 'Like what?' she found herself saying.

The PM, ever so slightly disconcerted, began to rehearse the familiar information about the number of policemen who were engaged in the search.

'I know, I know. I'm sorry, I don't want to sound cross. Of course there must be a search. It's just that I don't think they'll find David. I'm sure that this woman is tremendously clever. And she seems so considerate – she had a message sent to me only an hour ago from David – that I can't pretend to feel really anxious about his safety – anyway so long as people hurry up and work out a good ransom.'

Beta had not consciously formulated these ideas until now. Wet hair, a soapy eye, and a monopoly of the Prime Minister's attention had had a rapid catalytic effect.

'Oh, we aren't neglecting that, I can assure you. But of course there are difficulties in giving in to a kidnapper. We don't want to encourage others – and we don't know what price we have to pay, it's all so vague at present. But we're working out some ideas, indeed I'm seeing the Minister for the Environment later this morning.'

'Oh, good. I'm sure he'll have some ideas, there must be lots of schemes he knows about which could be hurried up. After all, everyone keeps saying that more has to be done about pollution and so on, and that it's urgent, and all this woman seems to be saying is "Get on with it". Really it seems different to me, not like giving in at all, if all you have to do is what you say you want to do anyway, don't you think?'

There was a moment's silence. 'Well,' said the PM, 'you're right, of course . . . in a way. It isn't easy, but we'll do our best. Anyway, I'm very glad to have talked to you. Perhaps I'll ring you up again in a day or two. And you can always ring me if you want.'

After a diminuendo passage of thanks and farewells the two receivers were replaced. Beta imagined the PM putting his down. She knew very well what he looked like. The PM did not know what Beta looked like, and exercised his imagination for a few seconds before reaching for the latest stack of telegrams. His imagination was surprisingly accurate. Later in the morning, when he saw the *Evening Standard*, which had a smudgy photograph of her peering through the window of her Mini, he was pleased to find that he had come so close. The small feat helped to coagulate the favourable but still fluid impressions which he retained from their telephone talk. Beta became established as a sensible and attractive figure, a significant pulse on which the PM's finger, unerring in selection and light in touch, uniquely rested. She was quoted to the Minister for the Environment before lunch, and offered to the President of the United States after lunch.

The President was showing his usual tendency to ignore the substance of the problem, or to seem to do so, in favour of what he called the publicity angles. Almost sleepy in tone, but purposive as a woodpecker, the slightly Southern voice buzzed away in the PM's right ear. The Irish story had been killed so quickly that it had made no impact. That was good, anything was good that kept Ireland out of anything. But the President was finding his public hard to read. Newspaper comment, and the first telegrams and telephone calls to the White House presented a whole spectrum of opinions, apparently unrelated to any of the familiar political or social groupings. 'They don't even add up sex-wise. All the analysts can say is that an awful lot of people are excited by the situation. So I'm being rather cautious in what I say. I think we all have to be cautious.' The President paused, and went on in a tone of self-indulgent discontent: 'But I surely wish there was some way I could show compassion to the victims, something personalised. Our man Grannery just has no relations nearer than a cousin. Truly a lone rider. I have such fine messages I could send, but there's no one to send them to.'

The PM shifted the phone to his other ear. 'Well, look, our man has a wife, and a very nice one too. I talked to her only today. She's sensible and has ideas – what's more she's a sort of representative of all the wives and families. Why don't you send her a message, or ring her up for that matter – I can give you the number.'

The PM smiled when this idea was well received. He

listened patiently to the Presidential thanks. He had already doodled a rough caricature of the President on his blotter, with an enormous balloon issuing from his mouth within which during the earlier part of their conversation he had time to write the word yak neatly twenty seven times. Now he drew another, and began filling the second balloon: ta, mate; thanks, bud; merci mille fois . . .

'Merci mille fois,' the Chairman was saying to the Belgian, who had offered to chair the work on marine waters pollution. The courtesy paid, he switched back to English. 'So, gentlemen, we have our sub-committees and we shall all be busy . . . except for myself. What is your wish? Do I take a holiday for the next three days while your prepare your drafts? Or is there some task which I should perform? You know, I am not a member of any sub-committee, and I should not interfere with their work, but I should like to be of use. Should I perhaps take over the library work, doing research for each group as it needs some?'

Piet jerked forward in his chair. 'No, no, Mr Chairman, there is no need. From tomorrow, when everything will be organised, we will all be able to use it freely; and as for the liaison with the librarian it is best that I continue to do it. I am quite familiar with her methods now. What you must do, Mr Chairman – I am sorry, I mean to say what I suggest you do – is to observe the work of the sub-committees, to see how their contributions are taking shape and to reflect on the presentation of the whole package. When we make our report to Mevrouw Anna it must be coherent, the elements must be in proportion, you see what I mean? This is where we will need your help.'

There was a murmur of approval, and the Chairman inclined his head in agreement.

Grannery said: 'Sure, that's a good point. What bothers me is whether we can find proposals that are really practical but seem big enough to suit Anna. We're all good bureaucrats, and we're not going to come up with anything which we know is out of the question. But if we stick to things which we can imagine our governments actually doing we'll have a pretty small row of beans to show her. We certainly need someone to monitor the work and check that some of the beans, anyway, are going to be knee-high.'

The Canadian nodded. 'Yes, and even better, you might plan to talk to Anna while we're working, give her the rationale and sound her out a bit. After all she did say that she had some ideas of her own. I suppose she's planning to give us them over the loudspeaker, but it would be more practical to have a kind of dialogue with her. If you could . . .' He glanced at Secunda, who was on duty in a corner of the hall. She smiled but said nothing. It looked as though she had not understood.

'I should like to meet Anna,' said the Chairman distinctly, 'and I am sure that it would be useful if I could talk to her. It might save us from wasting a lot of time. I will see what I can do. Now, gentlemen, I suggest that you start work.'

Upstairs, Anna left the speaker on long enough to hear the sound of chairs being moved and Piet's gruff voice herding the other two members of his sub-committee. He really seemed rather an odd choice to head the sub-committee on noise, she thought, since he and Portentoso were noticeably the noisiest of the captives. She clicked the machine off and looked at Alexander the Great.

'Will you see him? I mean talk to him. He mustn't see you of course, but we can fix up a screen or something and have you properly guarded.'

'I'm not sure. It may be necessary. That American was quite right. But . . . it's one thing to address them on the loudspeaker, that's quite enough to distort the voice, but it would be different just talking to one of them.'

'You mean you might come across him again, outside, and he might recognise your voice? One of us could do the speaking for you. Better not run the risk.'

'Oh, no, if I have any dealings with him it will be just the two of us. I must think about it. But do have a screen made, just a little one that could go on a table. And let me know if he asks for an interview. I think he will, but not till tomorrow.'

Alexander departed, with his elastic stride, somehow suggestive of a clergyman, and Anna reached for the daily press summary which Tim had brought her. She noted with pleasure that the *Algemeen Dagblad* editorial had been headed, 'Why Not Pay the Price?'. But her mind was only half on the typed sheet. She was also wondering how a screen could be arranged so that she was partly visible and yet safe from recognition. Perhaps a fan would be better. One could play gracefully with a fan. The Chairman sounded reassuringly courteous and mature. The students were behaving very well, and their youthful enthusiasm had been essential to her scheme; but it would be pleasant to talk about it to someone a bit older. Anna realised that she was feeling lonely, and that her mental manoeuvres with imaginary screens and fans had been taking up valuable time. She filed the press report and stepped quickly out towards the stair-case. Sister Agnes was coming up the stairs, and they hesitated, looking at each other.

'Were you coming to see me?'

'Oh, no . . . I mean yes, but there's no hurry. Perhaps I could see you tomorrow?' Sister Agnes realised that she was kneading her hands together, and stopped. She turned round and preceded Anna down the stairs. 'Anyway, I really ought to go to the clinic and get some things ready for this evening. It's surprising how many requests we get.'

They parted at the kitchen door, through which they could hear Elizabeth being briefed by Françoise about the sanglier.

'I'll see you tomorrow, then. You must tell me how you are managing with the Dutchman. You seem to have transformed him. I hope that you can keep him under control.'

'There are problems . . . but I know how to solve them.'

Fibber, hissed Sister Agnes to herself as she walked away, that's just what you don't know.

Chapter 10

'Only another ten kilometres or so,' called Marie over her shoulder as she and Felix pedalled through Bièvre.

It was drizzling, and Felix thought that ten kilometres sounded like a long way. But he was cheered by the thought of the welcome which awaited them in the cottage where Marie's uncle lived. Even with allowance made for Marie's incurable exaggeration it was plain that they could expect shelter from the rain, a blazing fire and plenty to eat.

They rounded a corner by a sawmill, picking up damp sawdust on their tyres, and came to a long straight stretch of road which ran ahead through the wet woods as far as their eyes could see. There was no traffic, and the silence somehow suggested that there would be none. Felix pulled up abreast of Marie.

'Look,' he said, 'let me get myself straight about your uncle. He was in the Resistance in the war, but what did that mean? Did he hide in the woods, and shoot at Germans, or what?'

'Listen, we do not speak of the Resistance here. That is a French word. They need it to distinguish those who resisted from those who collaborated. But here everyone resisted. Well, in Belgium it was almost everyone, and here in the Ardennes it was absolutely everyone. You must understand that the Germans did not dare to drive down these roads – the garrisons here were small and they had to stay in the towns and the open country. The woods and the hills were under Belgian control all the time, not the army of course, that did not exist any more, but the local people. They were all resisting, but only some of them had arms – like my uncle who was in command of a small group here – he will tell you all about it, he remembers every detail, and he is very friendly to British people, naturally, because it was British aircraft which flew over at night and dropped rifles and things. Some of the pilots still come back and visit my uncle, and they sit up half the night talking about the war.'

'But was there really no danger that someone would give him away? I mean, everyone round here must have known about the arms and who was using them, and you'd think that someone would be, well, indiscreet sooner or later.'

Marie laughed. 'Hah, you can imagine an Ardennais being indiscreet. That shows that you do not know them. Believe me they do not waste words even in peacetime, not to strangers, and in war – why you cannot imagine how silent they were, like these bare winter trees. They are cunning too, they can outwit the authorities every day of the week. Truly, the map says that we are in Belgium, but do not think that the Belgian Government rules the Ardennais.'

The straight stretch came to an end, and they free-wheeled down a curving village street. Many of the cottages still had the traditional manure heap or fumier out in front, steaming damply in the autumn air. A farmer stood beside one and regarded them impassively as they went by.

'Well, this all makes me think that we were on the right track yesterday when we thought of the Committee being held prisoner here. You said it would be difficult to hide what was going on from the local people – but now it sounds as though they wouldn't say anything even if they did know.'

Marie considered this. 'Yes, if the kidnapper belonged here. Then they would say nothing. But the people who belong here are not the types to do this . . . However we must ask Mononk. We're almost there. Are you hungry? Remember, if he invites you for a walk you must say yes. He will offer to lend you boots. Accept them. He does not like to walk on roads.'

'Mononk, did you say?'

'Yes, the old Brussels word for "my uncle". Haven't you come across that one yet? You call him that too, he's used to it.'

The drizzle stopped as they approached a tiny hump-backed bridge with a road junction at the other side. The sign to the right said 'Vresse 3', but Marie dismounted and pointed to a track leading off up the hill through the trees. 'That is where we go, and we must walk. But come and sit on the side of the bridge.'

The stream, swollen by the recent rains, gurgled busily below, and the parapet of the bridge was pleasantly over-grown with grey-green lichen and tiny ferns. But it was damp. Felix tucked his raincoat well under him as he sat down. Wondering how accessible she would be once under Mononk's roof, he kissed her. She purred and rubbed her cold wet cheek against him. 'When I was sixteen I was kissed right here on this exact bit of the bridge by a young Frenchman.'

'Oh, really, are you just reviving romantic memories?'

'Oh no, you need not be jealous. I was fighting him like a tiger, and he finished up down in the stream below. It was not at all romantic. But then nothing is here, it is a silly word to use in the Ardennes. My uncle would never say it.'

Felix kissed her again, more cautiously in view of what had happened to the young Frenchman.

'Talking of Mononk, who does he think I am? I mean are we supposed to be . . .?'

Marie laughed. 'Whatever we choose to be. Do not be so preoccupied by questions about what role you should play. It is better to follow your instincts, if you have any left, than to go round asking people to help you write a script for yourself.'

'Oh, I have a splendid script all ready, one hundred per cent instinctive. I was just wondering . . .'

The crack of a shot interrupted him. 'The hunters are out,' said Marie. 'Come on, let's get up that hill.'

Mononk's house was low-built, perched on a shelf of the hill, with a small plot of grass in front of it and two flag-poles. The Union Jack hung limply from one, the Belgian flag from the other. Mononk stood in his doorway, a slight figure in brown cord breeches and a faded green jacket. He stood to attention and saluted as they approached. Felix, pushing his bicycle, stopped and responded with some difficulty, while Marie rushed forward, leaned her bicycle against the wall and embraced her uncle.

'This is my friend Félix, the one I told you about who lives with me in Brussels.'

'Be welcome, Monsieur Félix, I hope that I have put your flag the right way up. Do you know that this same flag was given to me by the Pilot Officer William George Fairweather at a ceremony on the 20th of October 1944 at which the Governor of the Province was present? I must show you the photograph. But come in, come in, leave your bicycles in the porch, we will install you in the owls' room and then you must have a drink before lunch. I have a little surprise for Monsieur Félix in my cellar. Marie, you are wet, you must come quickly and sit by the fire.'

Felix was indeed surprised by his apéritif. The dusty unlabelled bottle, announced as the gift of the Squadron Leader Alistair Colin Anderson, on the occasion of his official visit to the village of Vresse on the 3rd of June 1945, turned out to be straight malt whisky, brewed in some remote part of Scotland by the Squadron Leader's father. It was surprisingly welcome. Mononk explained that it had only been offered once before, to the Colonel John Stuart Mill on the occasion of the official celebration of the tenth anniversary of the liberation, when the Colonel Mill and Madame Mill had been the guests of the Mayor of Vresse for three days. Felix felt that he was finding a new perspective on Anglo-Belgian relations. They seemed to have reached a pitch of intensity in this remote valley which it would be hard to match in, say, Brussels. He took a second glass of whisky, and was led to table and served vegetable soup from a large white tureen. The main course was equally simple and filling – a large round pain d'Ardenne, farm butter (very white at this time of the year, explained uncle, but none the worse for that), and a jambon d'Ardenne. It was all more robust in taste than the Ardennais foods on sale in Brussels. Finally there was a tarte au sucre from the local baker, and coffee.

Mononk produced an obscene crinkled pouch from his pocket, explaining that it was the bladder of the pig which he had killed in September, and extracted from it a fill of Semois tobacco for his pipe. Lighting it with a spill from the log fire he soon created a bluish haze all round the group, and began making plans.

'How did you come, then? On the road from Bièvre? Ah, well you will have seen the place of the famous ambush. I hope you explained it properly, Marie. Then this afternoon we could go up to the *champ de parachutage*, so familiar to

Fairweather and Anderson, and come back along the ridge and through the badgers' copse, so that you can see number four camp – it is the best preserved. How is that?'

'Fine,' said Felix dutifully, 'but I hope that you can lend me a pair of boots if we're going to walk through the woods.'

'Of course, of course. Then tonight we will talk about this problem which you have mentioned. We will need maps and perhaps my history books, the ones of this region. I have already thought of some places where your friends might be imprisoned. But do you not wish to hear the news before we set out?'

The announcer in Brussels sounded glib and brilliantined as he rattled off the latest items. The North Atlantic Council had met again in the morning, but issued no statement. A source close to the Secretary-General had indicated that there were grounds for expecting new developments. The Sixth Fleet had left Naples unexpectedly. The Prime Minister of Malta had demanded that NATO should consult him about the ransom terms and had said that he could not accept any proposals which ignored pollution in the Mediterranean. An article in *Pravda* stated that certain diseased hyenas in the United States, animated by their discredited revanchism, were slandering the Soviet Union, whereas it was well-known that the socialist countries regarded kidnapping as inadmissible. The fact that the missing diplomats had last been seen in what appeared to be a SHAPE bus was emphasised, with a strong implication that the Generals at SHAPE had abducted them to express dissatisfaction at political interference with their warmongering plans. In London the *Daily Express* was offering a prize to its readers for the best set of ransom terms in under 1,000 words.

When they clumped off up the woodland path behind the house Felix was sleepy. But the concentration needed to keep up with uncle, without slipping on the wet bracken, kept him awake. Mononk wore an ancient Loden cape, on the front of which was pinned the emblem of the Armée Secrète and used a heavy rowan-wood stick to help him up the slippier slopes. He talked the whole time, pointing out traces of wild boar and imparting Ardennais lore, but was never out of breath. Felix, to his annoyance, was panting slightly by the time they reached the plateau above the woods and inspected the champ de parachutage. It was a large field on top of the hill, cultivated but bare at this season. The woods dropped away steeply on all sides. One church spire could be seen above a hilltop in the distance, but otherwise there was no sign of human presence. Nor was there any noise, except for an aircraft thirty thousand feet up, which could just be seen and heard.

'Our aeroplanes were not so high,' said Mononk. 'On the contrary they flew in at about eight hundred metres, looking for the flare which we lit in that little cairn. It would burn for five minutes only, so punctual were they. By the time they were back in England we had collected the parachutes and buried them and carried the guns and radio equipment down into the woods where they could safely be hidden. The Germans were only five kilometres away, and they knew very well what was happening, but they could do nothing. It was death for them to come into these parts, even by day. By night . . . hah!' He snapped his fingers to indicate the speed with which they would have been despatched.

'There certainly isn't much pollution up here,' said Felix, after a pause.

'No, naturally, there is no one to cause it. I doubt whether anyone has been up here for the last month. Even in the summer, when there are tourists and campers, a place like this is deserted. But you must not think that we Ardennais are champions of the environment, not at all, we still have a good environment but only because there are not many people, not because they are willing to lift a finger to keep it. Oh, I could show you some rubbish dumps which would fill you with horror, spilling down a bank at the edge of a village when there is a suitable site only two hundred metres further away. This did not matter so much when the rubbish disappeared into the earth, but now with all these plastic containers and things it is terrible, terrible. And bits of motor cars, they are the worst of all.'

The sun was shining, pale but bright. Marie pushed back her hood and shook her hair. 'Well, what can be done? They will think about it when the rubbish is all round them in smelly mountains, but that is too late. How can we make them do something now?'

Mononk reached into his pocket, pulled out a leather purse and extracted from it a large gold coin. He held this up, smiling. 'There is your answer. Make it profitable for them to be tidy, to keep their woods and rivers clean, and you will find a change in a single day. Your Ardennais will never resist gold, he will look after his countryside if you pay him. Offer him a price for his rubbish, and he will save every scrap for you. Is he so different from other Belgians in this? I wonder.'

Felix considered this. 'Probably not, I suppose. But this is very discouraging. We gain collectively if we restore our environment, but how can we possibly fix things so that each person gains individually? Or rather so that he sees his individual gain? What would this woman kidnapper say? She can hardly expect gold pieces to be handed out to everyone who disposes of his rubbish properly. She's probably thinking of taking gold pieces from those who don't – lots of new laws and heavy fines.'

Mononk put the coin back in his purse. 'Then she will have to do some more thinking. The Ardennais pay no attention to such laws, and do not allow themselves to be fined. But there is a flaw in your argument. It is not necessary to postulate the certainty of a gold piece for correct handling of rubbish. It would be enough that the possibility should exist, and that the neighbours should be showing interest in this possibility. Your Ardennais will not allow his neighbour to gain something which he might gain himself.'

'Oh, bother the Ardennais,' said Marie, 'you make them sound utterly maddening, and really how could one have a sort of rubbish competition – with the poubelle men as judges, I suppose – and a prize for every hundredth housewife who makes up neat little parcels of stuff to be recycled? This has nothing to do with reality, it is pure djoumdjoumerie.'

'You are right, my dear, it is hardly realistic. But if you look with sympathy at my grotesque notions you may find an element of truth among the absurdities. Remember, it is a graduate in philosophy of the University of Louvain who addresses you. It has been the habit of that institution to produce men who perceive truths which they are then unable, because of faulty training in rhetoric, to convey to their fellows.'

Marie kissed her uncle. 'You win. I will search for your truth and then express it back to you, using the superb rhetoric which I learned in the Ecole Communale of St

Gilles. Now let's go and see your old camp and then hurry back to supper.'

The maps of the region were beautiful. They came from the Belgian Army, who sold them, incongruously, in the Abbaye de la Cambre in Brussels. The scale was 1 to 25,000 and every building was shown. Mononk pieced together ten of the sheets on the huge pine dining table and unlocked an old oak bible box which was half filled with gold coins. 'A souvenir of the events of 1940,' he said mysteriously. 'I like to use them as counters.' One by one he placed them on all the large châteaux and château-fermes over an area which stretched from the French frontier, only eight kilometres westwards, to Bastogne in the east. When he had finished there were more than seventy gold pieces on the maps.

'Now for the elimination.' He began to remove them, explaining as he went. 'This Count thinks only of money; here there are no hiding-places – I know because I tried to hide there once; this man is not liked by the villagers, he is a Gantois; this one is empty, I know, and the police visit it; this one is remote, but no, it is too small for so many prisoners; here is my friend Michel, I know he is up to no tricks; that is an institute for forestry, and the students are even sleeping in the cellars . . .'

After twenty minutes, and some references to books and a folio of prints, there were only three gold pieces left. Uncle pondered, then removed two of them. 'Here,' he said, pointing to the sole survivor, 'here is the best place. Close to the Semois valley but secluded from all traffic. It is bigger than you would think, because there are rooms built in the solid rock – I have been into them while the Baron was still alive. Now he is dead, since, let me see, since four years ago, and they tell me that . . .' He paused significantly.

'Yes, go on.'

'. . . that his daughter – how well I remember her as a child – is keeping the place going by renting it to hunting parties, who are of course installed in the comfortable rooms, the ones which you see from outside. Look, I will show you a drawing of the place in – where is it? – Duchamp's *Promenades dans les Ardennes*, of 1913, but the changes since then are superficial only.'

Marie had no doubts once she saw the engraving; she was sure that uncle had, by a purely cerebral feat of tracking, located the kidnappers' headquarters; and almost equally convinced that the daughter of whom she would not hear a good word (although her uncle offered her some) was the culprit. Even Felix, although he muttered cautionary words about the lack of real evidence that they should be looking in Belgium at all, let alone this particular corner of it, showed signs of being convinced as uncle traced with his pipe-stem the outline of the storerooms concealed in the cliff, and identified as a lift the iron structure which ran from the château above to the tobacco-drying sheds below.

It was quickly settled that Felix and Marie would bicycle over to the vicinity of the château on the following afternoon, take a walk through the woods to the west of it, which would give them intermittent views of the driveway and front entrance, and then return from the south at dusk. Uncle showed them on the map that there was a certain crag from which they could watch the building with no fear of being seen. Then in the evening, if their suspicions were not disarmed, they could puncture one of Marie's tyres and present themselves at the door, asking for help.

'It is possible that they will offer you beds,' said Mononk, 'if you arrive quite late and pretend to be exhausted, and if they are innocent. So I will not be surprised if you fail to return. On the other hand there may be danger. Perhaps I should go down to Vresse and tell the policeman if you are not back by midnight? Not that he would do anything at that hour. What do you think?'

Marie was quite clear about this. 'No policeman, please, Mononk. We will look after ourselves. It's a pity that we can't be sure of letting you know that we're all right, but you mustn't worry. Anyway we'll probably be back – it really would be extraordinary if this turned out to be the place, and we were able to get in at first try.' She set to work making a sketch map which they could take with them, and Felix took another sheet of paper on which he began to write, between sips of malt whisky. Marie came and looked over his shoulder when her sketch was finished.

'I'm doing your job for you, as surrogate sophist.'

The sheet was headed:

An Enquiry into the Dynamics of Group Remotivation in the Field of Environmental Pollution – Models constructed on the Basis of Psychological and Sociological Phenomena observed in the Communities of the Ardennes (Belgium) – by a Former Student of Rhetoric in Kirby Lonsdale Elementary School (3rd prize in Miss Warburton's speech class, 1944; aegrot, 1945; 4th prize 1946).

1. Bag of gold for good behaviour.
   Criticism – unnecessary, too costly.
2. Possibility of bag of gold.
   Better, but must it be gold?
3. Possibility of something which (may or may not be a bag of gold but) will be perceived as an individual benefit.
   Better still, but what are other such benefits?

(a) Feeling virtuous (not applicable in the Ardennes)
(b) Being praised
(c) Higher social status
(d)

'Marvellous,' said Marie, 'this is so penetrating. I have never seen an analysis of such subtlety. But I hope that it will not go on for ever. Why do you not complete (d) and stop there?'

Felix rapidly added:

(d) Enhanced attraction to other sex

and they departed to the owls' room.

Chapter 11

'. . . Meanwhile the silence of the kidnappers, since their first message two days ago, has caused speculation. Asked whether he thought this silence a good sign, a State Department spokesman replied: "Hard to tell – you could read it several ways." In Brussels the NATO Council has issued no further statement. Unofficial reports suggest that some of the Allies are unwilling to discuss ransom terms so long as there is no real evidence of a threat to the captured diplomats. At ten past nine there will be a report from the BBC correspondent in Brussels.'

Tim turned the radio down and signalled bafflement to Pete with his eyebrows.

'Our sinister silence doesn't seem to be having quite the right effect. You've got press officers, so use them, that's what I said to Anna last night. If we stay dumb we'll be off the front pages in no time flat.'

'Well, maybe. But we can't issue threats – that's been agreed all along – and there isn't much else to say, is there, unless we start giving bulletins on the prisoners' health, and I don't see any future in telling the world how fit and happy they are. Let's listen to this Brussels report.'

'. . . Underneath the arguments about whether the captured diplomats are really in danger or not, which have split the NATO Council into two factions, is an even more fundamental division of opinion. Could the NATO Allies, if necessary, put together a package of measures which would satisfy the mysterious kidnapper? Some Delegations are letting it be known that they think this could be done. Others argue that the problems of pollution are so complicated and the work already being done so comprehensive that no one could think of new measures which would be both dramatic and practical. The Secretary-General himself gave a carefully worded briefing to the press last night. He pointed out that NATO as an organisation is powerless to affect the environment. This can only be done by national and local authorities. However, he added with some emphasis that to draw attention to the difficulties was not to say that they were insurmountable.'

Tim realised that Anna was standing in the doorway, listening, and turned the volume up. But the commentator had nothing more to say about what was going on inside the NATO building, and went on to describe a student demonstration taking place in front of the gates. It didn't sound like a very big demonstration, and rain was falling on it. Tim switched off.

'Hi, Anna, how are you today? Don't forget we have that Bonn channel greased ready for the next announcement.'

Anna smiled. 'Keep it greased. I am sure we will need it before long. But every time we say something we must let it sink in. Anyway, that's what I think, and I'm sure you'll both be patient with me.'

'Oh, sure.' Anna's candid and earnest manner, as always, brought Pete under her spell. 'Don't think we're fussing – I mean I guess we do fuss, sort of, but pay no attention, just think it shows how keen we are.'

Anna left them, to continue her rounds. She looked modestly serene as she passed into the kitchen, but in fact she was worried. She could sense a certain restlessness developing, and was beginning to wonder how all her team would hold together after another week or two. But the scene in the kitchen reassured her. Françoise and Elizabeth were working hard, and Ingrid, perched on the high oak kitchen stool, was encouraging them.

'They did their exercises beautifully this morning. Some of them seem to be really interested in getting fit. The Portuguese has started going on about how he was a champion swimmer when he was a boy, and the American is planning to lose eight pounds while he's here. I think he'll be quite disappointed if he's released before he's managed to do it. He says that he's never had time before to think about his health, and he's simply lapping up advice now that he's found someone to give it to him.' She stretched her arms above her head and shook her hair back with a pleased smile. 'At first he thought I could only teach gym, but now he's discovered that I qualified in dietetics he shoots at me hundreds of questions about calories and nutrients, such a good pupil.'

Françoise smiled as she set up a row of six charlotte moulds. 'Today's lunch won't help him. Elizabeth is making some crazy English pie – what is it called? – a double-crust pigeon pie, the amount of pastry is fantastic, and then we are having my special charlotte. But do not worry, Anna, we have taken wine off the menu and will give them very strong coffee, so they will stay awake all right in the afternoon.'

Secunda and Tertia scampered into the kitchen. 'Oops,' gasped Secunda, 'we just got away in time.'

'Nonsense,' said Tertia, collapsing into a huge wicker chair by the hearth and taking off her black mask, 'it would have been quite safe to play with him a little longer.' She saw Anna's eyebrows ascending, and added maliciously, 'Besides none of them can run properly in those nightgown things, they're marvellously vulnerable.'

Secunda too saw the raised eyebrows, and choked back her giggles. 'Oh Anna, you look so severe, but it was nothing to make you worry. Truly, we did no harm. But we can't help getting to know them a little after three days of feeding them, and this one is so jolly.'

Anna wondered which one was so jolly. She was surprised to discover that she was at once excluding the Chairman from the range of possibilities. However, she let the matter drop. She was not worried about Secunda, who was guileless; and she thought it unwise to check Tertia, except with the lightest of reins. 'Well, do watch out,' she said, 'and remember that security comes first. Now let's all look at this strange pie, I am curious about it.'

Later she spoke to Franz about the incident, and asked him to increase surveillance in the area of confinement. Franz said that he would speak to Kemalettin. But he added that it was all he could do to maintain security at its present level. Kemalettin's attitude was splendidly suspicious and wary, but Jacopo and Giovanni were already a shade less alert and single-minded than they had been on the first couple of days. 'The trouble is, it's so obvious that these fellows aren't trying to escape. Some of them are actually enjoying themselves – you can tell when you observe them all day long – and just about all of them are working hard in their sub-committees. Of course if we left the door open they'd probably leave. But it isn't realistic to continue as though we were guarding a bunch of James Bonds. Besides, there's a spirit of fraternisation – on both sides. This business of Secunda and Tertia is just a foretaste of what we may have later. If we try to kill it dead, and keep up a prisoner and gaoler situation, we'll be in trouble. Much better to go along with the change in atmosphere, maybe even show a lead – hold a dance or something – but make sure that the basic security drills are followed. That's what matters, and that's where we must be grateful for Kemalettin. Anyway I'll go and see him now.'

Anna thought the suggestion of a dance rather strange, but played with it for a minute. It would have to be a masked affair, certainly if she was going to attend – and it would be proper, surely, for the Chairman to lead off the dance with her, so she would have to be there. She shook herself in sudden impatience and went to join Alexander the Great.

He had tuned in to the sub-committee on air pollution. The Norwegian was droning away about the need for a global monitoring system, such as the United Nations had been talking about, and suggesting that until this was set up no one could tell exactly what new regulations were needed. It was all very sensible, but dampening, and Anna was glad when she recognized the Chairman's voice, interrupting him.

'Look, I mustn't interfere with your work, but I have this job of co-ordination, and I must say that I wonder what conclusions you will reach if you take this line. Trygve, we all agree with you about the need for data, but what exactly are you going to suggest in the way of immediate action? This is what we need if we're going to be home for Christmas, isn't it, and the other sub-committees are managing to concentrate on positive ideas . . .'

'Well, of course. Yes we must have positive ideas. But these ideas have to be related to the problems, and the problems must therefore be defined. What I am saying is that the problems are not yet defined with accuracy. Sometimes red rain falls on my country, coming from the Ruhr, and we all think this is bad, but we do not know whether it all comes from the Ruhr, nor from which factories, and we have not yet measured the effect of it on the growth of our trees. All this is being worked on, but it takes time. What are we to say now, which will not make the scientists laugh at our ignorance.'

An American voice intervened. 'I can think of things which won't make the scientists laugh. OK, they're still playing around with test tubes of red rain. But I don't have to wait for them to fell me that red rain does trees no good. I can figure that out all by myself. Let's have it stopped, just like that . . .' There was a sound of fingers being snapped. 'Why don't we say that the German Government has to levy sums from the Ruhr which will be forfeit if there's any more red rain and given back if it stops? How about that, huh?'

Alexander the Great wrinkled his upper lip in approval and nodded vigorously at Anna. But she held up her finger for silence as the loudspeaker reproduced the sound of a door banging and rapid footsteps.

'Hallo, Luis, what brings you here? I thought you were busy on noise. Have you finished already?'

'Listen, I want to make an exchange, I can't work in that group, it is impossible. Mr Chairman, you are here, can't you transfer me to air pollution?'

'But what's the trouble, you asked to work on noise, didn't you?'

The voice of the Portuguese remained soft, as always, but it was sibilant with emotion. 'Yes, yes, I like quiet, but that is why I must leave. Piet is shouting at us all the time, I think he is going mad, we can't work fast enough for him, and . . .'

Another bang, and then what was unmistakably Piet's voice boomed loud and harsh. 'So this is where you are hiding. I knew that you didn't want to go to the lavatory, you're shirking, don't you realise that we must get *on*, get on, we have to finish quickly . . . No, *come*, Luis, my God must I carry you . . .?'

There was a scuffling noise, and then the door banged again.

'Shall I switch over to the noise room and see what happens?'

'No,' said Anna, 'I've heard quite enough. This is serious. How can they work if Piet carries on like this? I must think what to do. You go on listening. Oh, and don't forget to tell me if there's a message from the Chairman. I'm half expecting one.'

Anna would have liked to make herself some tea when she got back to the tower room, and to drink it all by herself. But Sister Agnes was waiting there for her. Anna sensed at once from her posture, just perceptibly awkward and rigid, that the interview was not going to be easy.

'Oh, hallo, Agnes, I hope you haven't been waiting long. I hadn't forgotten about our talk, but I was held up listening to the men discussing noise. Your friend Piet was making a lot; I am quite worried by the way he goes on. But will you have some tea?'

Sister Agnes shrugged, in gawky fashion, and said, 'I don't mind. But I came for a talk. It's about Piet.'

Anna was considering which teacups to use. She possessed a pair of the *Linnaea borealis* set made for Linnaeus, and had been wondering whether it would please Sister Agnes and smooth the interview if she used something so delicate and patently valuable. The tone of the girl's voice, almost harsh with suppressed tension, dissuaded her. She reached further and selected a pair of strong Sunderland lustre-ware cups and put them on the little oak chest by her chair. Points of gold flickered where the light caught the purple bands. Anna opened the tea caddy, poured hot water into the brown Chinese teapot, and waited for the kettle to boil.

'Yes, I think you have been having a difficult time. But what about Piet, exactly?'

'It can't go on. Not like we have to, just meeting in the library with a guard outside. When it's Giovanni he always finds an excuse to knock on the door and interrupt us. Can't you see what a state Piet's in, he's fit to explode, it's all got out of hand.'

The kettle boiled, and Anna made the tea. 'Hmm, I agree about him being in a state. I was wondering whether it would be better for you to stop seeing him for a bit . . .'

'Oh, no, you must be crazy. No one else can control him, he'd start tearing the place apart. Oh, I know Kemalettin and Jacopo could overpower him and lock him up or something, but don't you see the whole plan would be wrecked if something like that happened?'

Anna poured the tea. 'All right. What do you propose? I will listen.'

Sister Agnes held Anna's gaze defiantly. 'We've got to have an evening out together. This evening.'

'*Out?* You mean let him out of the confinement zone? Now it is you who must be mad. Think, he could escape and undo everything. Even if he didn't escape he would see too much. And what about . . . No, there are so many objections I cannot even list them. Surely you see it is out of the question?'

'No, I don't see. You've got it all wrong. Of course he won't escape. He'll only run one way, and that's after me. And so far I've no plans to leave. Oh, I see all the problems, and I've worked out the answers, but it's no good telling you if you can't even see that something's got to be done. Look, you put me on this horse, and it's bucking, and I know how to handle it, but all you can say is keep it in the stable.'

Sister Agnes was pleased by her metaphor. She went on, more calmly, 'A good gallop is all it needs. Anyone who knows about riding would know that.'

Anna sipped her tea. She was tempted to say that she too knew a lot about riding. But her knowledge applied to horses. She was not disposed to pursue a subject which could shift disconcertingly from the metaphorical to the not. She reflected on the threat faintly implied in one of Sister Agnes' remarks, and on the charge of inflexibility which was implicit in all of them. Franz had been warning her against just this.

'Well,' she said at length, 'tell me your plan.'

Sister Agnes told her. Her voice was flat now, almost relaxed. She knew that the plan was a good one, and she knew that Anna was honest and would admit it.

Anna did. But she still had questions. 'Who thought of this, to begin with? And what about you, are you looking forward to it very much?'

'Well, we sort of thought of it together. I don't mind going out with him, since it's got to be done.'

The questioning light did not fade from Anna's eyes. Sister Agnes tried again. 'Yes, I am looking forward to it.' Suddenly she began to sob. 'I won't see him again, afterwards . . . He's the first man to . . . He's . . .'

Disarmed by this exhibition of weakness (which, logically, should have alarmed her further), Anna put her hand on the girl's shoulder. 'Well, you will have your evening together, and perhaps it will calm you both. We should never have let you in for this but we must make the best of it.'

The light was beginning to fail, although there was a full hour to dusk. Anna switched on the tablelamp, crossed to the corner window, peered for a few moments at the outside world into which her vehement prisoner and anguished aide were shortly to be released, drew the curtains and reached for the telephone. She preferred to dissemble on the telephone because she knew that face to face her eyes would give her away.

'Kemalettin? Anna here . . ., Yes, fine, but listen, we have one problem. The Dutchman is becoming impossible, and I've decided to give everyone a rest from him . . . You've noticed too? Well, I don't need to explain why, but listen while I tell you how. He's going to clinic in a few minutes to see Agnes – you know, that's the trouble, he is too excited by her. Anyway, he's been too clever this time, he's invented some illness as an excuse for seeing her again, and she's promised to give him medicine . . . Yes, how quick you are, it should knock him out in a couple of minutes. Now once he's knocked out I want him strapped to the first aid stretcher and brought up here to me. He'll have to be kept right out of the way for five or six hours, we can't have the others seeing him unconscious in the clinic and there's really nowhere else to put him . . . What? No, no, there's plenty of space here, he can be left behind the screen. Anyway, I may want to talk to him when he wakes up. All right? . . . But listen, I want him removed discreetly, you must choose a moment when the others are all out of the way – get Jacopo to help you.'

Piet made plausible snoring noises while Sister Agnes pulled the strap tight over his ankles.

'Goodness, he makes almost as much noise asleep as awake,' she said to Kemalettin and Jacopo as they came into the clinic.

'So, the parcel is all ready for us.' Kemalettin tested the straps.

'Yes, off you go, and tell Anna there's no hurry about sending him back. We could all use a bit of peace. I've left a bit of paper in his pocket saying what I've given him and when he might start waking up. Oh, and take this sleep mask, Anna had better put it on him before he wakes, otherwise he might see something he shouldn't. Look, I'll stick it in his hand.'

The conspiratorial pressure of her finger tip in the palm of his hand inspired Piet to give an even more convincing snore as the stretcher was lifted up and carried, joggling, away.

Sister Agnes retained her nursely habits faithfully. Although she had only given Piet a mock injection she washed her hands carefully, humming to herself, and then patted her hair into place in front of the old rosewood cheval mirror which someone had left in the clinic. When Jacopo came back and winked at her, to signify that Piet had been delivered, she winked back. 'Remember you promised me a ride in the lift?' she asked. 'I'm free for a bit now, and feel like some fresh air. How about letting me down in the lift?' She slipped off her white tunic and donned in its place an olive green raincoat with a hood.

'Yes, you mean right now? Suppose I come too? I could get Giovanni to take over from me for a bit.'

'Mmm, you are nice. No, don't come this time, I have one of those moods, I want to be alone, but if it's nice down in the valley we can go together next time.'

Oh scarlet, vermilion, ultra-crimson fibber, she thought, how can you deceive the poor man so? Does he really think I want to walk in the damp all by myself, I'm sure if I was an Italian girl he'd think I was potty. I am, too. Proper potty.

She followed him through the two security doors to the guard chamber, and pulled the green hood over her hair as she stepped on to the lift platform.

Perched just below the lip of their crag, close together on a fragment of groundsheet which uncle had given them, Felix and Marie were watching. Felix saw Anna in the window for a moment, having swivelled his binoculars in that direction when her light went on. 'A girl,' he announced to Marie, 'I bet that's the one who owns the place. The room she's in looks quite big, and it must be above one end of those store-rooms your uncle talked about. I suppose the lift marks the other end.'

Marie edged forward cautiously and peered down into the complex of sheds and yards which lay between them and the cliff on which the château stood. The bottom of the lift run was clearly visible, but the lift itself was evidently in the up position, unless it had been removed altogether. The iron framework in which it would run up and down looked as though it could be climbed by an expert, but not easily. She took the binoculars from Felix and examined the room in which he had seen the girl. It jutted out slightly from the cliff, like a turret, marking one corner of the whole building. On the store-room side the drop was sheer, and there could be no hope of reaching the windows from below. Round the corner, where Marie could not see so well, there seemed to be a grassy ledge about ten feet below, running back and down in a gentle curve until it reached a small ravine in which young pines were growing closely together. Marie could see that it would be possible to scramble up through the ravine and reach the grassy ledge, but that the windows of the room would still be well out of reach for anyone without a ladder. Like me, she thought, I certainly don't have a ladder; it's the front door for us.

'Marie,' whispered Felix.

'Yes?'

'I've been thinking about all this motivation business. You know, how to make people take more care of the environment.'

'Really, Felix, you are strange. I thought you were going to say something quite different. Still, go on, so long as we keep watching.'

'Well, I was thinking we've been unfair. It must be the influence of the Ardennes. I reckon most people would be a lot more careful if they just knew, I mean really knew, what's important. It's too muddling at present, people only get little bits of the picture at a time, they don't know whether it's good to use electricity or bad, they don't know how many babies they ought to have, they hear wildly different stories about car pollution, they can never remember how much aluminium is left in the world or whether it's something else that's going to run out at the end of the century. You see what I mean? They haven't even got a basis for a code of conduct, let alone a code, so they mostly go on as before. You can't blame them. I think most of them just need more information and advice, not bags of gold or anything like that. Way back in the war, in England, when I was a boy, the papers used to carry big notices from the government saying what kind of refuse to save and what to do with it, and lots of things like that. I remember my mother was an absolute fanatic about doing everything they said, even things that seemed a bit ridiculous – and she wasn't exceptional at all.'

Marie stroked his calf with one hand, while keeping the binoculars to her eyes with the other. 'Mmm, you are so trusting and hopeful. Maybe you are right. But look, the light is almost gone, what are we going to do? We haven't really seen anything from here. Shall we . . . Oh, wait a minute, *look*.'

Even without binoculars Felix could plainly see the lift travelling downwards, with a solitary cloaked figure standing on the platform. The still air carried sound well, and they could even hear what sounded like a window being shut in the château; but there was no noise at all from the lift machinery. As soon as the figure stepped off the lift at the bottom of the hoist they could see that it was a girl. She waved upwards, then in pantomime tugged at a rope running down the side of the hoist, gave the thumbs-up sign and blew a kiss to the unseen figure at the top of the shaft. The lift began to travel silently upwards. Once it was well on the way the girl darted off through the yard, passing in front of them, and made for the ravine which climbed up the side of the château on the right.

Marie passed the binoculars to Felix. 'Strange. What is she doing, is it the woman we saw in the window?'

'No, I don't think so, but I can't be sure. She seems to be in a real hurry.'

The girl disappeared into the tangle of trees in the ravine, then reappeared higher up and paused, not far from the grassy slope which curved up in the lee of the château and ended below the turret room. Felix and Marie could just hear a faint whistle. Then the girl resumed her climb.

'Look at the window.' Felix gripped Marie's arm. They could just make out what appeared to be a rope dangling from the turret room and gradually being lowered until it reached the grassy slope. A moment later a bulky figure slid rapidly down it, hand over hand, and stood at the bottom, still holding on to the rope and gazing sightlessly across the valley at them. The figure was wearing a black mask.

Meanwhile the girl was running up the slope. When she reached the man the two shapes coalesced into one and stayed thus for a full minute. then she stepped back and tugged on the rope. At once a large bundle dropped down into her arms. Fitting this somehow on to her back she began to lead the man carefully down the slope, and they soon disappeared into the ravine.

Felix and Marie looked at each other, left speechless by their total inability to interpret these events. Then they swung their gaze back on to the lower end of the ravine, and watched the couple emerge. The girl picked some twigs off the man's clothes, and they could hear her saying something to him. The man opened his arms, and she was in them, bundle and all, in a flash. Another minute passed before this second clinch was broken. Then the pair moved rapidly, always with her guiding arm linked in his, to the courtyard below and moved crabwise around it, seeming to shelter from sight in the shadow of the sheds. Outside the least ruined shed they stopped again and the man was given the bundle to hold. Some words floated up. '. . . . blankets, darling, I insisted we'd need some . . . inside quickly . . . the handle's stuck, no here we go . . .'

◇◇◇

Anna coiled up the rope and laid it lengthwise on the stretcher, then put a blanket over it. In the dim light behind the screen it passed for a recumbent figure. She closed the window, put on d'Indy's *Variations on a French Mountaineer's Air* on the record player and lay on the chaise longue, thinking. Franz found her thus when he came in with a folded piece of paper. He held it up so that she could see written on it, in green capitals, 'Anna'.

'From the Chairman?'

'Yes, as we expected. He gave it to Tertia just now, and didn't say what was in it. But I'm sure he's asking to see you.'

Anna read the paper rapidly. Franz waited, noticing the colour in her cheeks and wondering whether she had been out with the hunting party.

'Yes, quite right. He says what about this evening, and can I arrange it so that he sees me alone, but in – what does he say? – "in conditions which will meet my security requirements". Oh, I am glad, I feel sure that this will help. Now what about the arrangements, we must think them out before I reply. I trust him, myself, but everything must be planned so that he can do no harm even if it is all a trick.'

It was quite dark by the time Marie slithered back into place at Felix' side after her reconnaissance.

'I didn't see anything while you were down there, except for those lights coming on.' Felix pointed to several lit windows in the château. 'What did you find out?'

'Nothing really. They're still in that shed. They weren't doing much talking – just murmurs. If you ask me, they're stretched out on that blanket she had, having a good time, although it must be damp in there – I sniffed through the cracks, and the smell was all of rotting wood, you know, not very romantic.' Marie mused for a moment. 'Could the man be one of the prisoners, do you think?'

'Hardly – I mean, the chaps in the SPC don't usually behave like that.'

'I'm sure they don't. But who does? Do you think he still has that mask on?'

'Goodness knows, people have such odd habits – though I must say I can't imagine why they'd choose a damp shed. Still, I suppose that's their business. The main thing is that they're out of action for a bit, and meanwhile whoever's in charge of the lift is just waiting for a tug on the rope. Let's go and tug it and see what we find at the top, what do you think?'

'D'acc. Much better than having a puncture. But I wonder, is this the right place? Those two down in the shed are so weird. I mean, the way they were acting before they got in there. It all seems more like a lunatic asylum or something.'

'Don't worry. I've got that Brigham Young feeling, clear and strong. You know, *this is the place*! Kop af. I really know. Come on, or those crackpots will be crawling back out of their rotting woodwork.'

Chapter 12

Jacopo was wearing his Polizia Stradale uniform, complete with goggles. He was due to go through to check with Giovanni in the confinement area in a few minutes, at five o'clock, and he liked to be clad in chic, authoritarian clothes when he walked among the prisoners. But as he turned the giant handle and watched the counterweight sink out of sight he felt less sure that these were the best clothes for impressing Sister Agnes. He wondered whether she would be pining for company after her solitary walk. In the twenty five seconds which it took to wind the lift all the way up he managed to develop this line of thought quite considerably. He hurried to lock the wheel in position and turn round so that it would be easy for the inflamed nurse to fling herself sobbing into his arms. But two people were flinging themselves at him. In the second available to him he managed to observe that one of them was indeed a beautiful female, and had automatically begun to construct a new sexual fantasy around her: then his head bounced off the brass wheel and the rest of the drama was lost to him.

'Goodness, a policeman. Italian, too. We haven't killed him have we?'

'No, he's OK, but let's get these clothes off him quickly. They'll fit me and I can go on in wearing them.'

'*We* can,' said Marie, eyeing a second uniform hanging on the wall while she helped to peel Jacopo's trousers off. 'Here, you tie him to the wheel with that rope and gag him while I try these on.'

Felix found the keys in the jacket pocket and they both read the notice on the thick oak door. 'Procedure for entering the area of confinement', it said; there were four paragraphs, very clear and detailed.

Secunda was clearing away the tea things, and the Committee were about to start work again. They felt rather jolly. No one had said anything about Piet's absence, but they had all noticed it and were enjoying the more relaxed and tranquil atmosphere. The Chairman seemed to be in a particularly good mood, and hummed as he shook cake crumbs off the plates and stacked them up to help Secunda. In his pocket he had a note from the Belgian. It read 'I looked. Erable plane (*Acer platanoides* Linnaeus)'.

'I've really enjoyed today,' said the Canadian. 'I guess I want out, like everyone, but if you think about it this is really a lot better than Evère – better working conditions, far better food – remember those NATO menus, huh? But what's really best is having no instruction from our governments. I know mine would foam at the mouth if they could see some of the bits in our marine pollution paper, I guess they will too . . .' He laughed with deep pleasure, imagining scenes in Ottawa.

Portentoso laughed too. 'What I like best is that we are free from our Permanent Representatives. Oh, I have been discreet about mine, I have never said a word to his discredit, is that not so?' The others nodded. 'Yet there is much to say – his laziness is incredible – I must tell you some stories at dinner which will surprise you. And now the good man is running in and out of NATO all day long, working like a maniac, and all to free Portentoso. I call this the justice of the poets.'

Giovanni, at the side of the room, beamed; he liked to see his fellow-countryman happy. His goggles were misting over and he lifted them slightly forward to check the time on his wrist-watch. He saw that Jacopo was due any moment now. He moved over towards the security door and saw the blue light above it start winking. The Chairman followed him, thinking that whoever came in might bring Anna's reply, but stood at a tactful distance while Giovanni opened the control panel in the wall and signalled 'all clear to come in' to his unseen partner. The door jerked open, and two uniformed figures, instead of one, leapt into the room, swivelling their heads from side to side to take in the whole scene, and then, within an instant, focussing on Giovanni. 'Hands up', croaked one in a high-pitched voice, pointing a gun at him. Giovanni hesitated, mouth agape, then began to raise his hands. The other intruder jumped forward into the middle of the room. 'You're free,' he said. 'We've come to rescue you. Quick, overpower that guard, and follow us.'

There was an equivocal silence. 'Rescue us?' said the Canadian, 'What do you mean? Who the hell are you, bursting in like this?'

Felix supposed that they had not understood. 'I'm from NATO,' he hissed. 'Come on, get out of here fast, there may be other guards.'

The dozen or more faces which he could see through his goggles registered growing hostility. No one moved forward. They seemed to be waiting for something to happen. Too late, Felix realised that there was someone behind him. The chair crashed on to his head and he fell at the Chairman's feet. There was a growl of approval from the Committee. 'Get the other one,' shouted the Canadian as Lute launched himself across the room in a rugby tackle which took Marie by surprise. Her gun went off with a kindergarten plop as she fell. Lute realised that it was a woman as they landed on the floor together. He also heard a hissing noise, and then his thoughts began to blur. One loud crash pierced his consciousness just before he passed out: this represented the laden tea-tray which Secunda dropped as she melted downwards across the already recumbent body of the Dane.

Upstairs Franz went on counting until he had reached a hundred, then pushed the gas lever back and reached for the microphone. 'Franz here, Emergency, Emergency, someone has broken into the confinement area, draw gas masks. Repeat, Franz here, Emergency in the confinement area, gas released in minimum quantity, everyone assemble with gas masks, Tim and Sister Agnes to take charge of resuscitation, Kemalettin to cope with intruders, Pete to check outside château for any more of them. Repeat, Franz here in the control room, Emergency . . .'

Anna crossed swiftly but calmly to her windows. While she checked from each in turn that there was no sign of life outside, she mentally listed the problems. Who were the intruders, and did anyone know that they had come to the château? The plans for a mass evacuation at short notice existed, but they were rather sketchy. Where to imprison the new prisoners?

Well, first things first, what sort of people were they? Alexander had better interrogate them, the sooner the better. Tell Tim and Sister Agnes to bring them round first. Sister Agnes? Of course, what a nuisance. The others would want to know where she was. Oh well, that was a minor problem, so long as the two of them got back in all right.

Anna was hastening along the narrow corridor which led from her room to the main hallway of the château. She stopped suddenly, walked back and locked her door. It would not do if anyone went in and took a good look behind the screen. Back down the corridor, into the hallway.

'Oh, good afternoon Monsieur le Baron, are you having your apéritif all alone?' There was laughter in her voice, but no trace of tension. 'No, I won't join you, although it is so peaceful here that I should like to. Let me see, is there any sign of the others coming back?'

Anna looked quickly down the driveway, then at the pine-clad slopes beyond, more slowly. Again, no sign of life. She stepped outside and listened for a moment. Silence, except for the noise of a lorry climbing up from the bridge two kilometres away. Or a bus – yes, the 5.30 from Bouillon.

'Yes, it really *is* quiet. But we are quite busy in the kitchens. Tonight you are having Patakukko, and pancakes with cloudberry jam – yes, I have a friend who lives just above the Arctic Circle and sends me food parcels. I hope to join you for dinner, but I'll be busy until then.'

Anna thought that it was just as well that she had found the Baron there. It was useful to have him anchored to his bottle of Scotch near the front door. And she might have forgotten about the dinner. Françoise and Elizabeth simply must stay in the kitchen and finish that pie. Ingrid must take over Sister Agnes' duties.

Halfway back down the corridor she turned off into an empty bedroom, went through another almost filled with furniture under dust sheets, unlocked the door of the strange Biedermeier bathroom which her aunt Ermesinda had always used, unlocked the door on the far side of it – goodness, it still smelled of that essence which Ermesinda had distilled from pine cones in the brewery – and down the spiral staircase into the store-room office, beside the lobby in front of the confinement area doors. Both doors were open, and a faint ammoniac smell was coming through them. Anna slipped on one of the few gas masks left on the rack and went on in.

The team was behaving beautifully. They had already sorted out all the bodies, laying the Committee members down one side of the main room in a neat row. Anna observed the Chairman at the near end of the row, distinctively clothed in his blue djebbah. She noticed that his incipient beard was fair, and looked silky rather than stubbly like some of the others. Tim was working on Secunda and Giovanni, and Ingrid was helping him; they hadn't needed to be told. Kemalettin and Pete were stripping police uniforms off two more bodies in another corner of the room, while Franz collected things out of the inner and outer pockets. Anna moved over to this group. Franz reported, while continuing his search.

'I've left Alexander in the control room. Extractors full on for two minutes now, the air must be almost all right again. These are the two who got in, we still don't know how or what happened exactly. Jacopo had been knocked out and tied to the lift wheel, he's in the clinic, still a little groggy but nothing broken. Look, do we want Pete to go and look outside? There hasn't been time to let him down in the lift yet. We're two men short, will be for another hour or two, and both the Jameses are away shopping, that makes four down. What do you think?'

'No, I've looked out myself. It's all quiet, and that big Baron is at the front door like a watchman. How quickly can you wake these two up? Goodness, one of them's a girl.

This is really odd . . . I don't like her clothes at all, do you? . . . but it may make it easier to find out who they are. That's the top priority, don't you think? What about having Alexander question them, separately of course?'

Pete objected. 'Too slow. We've got to get their story fast. Why don't I take the man and Alex can have the girl. I bet I get results first. But where can we take them? Here, take her stockings off, we can use them to tie her wrists. Don't you have a dungeon here in the château?'

'Yes, but one of my enlightened ancestors bricked it up in the seventeenth century.' Anna added pointedly, 'We have a long tradition of humanitarian behaviour here, which I don't intend to break. Anyway, the man looks quite nice. I expect they're just hikers or something. The problem is going to be how to conceal their disappearance, or make sure they don't talk if we have to let them go.'

Franz shook his head, holding up an open wallet. 'It's not as easy as that. I heard him say he was from NATO and had come to rescue them. They know all right, and look at this – "Ministère des Affaires Etrangères, Monsieur Felix Blayne, Premier Secrétaire, Délégation du Royaume Uni auprès de l'OTAN" – oh, good, marital status, bachelor, that's something. No, there's only one thing we can do – lock them up and hope that no one can trace them to this area.' He finished tying Felix' feet together. 'Anna, you can leave all this to us, we'll tidy up. Why don't you go and see Alexander? Make sure he's listening to the news bulletins – he'd better listen in on the police network too, don't you think? We'll come and report after a bit, and let Alex come down for the questioning.'

'All right, but make sure that the girls have dinner ready on time even if this lot can't eat any. And what about the

Chairman – can you have him on his feet again for our talk this evening?'

'Yes, he ought to be all right. Where's Agnes by the way? We need her, but she's vanished.'

'Oh, I think she had a headache and went for a walk. She's a funny girl. I'll send her down if I see her, but if she's gone down to the village she won't be back for a while.'

Sister Agnes and Piet had been enjoying themselves in the shed, so long as they stayed on their feet. But after twenty minutes they both felt a need to be on the ground, and ran into trouble. Sister Agnes had brought a pencil torch which gave enough light for unrolling the blankets; but the blankets were unexpectedly small, almost like crib blankets, and it was difficult to find a good place for them. 'Here, you hold the torch. No, don't shine it on me, my sweet; on the *ground*, I must see what I'm doing. Oh! What are those things, no, don't tread on them, they'll come off on the blanket. Wait a minute, point the torch further over, there may be a drier patch – no, I hadn't seen that fungus, it's even worse on that side. Oh, Piet, I'm so furious, kiss me again.'

They enjoyed themselves for a few minutes more, until the strain of the embrace began to tell on them both, but especially on Piet.

'Agnes, Agnes, have you no better place for us to go? Where is the torch, let me look, give me that blanket . . .'

They heard a rumbling noise, and thin lines of light suddenly formed in the shed, quivering and shifting along across their bodies.

'The van, they may be going to put it in here. Quick, up to the end.'

They stumbled to the far end of the shed and ducked down behind a pile of mouldering logs. Sister Agnes arranged a blanket over each of them. As the damp penetrated her skirt she wished that there was blanket underneath her as well. But they could hear the big end-door opening, and voices. 'Back her in then, dead straight.'

Two white and two red eyes approached their hiding place and stopped just short of the logs. The engine revved up and nauseous blasts of exhaust smoke played over them for a full minute. Then the engine was cut and the lights switched off. They heard the van door slam and footsteps retreating.

Sister Agnes was half-crying and half-giggling as they rose to their feet and uncreased their aching legs.

'What about inside the van?' she whispered. 'It must be warm and dry.'

They had been inside for two minutes and had managed to spread the little blankets across the floor, just behind the driver's seat, where it was warmest, when they heard footsteps returning. A minute later the van started up and lurched out of the shed, bouncing so violently across the rutted yard that they had to brace themselves against both sides. The ride was mercifully short. When it was over they heard a whistle, and an English voice said, 'Here's the dustbin man. I nearly forgot to come round. Back at 9, OK? Put it in neatly, and make sure those bags are tied, I don't want any more spills.' A female voice replied, 'OK, but come in, James, I bet you don't know what's happened . . .'

Pete and Alexander the Great came in together to report to

Anna and Franz at a quarter to seven. Neither looked triumphant.

'The man's conscious,' said Pete. 'Doesn't seem at all scared. Won't tell me anything except his name and address, which we've got already. But he hasn't said anything about anyone knowing where he was going, or sending him here. And he keeps asking *me* questions, like why didn't the prisoners escape when he gave them the chance, and was it one of them who hit him on the head.'

'How much did you give away?' asked Franz ironically.

Pete flushed. 'What do you mean, give away? I thought it would help if I told him a bit of the truth, that the prisoners don't want to be rescued, that they're working with us. And I did say that it was one of them who hit him. I think he's gotten the picture now, and he made some crack about maybe he was on the wrong side. But he says he won't decide what to do until he and the girl can talk to one of the Committee together.'

'What does he mean, *he* won't decide what to do? *We* decide. We've got him locked up. Haven't we?'

'Sure, and handcuffed too, James Minor got back in time to tell us where to find them. But you try talking to him. He just doesn't see things that way.'

Alexander the Great nodded. 'The girl has similar characteristics. She asked me innumerable questions. I was unable to stop her. But I have her name – it is Marie – and I have established that she is concerned for the environment. I think she would co-operate if we approached her properly. She has already hinted that we need a new impetus in our work. She speaks with contempt of what we have done so far, dismissing it as inadequate . . . But she too demands the right to be with her man. I soothed her by saying that his head needed attention, but I must tell you she will be like a tigress soon if we keep them apart.'

Anna glanced at the clock and put on her evening stole. 'I must go. Thank you, both of you. I'll have to talk to the Chairman about this after dinner. If he would see them together perhaps it would all work out quite well – but I must be sure that he'd say the right things. You're sure it was he who hit the man on the head? . . . Well, that's certainly a hopeful sign, though I do find it disturbing. Franz, you're in charge, I'll be back by nine.'

She went upstairs to her room and checked that the door was still locked before passing along the corridor to join her hunting guests. The fish pie and the potatoes with dill were admirable, and the conversation was such that she could keep up her end charmingly while devoting all her thought to the problems ahead and her meeting with the Chairman. She enjoyed her dinner. She hoped that he had managed to eat some dinner. Perhaps she could make him a cup of tea if his stomach was still upset from the gas?

Anna declined coffee afterwards. She would have liked to take a cup, but the smell of cigars displeased her. As she made her adieux in the hall, where the hunters were clearly going to settle down for an evening's drinking in front of the TV, she heard a car engine starting up outside and automatically related it to the evening routine. James Minor, setting off from the kitchen entrance with the garbage. She had arranged for him to take it nightly, in bio-degradable bags, to the official dump on the road to Bouillon. Otherwise they would have had trouble with rats. It was reassuring that he was going off as usual; Franz would have kept him back if he needed him.

Anna walked back along the stone-flagged corridor, slowly since her black evening skirt was a tight fit. She noticed a row of dark, shining spots extending across several flags, but did not pause to investigate them. Once she had unlocked her door and switched on the chandelier she spoke to Franz on the telephone. '. . . In ten minutes. Fine. I'll have everything ready. I want Kemalettin to stay while I explain the conditions, then if he agrees Kemalettin can wait outside until I ring the bell. Yes, I know it's a bit risky, but we really need his help now and we'll have to show some confidence in him. Leave it to me. What about the radio? Has there been anything new? . . . Good. And you'd better tell this Marie that she'll see the man – what's his name, Blayne? – in the morning, I think it's clear that we'll have to put them together. Can you give them sleeping pills tonight? . . . No, she hasn't come back, but surely Ingrid can do it? . . . Well, let her try, anyway, we can't have two of the men staying awake all night to guard them. How's Jacopo? . . . Well, he must have a night's sleep, if no one else does. I should really have come down to see him. Tell him I hope the headache disappears soon. Good, well ten minutes from now . . .'

The Chairman gravely agreed to stay in the chair into which Kemalettin had guided him, and blinked as the bandage was removed from his eyes. A single candle burned on a low table in front of him, casting almost all its light on his side and illuminating the chair back which shielded the rest of the room from its light. Beyond, as his eyes became accustomed to the conditions, he could make out the silhouette of a woman seated in a high-backed chair, apparently clad in black and wearing some kind of bonnet. He waited.

'Good evening, Chairman, you wanted to talk to me. I want to talk to you too, about what has been happening today, but you can start.' The voice was low and clear, free of any recognisable accent and touchingly solemn. The version which he had heard over the loudspeaker had been older, more formal.

'Thank you. I've some things to say, and a question to ask.

'First of all, I hope that you realise what a change there is in the Committee's attitude. I congratulate you. They – we, I should say – are really on your side now. We're honestly trying to work out a package of measures which would do good. Of course we all want to get back home, but not till we've finished what we're doing. Most of the Committee really think that NATO will buy them out on your terms.'

'Most of the Committee?'

'Most; but I'm afraid that I don't. I'm not sure whether you really know anything about NATO . . .' The bonnet shook slightly, as if disowning any detailed knowledge. 'Well, I don't claim to understand it completely, but I can tell you one thing about how it works. It can't deal with details in a hurry. It's all a question of how they get instructions. On big, broad, urgent questions they get quick, political decisions from their capitals. But if they ask for instructions on more finicky things then they've got to wait while the finicky things are handed round among experts, you know, civil servants and scientific advisers and those kind of people. The politicians aren't going to touch this sort of thing without expert briefing, and some of them are going to wait a long time for it. Do you see what I mean? It's really the Ministers for Foreign Affairs, or even the Prime Ministers, who are going to decide; but they can only decide quickly on something they understand. They're not going to understand the things we're working on. Tell them that by two years from now the lead content in exhaust emissions must be down to 0.05 or whatever we think it should be, and they have to find out what that means – in terms of the effect on industry, legislation, all kinds of things. They do talk about this sort of thing in NATO, they have for years now, but they do it slowly and it can't be speeded up more than a little.'

After a silence Anna said, 'And what is your question?'

'Just this. What are your terms? You must know what you want. If I knew too I could guide the Committee along, and we might even come up with some ideas which would help you. Also . . .'

'Yes, also what?'

'Also I could give you some advice about your terms. I'd know fairly well what the governments might swallow and what they'd choke over. But I wouldn't want to talk to you this way unless you accepted that I was trying to help. I am, but do you believe me?'

'I don't disbelieve you. But you're very discouraging.'

Anna pondered. It would not do to let him know just how discouraging he had been, that she had never had a really exact idea of what the ransom terms should be. In some ways she was still the same girl who had found a way into the campanile and set the bells ringing, with only rather general expectations of what would ensue. She had hoped on the present occasion to bluff the Committee or the governments into making proposals which she could not formulate precisely herself. Now she was not so sure. And she was uneasily aware that the students, including even Franz, all believed that she was ready to state her terms whenever the need emerged.

'I'll think about what you said. We could talk again tomorrow. But I need your help on something else, these people who burst in this afternoon. Are you feeling all right, by the way? I'm sorry we had to lay you all out.'

'We all felt awful when we woke up, but it's passing away. Tell me about the man. Did I hit him too hard? And Lute says the other one was a girl. Was she?'

'Yes, they're all right, and safely asleep for the night. But I have a problem. They know where they are, obviously. We've got to make sure that they don't tell anyone when they're released. This is important for me personally. Now did they say anything which would have given the Committee a clue? My team say no, but I'm not sure they heard everything.'

'No, there was no clue. I was afraid they'd say something – that's partly why I hit him.'

'So you're all still quite in the dark about where you are?'

The Chairman hesitated. 'So far as I can tell, none of my colleagues knows where we are.'

Anna examined this sentence and found it unsatisfactory. 'And you – are you included in this statement?'

It took her several minutes to establish that the Chairman knew where he was, within ten kilometres, and to find out about the cry of the grive mauvis and the leaf of the érable plane. Her hands fluttered in her lap.

'This is awkward . . . for me. I must ask you to keep the secret. Please tell me, will you?'

'I've told no one else. The Belgian knows about the leaf, but it doesn't tell him much by itself. It's characteristic of the Semois Valley, but it grows in other regions too.' He paused. 'I'll make no promise to you – I once had to break a promise which I shouldn't have made – but I tell you this, if you trust me I will help you.'

The Chairman spoke with an edge of roughness to his voice, as though he was recalling something in his past which still troubled him. Risking a glimpse round the trimmings of Ermesinda's bonnet Anna saw that his face was hard in the candle-light, the face of a man who wanted something on his own terms. Yet he asked only for trust. Suddenly she thought that she understood his need.

'I trust you,' she said. 'Look, put your hands over your eyes, no just close them, that's right.'

He heard a rustling of silk and the sound of a chair being moved.

'Now keep your eyes closed and listen. If you see me, so that you would know me again, I will be in terrible trouble. I wish passionately, and for your sake too, that you shouldn't see me. And here I am sitting a foot away from you – here, feel my hand – and relying on you not to open your eyes. That is how I trust you.'

A smile with closed eyes is only half a smile, but this one was enough to tell Anna that she had met his need.

'Thank you, Anna. Now let's settle how to deal with these intruders. But stay where you are. I'll keep my eyes closed a little longer, long enough for you to blow out the candle.'

When the bell rang for Kemalettin forty minutes later he found everything as he had left it, and he failed to notice that the candle had scarcely burned down at all.

Anna had said nothing to the Chairman about Sister Agnes and Piet, but she had not forgotten about them. For all the charity which welled steadily within her she wished that she had hardened her heart in the afternoon and vetoed their sortie. With a sense of foreboding she crossed to the window and leaned out. There was no one below, although it was already five minutes past the appointed time. The night air was chilly and damp. Anna let her mind play over some of the things which could have gone wrong. The possibilities were endless. She let the rope down, but without much hope that Piet would reappear and climb up it, half closed the window and drew the curtains again. If she left the room locked Piet would be safe enough in it until morning, and then she could think of some way of disposing of him. But meanwhile what could she say to Kemalettin when he came back? She wished now that she had consulted the Chairman – he had such good ideas about the other two, he would surely have thought of some solution which would have let Anna go off and have a night's sleep. She realised suddenly that she was very tired.

Outside in the corridor Sister Agnes stood uncertainly at the door. All right, Agnes, she thought, in you go. Tell the headmistress – che sara sara, and it's no good putting it off, is it? She tapped.

'Goodness, what *has* happened to you? Look at your clothes, where has that blood come from – oh, my dear, have you had an accident? Come in, let me sponge your face, you've been crying.'

Sister Agnes was both relieved and taken aback at this reception. She had not seen herself in a mirror for some time.

'No, I'm all right, but Piet had an accident. We were running through some bushes – we had to get out of the van before they put the garbage in on top of us – and Piet had his mask on again and he slipped and put his thumb through one of those bird snares, you know, what they hang on bushes round here, it nearly cut his thumb off, oh it was awful – he was bleeding such a lot, and I couldn't dig the snare out of his flesh in the dark . . .'

Even if Anna had been less tired she would have found the recital puzzling. But she knew very well the snares which Belgians used, of double or even triple horse hair, and that the boys from the village sometimes set them in her grounds. And she remembered a row of dark spots in the corridor.

'Agnes, just a minute, first tell me one thing – where is he now?'

'Well, I think it's what you call the bridal suite, you know, that big room above the dining room, the one where that German count was last week. I knew it was empty, and I had to put him somewhere, hadn't I? I wrapped his hand up in the bottom of his djebbah and ran him along the corridor and upstairs. You were all having dinner, and no one saw us, and he's locked in and I've bandaged him up a bit, but I've got to get some things out of the first aid room to do it properly, I just thought I'd tell you first.'

Anna raised a hand to her head. 'Listen, a lot has been happening here. Two people broke in, the whole Committee had to be gassed, oh dear I can't tell you everything now. But could you just leave Piet where he is for the night? You can take my first aid box if that's any good. You see, there's someone in the clinic, being guarded . . .' With a final flicker of inspiration, Anna added, 'you can stay with him of course, make sure he's all right. Just lock yourselves in and keep the curtains drawn and don't come out till I come and see you in the morning.'

'Oh, you are kind, Anna . . . I'm sorry. I'm afraid we've been an awful nuisance. But we'll just stay there, out of the way, till you tell us.' She thought, I could just do with an hour in that lovely bathroom, and it's only his thumb that's out of action, isn't it, maybe the tide has turned for faithful little Agnes, get up there lass and let the good times start.

Anna made her last phone call short. 'No, they're definitely all right for the night and out of harm's way. It's a medical problem and she has to be on call. No, absolutely nothing more until tomorrow.' She went to bed, and fell quickly asleep, using the distant sound of bawdy hunting songs as her lullaby.

Chapter 13

Lady Lavenham usually took Pontifex for a walk in the woods before breakfast, a procedure which increased her appetite and the vigour of her conversation at the breakfast table.

'Have you decided yet, Ambrose?' she asked, as she tapped the top of her egg, 'I mean about the dinner next week. It's only five days away.'

Sir Ambrose swallowed tea and dabbed his mouth with an official napkin. 'I suppose we'd better call it off. It's a bore. We'll just have to do it some other time, in January I suppose, and I doubt if we'll get the Dean then. But it can't be helped. There's absolutely no sign of work slowing down. So far as I can see we'll be meeting two or three times a day for weeks to come, unless of course the police find this woman kidnapper.'

'All right, I'll tell Jean to ring round and explain. I don't mind. And if the Dean's away next time, the Dean's away.' She paused, assuming an expression of finality, as though allowing time for fates to be sealed in accordance with her decision. 'But I wish you'd tell me what you do at all these meetings. To judge by the papers you're just chattering. You haven't told the woman to go to blazes, you haven't worked out a ransom, you don't seem to have done anything.'

'Well, dear, the situation is very, ah, fluid. I really don't know from one day to the next what London are going to tell me to say; and most of the others are no better off. But today we're supposed to go through a paper which the International Staff have prepared – you know, one of these very non-committal documents, it's called something like "Measures which might be examined for possible consideration in the event of a decision that it would be desirable to consider measures".'

'Huh.' There was a tinge of tolerance in Lady Lavenham's ejaculation. She was mollified by her husband's willingness to poke fun at his own work. 'I must ring up Beta. Poor girl, I'll ask her round for coffee.'

As Sir Ambrose rode to the office he reflected that Georgina's questions were very much to the point. What were they all doing? There had been very little direction to their work in the last few days. Oh well, the department had told him on the telephone last night that he could expect a telegram in the morning with instructions approved by Ministers. Perhaps this would enable him to take a lead.

The telegram was waiting for him when he reached his office, on a long roll of coarse paper. Sir Ambrose read it with keen attention.

Your telegram No. 1149.

Ministers have now considered the report of the Special Interdepartmental Committee set up to consider possible ransom terms. The suggestions in your telegram No. 1132 were also before them.

2. The decisions taken are entirely without prejudice to the question whether there should be any ransom offer or not. You will have realised from the Prime Minister's recent message to the President (my telegram No. 9432 to Washington) that we are still not in a position to instruct you on this point. But you may tell the Council that, subject to this general reservation, HMG would be prepared to consider including the following in ransom terms:

(A) Provided that our allies were prepared to act likewise we would be willing to introduce legislation at an early date

to implement the supplementary safeguards against oil spills recommended at the IMCO meeting last February (and of which the text was sent to you last week).

(B) *We are willing to make available to our allies full information about the successful clean air measures taken in the UK during the last decade. Our hope would be that British achievements in this field might be taken as a yardstick of what the allies collectively could agree to implement by, say, two years from now. (For your own information only at this stage we might be able to send a small team of experts over to brief the Council if this was desired.)*

(C) *Subject to general agreement in the alliance and to further detailed study by the Treasury we would envisage increasing our contributions to United Nations projects on environmental problems by 3%. Alternatively, but only on the assumption that others would make parallel gestures, we could offer the United Nations Secretary-General a special once-for-all contribution of ninety thousand pounds sterling to be used at his discretion in environmental work. (If asked how we arrived at the figure of ninety thousand you should merely undertake to refer the question to London.)*

(D) *We could agree to doubling the size of the section of the NATO International Staff which deals with the Environment, and to the upgrading of the post of Director (Environmental Studies) by one grade. This would of course be conditional on the achievement of corresponding economies elsewhere in the International Staff.*

3. *Ministers recognise that in the event of negotiations over a ransom the kidnapper may well hold out for measures which would appear more substantial than the above. They believe however that a practical set of proposals of this kind would make a suitable opening offer, and that (A) (B) and (C) in particular*

would offer convincing proof of NATO's willingness to accelerate and intensify work on the problems of the environment. (D) is less substantial, in view of the very small number of staff involved, but we think it worth including for cosmetic reasons and also because we understand that the Belgians will be making a similar but disproportionately sweeping proposal, which we should prefer to anticipate rather than oppose.

4. Other points which may come up in the Council discussion have been covered in my telegrams Nos. 947 and 948, by which you should continue to be guided as necessary. In addition, however, you should know that the Dutch Minister called on the Head of Western European Department this evening and (with some embarrassment) enquired whether we were recommending a decoration or other honour for Lute. It appears that The Queen of the Netherlands has shown interest in a proposal to bestow a high honour on the Netherlands member of the SPC immediately, while he is in captivity. If your Netherlands colleague raises this in Council, or consults you informally, you should follow the line taken by Entwhistle with the Minister, namely that there is no present intention on our part to propose Lute for any honour and that while we would naturally see no objection to any of his colleagues being honoured by their sovereign or governments we are not ourselves convinced that this would affect their plight or seem appropriate to public opinion.

Sir Ambrose put the telegram down. In a voice which did not betray his dismay he asked his PA to get him the Permanent Under-Secretary in the Foreign Office on the telephone, and to ask the Head of Chancery to step in. While he waited he tried to translate the instruction mentally into a statement which he could imagine himself making; it was hard going.

As the PUS came on to the line the Head of Chancery skidded eagerly into the room. He was holding another copy of the telegram, on which he had pencilled 'HE – am having this turned into a statement for circulation in case you want your colleagues to have the text.'

'Good morning, James. Thanks for the instructions about the kidnapping.' While he spoke, Sir Ambrose neatly wrote 'Hold it, I can't hand this tripe out' on the Head of Chancery's copy and dismissed him with a motion of the head. 'All very clear, and I'm grateful. But there's a problem of presentation. I can see that I ought to have reported more about the atmosphere here in the last day or two. The thing is that the hardliners are going to be upset if we say anything at all about negotiation terms, and the others, frankly, are going to think our suggestions are, well, trivial. Now I'm not sure whether it's part of your tactics to draw fire from both sides and dig in in the middle, or whether Ministers are going to have an unpleasant surprise when everyone pounces on us . . .'

'I see, I see.' The PUS had a capacity for treating every event or item of news, however catastrophic or depressing, as though it were somehow personally welcome to him, not wholly unexpected and potentially rather jolly. 'Well, I did have a feeling that what we were sending you was rather a bag of peanuts, but I'd better warn you that there was a fearful struggle yesterday before we were allowed to send you even this much. I'm afraid you'll have to treat it as a serious contribution, and you'll certainly have to say it all, although I'm sure you can dress it up a bit so that it sounds better.'

'Ah, that's just what I wanted to say. How would it be if I started by saying that we just haven't made up our minds about tactics and so on, and await further views from our allies – then I could add that we had been doing some preliminary studies on the kind of thing we might offer if we ever did decide to negotiate, and that I could give the Council some examples if they liked – someone's bound to say they would like – but that so far we've been working on low-key offers suitable for use in a modest opening bid? Something like that, eh?'

'Well . . . that's playing it down rather far; I mean Ministers were sweating away late yesterday evening on all this and I don't think they'd be very happy if you put if just like that.'

'Mm, I see. Well, I'll play it fairly straight then. But if it doesn't go down well – and you can be sure it won't – I'll take the line I just suggested, more or less on a personal basis. How's that?'

'All right. But you can be pretty sure that all this will be lost in the wash by tomorrow. Don't say this, of course, but we're likely to get a decision from across the road by tonight, on the main question I mean, and my guess is that we'll be lined up firmly among the doves and what's more we'll have a really big olive branch in our mouth. A pity all this couldn't emerge sooner, but you know how it is when the PM's making up his mind – we can hardly tell him that it would make life easier for you if he hurried up, can we?'

Sir Ambrose echoed the laugh which came down the line, then hung up. 'Get me the Canadian Permanent Representative, please – he's probably in a briefing meeting, but say that I particularly want to speak to him before Council.'

'Was it you who hit me? asked Felix.

'Yes, I do apologise. A member of the International Staff should certainly not hit a member of the British or any other delegation. But I didn't know who you were, and anyway it looked as though you were going to spoil everything.'

Felix blinked. 'Look, where's the girl who was with me? You'll have to explain what's going on to me – I'm obviously on the wrong wavelength – and you might as well tell us together.'

The Chairman nodded to Franz, and Marie was escorted into the clinic. She seemed to be in vigorous mood. 'Who is this man? No, don't tell me, it's Mr Big, isn't it, a rotte boestring if every I saw one, let us out before the police arrive, your game is up . . .'

'Just a minute, darling, this is the Chairman of the Committee – yes, the Chairman of the Committee, one of the people kidnapped, not a kidnapper, and he's going to explain why they didn't want to be rescued yesterday.'

'Oh, is he? Well, I don't need any explanation, I could see they were paralysed by fear, goodness knows what's been done to them, but this man's obviously behind it.'

The Chairman held up his hand. 'Do sit down, and I will explain my guilt. Then you can judge me.'

He gave a very good explanation of what had been happening. Felix clearly found it perfectly reasonable and rather amusing. Marie accepted it less easily, but was influenced by Felix. 'All right,' she said, 'so you're on Anna's side now. Why not? You'll have a lot of explaining to do when you get out, but that's your business. What I want to know is what you're going to do with us. Are we supposed just to go away and say nothing about what we've seen? If you keep us here there's bound to be a search before long, and anyway we're supposed to be on holiday, aren't we, Felix?'

The Chairman pressed his fingertips together. 'You see, it is not a question of what are we going to do with you. You will have to work out with us, and with Anna, what happens. What she would like is for you to stay and help us, probably just for a few days, but of course this is not possible if you don't agree with her aims . . .'

Felix spoke. 'Aims, yes, they're fine. And her methods don't seem so bad now that we've heard about how you've been treated. But where are the others? I think that Marie, anyway, would like to hear from some more of them how things have been. After all, she hasn't ever met you before.'

'Here is the big problem. It is very important for Anna that her identity, and the use of this château, should be kept secret, even after everything is over. This I assure you. And I can also tell you that no other members of the Committee know where they are. Nor do they know that I know. But they know that you know – obviously, because you found your way here. Therefore they mustn't know who you are. You realise, don't you, that at present they have no idea? But if they talk to you at all they will want to know where they are – and if they discover who you are they will go on asking you afterwards, when we are all back at NATO, and the story is bound to come out in the end. Do you see? If you stay, you must be kept away from the Committee. Your, er, girl can mix with them, I suppose, if she is not likely to meet them again later in Brussels. But both of you will have to keep it a secret that you were ever here. When you go back to Brussels you must have a story to tell of your holiday, which can take you through this valley, of course, but without any mention of the château. Perhaps all this is too difficult. What do you think?'

'Why is it so important about Anna?' asked Marie. 'Why are you so concerned about her? What about the others – these handsome young men who watch over me all the time, for example?'

The Chairman looked anxious. 'The students will melt away when it is all over, they have no connection with this place – but for Anna it is different.' He added, 'I don't know who she is, and I'll take care not to make enquiries, but it's obvious that she could be traced through the chateau, isn't it?'

'It certainly is. Shall I tell you her name? I think I know it.'

'No, please.' The Chairman almost lost his composure. 'I must not know. You must think of the questioning when we are released. It will be hard enough for me to pretend that I don't know roughly where we have been kept . . .'

Marie smiled with satisfaction, the smile of a woman who has power in her hands. 'All right, I'll not tell you, not now anyway. And we'll stay, and help, on two conditions. First, you really must get a move on, we have to be back in Brussels quite soon. And second, if I'm going to help you'll have to think of something really big, something that people can understand. Now fix me up with a nice room, put Felix in it, leave us alone for a little and then lead me to these sub-committees and watch me wake them up.'

'What about me?' asked Felix. 'Do I just lurk in this nice room of yours? I've got some ideas too.'

'Of course, chéri, and I will be your mouthpiece. I'll pop up and see you every ten minutes, you can be the man behind the girl who's going to change the world. But Mr Big's quite right, you've got to be kept out of sight of the Committee.'

Franz had followed all these exchanges with attention. 'Good,' he said to Marie, 'there is a beautiful big room in the other part of the château which you can have. Your man will be comfortable there, and so will you. I will speak to Anna and take you there in a few minutes.'

'Tell Anna that I'd like to see her again soon,' said the Chairman. Catching Marie's puzzled look, he added 'I don't really see her, that wouldn't do, but we have found a way of talking together, and I must tell her what you have said. I know that she'll be pleased to have your help, but she may want it to be on her own terms.'

'I advise you strongly to persuade her to agree to mine. If I take over, success is sure.' Marie shrugged, indicating the alternative. 'By the way, what was that cheese I had for breakfast? It was good, and I'm hungry again. Ask someone to put some in our room. We will also need a supply of mineral water. Explain to the responsible person that I prefer Spa pétillant.'

Sister Agnes stepped out of the oval gilt bath, rubbed steam off the mirror with the corner of her towel and looked at herself. Nothing like a good night's rest, she thought, you were right cross when he fell asleep but the poor lad was weary, no wonder really, and it's all for the best, you looked a proper sight last night, and now, well, now you look all right, don't you? She dried herself, reached for her underwear, thought better of it and wrapped herself in a fresh lime green towel from the pile. 'Shan't be a minute,' she called through the keyhole, and winked at the mirror. Fibbing again, she thought, you need another five at least, but when he sees the Tyneside Venus come out he won't complain. Golly, what a set-up, I wonder when a real bride was last here.

She was attending to her wig when she heard Piet gruffing in the bedroom. 'Who is it, just a minute, we're not supposed to let anyone in . . . No, she's in the bathroom.'

A moment later there was a tap on the separate bathroom door. Sister Agnes crossed to it, already feeling apprehensive. 'Yes?'

'Agnes, it's Anna. I'm terribly sorry, but you'll have to move. It's too complicated to explain, but I've got to put some other people in here. Tell Piet to put his mask on and I'll take him up to the top floor nursery and shut him in there. Then can you tidy up *quickly*, and leave everything ready for the others?'

'Oh, no! Anna, you don't know what you're doing – we've hardly settled in, I've only just had my bath, can't you put these other people in the nursery?'

'No, it's all a terrible muddle, but they've got to be put in here. Agnes, I *am* sorry, but after all you've had all night here, haven't you?'

'Yes, but . . .' Agnes shrugged. The first waves of fury gave place to hope. Perhaps the nursery would be almost as good as the bridal suite. 'All right.' She adjusted her wig and went through to the bedroom. Piet leaped forward as if stung. She held up a hand to ward him off, and the towel flapped open. 'No, no,' she squeaked, racing round the back of the dressing table and fumbling with the towel, 'give over, not now, you've got to move upstairs.'

Chapter 14

'Now there will be a five minutes' break before you begin work,' called Ingrid. Panting slightly from the exercises, Portentoso crossed the hall and joined the group which was forming round Lute.

'What is happening? Where is the Chairman? First Piet disappears, then our leader, have you not noticed his absence?'

'I think he's been to see Anna again. He'll probably be back in a few minutes to tell us what's going on. I must say, I don't feel like settling down to committee work. Does anyone know what's happened to those two who tried to rescue us yesterday?'

Almost every member of the Committee had a scrap of gossip or speculation to contribute. Only Brasfort, who stood silent on the fringe of the group, saw the Chairman and Marie enter through the security door. He raised his eyebrows ever so slightly at the sight of Marie. Not French, he thought, but magnificent. The hubbub died down as the others noticed her too. Portentoso ostentatiously folded his arms, to express reserve. The German permitted himself an avuncular smile; Marie reminded him a little of a certain niece.

The Chairman could see that the situation would require a further application of his diplomatic skill. He had just been exercising this on Anna. It had been very necessary in that interview, for Anna showed a strong disinclination to accept the intervention of Marie. Eventually, disarmed by the impersonal manner in which the Chairman recommended exposing the Committee to what he called 'this unexpected catalyst', she had given her assent. 'We will see,' the Chairman had said, 'whether the reactions thus produced precipitate anything which you and I can refine and use.' He was pleased by his handling of the metaphor, and of Anna, whose pride was intact at the end of their talk.

Now the catalyst, vibrant at his side, was already producing reactions. He hastened to bring them under control.

'Gentlemen, I have good news for you. But first I must introduce you to our visitor. Marie, may I present Signor Portentoso, of the Italian Delegation . . . Mr Lute of the British Delegation . . .?'

The introductions took a little time, during which the sentence about good news hung in the air, creating uncertain but pleasant expectations.

'Now, gentlemen, that is done, and I must give you news of your friend Piet. He had a slight accident yesterday, very slight but sufficient to require medical attention, which he is receiving. He sends you his greetings and wishes you well in your work, in which he hopes to take part again before long. Which brings me to the programme for today. It is Anna's wish that our work this morning and this afternoon should be of a more general character than what we have done so far. Marie, our visitor, arrived yesterday with the intention of setting us free. Having discovered the benign nature and the praiseworthy aims of our confinement, she has resolved to share it with us and to take part in our work. So indeed has her companion. Both of them intend and expect to help us, but only Marie will take part in our meetings. Her ideas will be welcome, I am sure, the more so since I believe that they are likely to simplify rather than complicate our task.'

Portentoso, arms still sternly folded, shrugged. 'One must comprehend before one attempts to simplify. Is it proposed that we should begin by explaining to this lady the detailed and complicated work on which we are engaged, this work which she interrupted yesterday, no doubt with the best of intentions but in a manner which one might describe as both crude and unsuccessful?' He did not smile, but he was pleased by the crushing nature of his intervention.

'It will not be necessary to attempt any explanation.' Marie's voice was low in pitch, and powerful. 'Rattekwaker,' she added.

Portentoso wondered crossly what that meant. Nor did he like the word 'attempt'. 'If I described our work as detailed and complicated, it was not to imply that we could not explain, but rather to suggest that it would take a long time, time which we cannot afford to lose. Would it not be appropriate if you were to take your seat in one of the sub-committees and listen to the proceedings, aspiring in due course to contribute, perhaps, certain comments?'

'It would not be appropriate.' Marie's voice was huskier now, and almost casual. She let her eyes linger, dismissively, on Portentoso for a second or two, then moved her gaze away. She found herself returning the amused gaze of Brasfort, whose name she remembered without difficulty. 'You, Monsieur Brasfort, have the air of one who has not forgotten his Aristotle. You remember perhaps a certain passage in the *Nicomachaean Ethics* . . . that it is a fundamental error to go into more detail than a subject requires. The theme could be developed in our discussion. Are you willing to speak?'

'I am willing to listen,' replied Brasfort deftly.

The Chairman, like a wise pilot, caught the turning tide. 'I think we must all listen. It is true, what Portentoso says, that our work has been detailed, and it is not to be cast aside. But let us hear Marie's ideas before we go further. Was it not Plotinus who said that a synthesis could only be attempted when the constituent elements have been defined?'

'Right.' said Marie. 'If you wish to sit, you will arrange your stools in a circle. I speak best in an arena. Leave me room, to pace up and down . . . So, I will give you a first taste of thought. Cry out if you will when I rip the cobwebs from your eyes, to see is not always comfortable, but see you will.' She shook back her hair and swivelling on one heel raked the attentive committee members with a gaze of Tartaric wrath. The Norwegian remembered the thundering of a village preacher north of Tromso, and shifted uneasily in his chair.

Marie strode to and fro, soliloquising fiercely. 'Ah, which of them is a logician, which has studied psychology, which has mastered the theory of conflict? Not one, not one, not one. The answer stares out from their guileless eyes, it is like going into a forest and addressing the animals, I am mad to try. Why are their ankles so thick, their wrists so thin, what are these weak beards sprouting on their chins, this is no prison, it is an asylum, the horror of it grows every minute.'

She stopped opposite the Icelander. 'What have you been trying to do, man of the north, or what do you think you have been trying to do? I'll tell you what, you've been trying to make a blueprint without paper, without ink, without instruments and without light. You've been trying to do other people's work, the work of scientists, of bureaucrats, of parliamentary draftsmen, the work which goes into rule-making, work for which you are totally unfitted. And shall I tell you what you haven't been trying to do, what you have totally ignored, although it's the one thing you could do?

Shall I blind you with this revelation? Are your eyes which have survived the midnight sun strong for this too? Yes, I will tell you.'

The Chairman thought to himself that she had certainly claimed the attention of her audience, but that it was time to start delivering goods if she was to keep it.

'Your job is to change *attitudes*, to change the attitudes which are reflected in the rules. And how are you going to do that? By enlightenment? By penalties? By rewards? I can tell you, but why don't you tell me?' Her voice was lower now, and she was smiling at Lute. He responded.

'Not by penalties.'

'Exactly. Go on.'

'Well, what do you mean by rewards?'

'I mean big rewards, rewards so big that they will command attention, divert energies, harness new resources. I mean prizes which will glitter so brightly that none will be outside their field of attraction. I mean great big heavy bags of gold. Think – you are English, yes? – well, think of the structure of rewards in England, think of the little bags of silver you can get for doing this or that, think of the titles you can earn by a lifetime's work, all related to the past instead of the future. Now think what a difference it would make if the biggest rewards were for work on the environment.'

'Like Nobel prizes for environmental work?'

'No, no, the Nobel prizes are much too small. But multiply them many times, and you have the idea.'

The Chairman spoke. 'You make it all seem very easy. We demand the creation of these new prizes. They are huge. They glitter. They magnetise human resources. Is that all?'

'No, but it will do for this morning. I shall leave you to work out the details, since some of you are so gifted for detailed work.' She eyed Portentoso. 'Later we will speak of enlightenment. That is important too. But it is the prizes which will cause a stir. Most of them must be annual, to keep up the excitement. Make me a list and we'll look at it over lunch. What's for lunch, by the way, and when is it?'

'Maquereaux à la façon de Quimper and Kouign Amann,' said Secunda with a sidelong glance at Brasfort. 'At one o'clock.'

'Good. I will join you for your apéritif at twenty to.'

There was a silence. Marie raised her eyebrows.

'They don't give us an apéritif,' explained the Belgian, 'only a glass of wine with lunch.'

'Oh, êke and âke, of course you will have an apéritif. I cannot have one all by myself. Arrange it please, Mademoiselle.'

In the bridal suite Felix was sitting by the window putting the finishing touches to his list of rewards, of which there were eight. Marie read it with approval. 'Double number 6, and it's perfect. I'll take it down at lunch-time. Now, what about your reward?' She stroked his chin.

'I'm in a planning mood.'

'But what is there to plan? Unless you want to plan your reward. That might be pleasant. But I'd rather just give it to you.'

Felix removed her hand. 'There's plenty to plan. We've got to get the Committee back to NATO. Anna said something last night about dumping them in batches in back streets in Brussels with money for taxis, but that's feeble. She isn't happy about it herself. Let's think of something more dramatic, that would be good on TV.'

'All right, we've got an hour and a half. Half an hour for planning the drama. You start.'

'First requirement. They all arrive together. But they can't be taken nearer to NATO than about three kilometres. Otherwise they'd be spotted. It ought to be quiet enough to the north, maybe in a lay-by on the Liège road. But then what? It's a bit far to walk. Horses? That would be marvellous, but I bet some of them can't ride. A bus? Wrong image, they can't bowl up belching diesel fumes. I've got it, *bicycles.*'

'Oh, yes,' purred Marie, 'oh, yes and yes again, and we'll dress them in maillots of . . . what . . . black and gold, like wasps, I think. But where do we get the machines? I wonder if old Coppenfrons would have enough?'

'Surely, remember, he rented about twenty to the Scouts that Sunday. And he'd never give us away, I mean even if he said anything, which he wouldn't, no one would understand him outside the Marolles. But do they all know how to ride bikes?'

'I'll ask at lunch. But you'd better check with your Anna person first, I'm not sure that she has enough sense of the theatre.'

'Oh, come on, this whole thing is pure theatre, and she must have thought it up. She'll love the bicycle idea. I'll go find her now.'

'Bon, but dally not in her bower. Remember, this is the bridal suite, and it's time you played groom-groom-groom again.'

'Crotche, crotche, I'll be back in an uugske.'

'Don't you think Felix is clever? I adore this idea of bicycles. And if any of them can't ride they can learn here, there's plenty of room in their hall.'

Anna was taking pleasure in the new bout of planning, partly because it anticipated victory, thus pushing present doubts into the background, and partly because it was a relief to her to be back on familiar ground again.

Franz too was enjoying the discussion. 'It's mad,' he said with relish, 'but it ought to work. What worries me a bit is the stage before that, I mean fixing it so that they think they've been on a long journey, when they haven't. And they'll have to be wide awake for the cycling. Tim, do you have something that would do the trick?'

'No, if I put them to sleep they'll stay asleep for four hours at least. That's the minimum, and it's risky because the dose would be rather weak. Even then they wouldn't be ready to start cycling for six hours. Well, perhaps a little less if we gave them strong coffee.'

Anna looked concerned. 'Certainly they must have coffee, but I should think croissants too – it is bad to exert oneself without food.'

'Well, one croissant each, no more. We can't stage a full meal in the lay-by, and they'll have to be in and out in three or four minutes. But, look, we still haven't solved the main question. It's only a two hour drive to Brussels. They must be dead to the world when we load them into the camionettes and all bouncing with energy when we let them out.'

Alexander the Great leaned forward with glinting eyes. 'You have not stated the problem correctly. The journey *need* only take two hours. But that is not to say that it *will* take only two hours. It could take as long as we wished, provided that the Jameses would be willing to take a détour.'

'Of course, that's it.' Franz scribbled on the graph paper on his clipboard, reading aloud.

2200	*Victory celebration, drugs in wine, knockout dose for 10/12 hours.*
0600	*Load them into the camionettes – can't we just lay them on the floor, by the way, this time?*
0645	*Camionettes leave on four hour journey (check gasoline).*
0900	*They'll be waking up.*
1045	*Arrive at lay-by. Coffee and croissants (one only each).*
1110	*Arrive at NATO.*

'How's that? And I'll throw in a few mystification measures too, like letting them overhear someone saying it's Tuesday on the day before, when it's really Thursday.'

'But this is delicious,' said Marie, biting into the Kouign Amann. 'Give me some more Muscadet, if you will, Monsieur Brasfort.'

Brasfort was in high favour. During the debate on the prizes he had consistently argued for sums greater than some of his colleagues thought feasible. Marie had dubbed him her rat de chambre, and he had not been displeased when the term was explained.

'Now for enlightenment,' suggested Lute.

'Oh, yes, now bring me half a pint of steaming black coffee. Bring everyone half a pint, and a little cognac too, please. Now, here is the problem. Take the average person. She – he, if you will – is anxious about pollution, right? But confused, right? What are the priorities? Should one make durables last longer? Should one stop using plastics, or only some of them? Is the system of wrapping things in shops really so bad? What about noise, how much is safe? Is there any point in keeping one's own little corner clean if pollution is drifting about in the air? And so on, you see – their disquiet is all too vague, they have nothing to focus on, nothing they can *do*. Yet there is much goodwill, don't you agree? There are many who would change their habits if it was clear to them how they should change their habits and if everyone knew – that is important, they must not be alone, they must be acting in the mass, acting together, then they will have the pleasure of frowning at those who do not conform.'

'Fine,' said Grannery, 'there's certainly a lot of goodwill in the States, and plenty of people saying what's to be done. The trouble is they don't all say the same thing. I mean, take garbage disposal units. Some say they're good – it's easy to see why – but others say no, they have to be powered and that uses up natural fuels and that's bad. So where are you? Buying a unit and then taking it out, that's what happened to my aunt. Now who's going to weigh everything up and say yes or no; and will it be the same answer everywhere?'

'But this is what governments should be doing,' replied Marie. 'They must bend right down with a magnifying glass and look at the tiny decisions of everyday life and give advice. Of course they've got to look at the big things too, but they come in the them-and-us category, ordinary people just don't feel involved. Once you get it all working on the personal plane too you change the whole situation. Now, how to do it? I want to make the governments take a whole page in the papers once a month to explain what they're doing, mostly big-league stuff, and also to give advice on little matters, like, well like this business of garbage disposal.

Just think, if they had to fill a whole page every month, with the opposition waiting to pounce on any hollow claims or bad advice, they'd really have to think hard.'

'We don't all have an opposition,' commented one member of the Committee.

'Well, never mind, we can't attend to that too, can we? Anyway most of you have.'

The Norwegian cleared his throat and adjusted his djebbah over his knees. 'I, er, used to work in our Prime Minister's press office. I like this idea. Perhaps I could write something, a draft which you can all discuss. The idea needs to be expressed rather exactly.'

'Bravo, I swear we shall not alter a word, you are just the man we need. Where is the pretty milkmaid, let her exchange the cognac bottle for pencil and pad – go to a cubicle together, handsome pair, and confect some perfect paragraphs. Now, there is one thing more, a missing ingredient, we must not only . . .'

The Belgian raised his hand. 'One moment, please. Let me ask a question. This one thing more, will it cost money?'

The Turk had been silent for a long time. Now he spoke. 'We have spent enough already, perhaps too much. In Ankara they will not like this.'

'Well,' said Marie, with an unusual note of caution in her voice, 'it will and it won't. Cost money, I mean. Listen, I'll explain . . .' She thought damn, I should have got this one in first.

Franz turned the volume down when Anna came in with her cup of tea.

'It's fantastic,' he said, 'they're still swigging coffee and cognac and it's nearly four. Marie's been persuading them to include a model town – you know, pollution-free, no motor cars – and she's almost won them over. Listen . . .'

'Dear Monsieur Brasfort, you put it so well. Each government will hope to win the lottery and have this marvellous creation for about a third of the true price. So the cost will not really be reckoned. But look, we must finish going round the table. Everyone is entitled to define one feature of Nova Atlantis – that is what we will call it, eh? – and then I will add mine, which I implore you in advance to approve.'

The Greek laughed. 'I'm sure we will approve of yours, if it costs as little as mine. I stipulate that none of the inhabitants will smoke, I mean the volunteers will all be non-smokers. That removes at once much mess and smell.'

'Excellent. But that costs nothing at all. I'm afraid that my idea isn't quite so cheap.' She thought, it certainly isn't, I wish they'd take their minds off the money . . . Aloud she added, 'I think that was really a brilliant idea, it is the best yet . . . Now Italy.'

Franz tuned Italy out. 'What do you think? I'm a bit dubious.'

'It all depends on the scale and quality. Let's wait and see what it looks like on paper. At this rate they'll have the whole document drafted by tonight. Then I suppose we'd better have our own committee meeting in the morning and perhaps change it a bit. The students must all have their say. But really, we may be able to give it to the world tomorrow night. Have Tim and Pete got their channels clear?'

'Yes, Tim's going to catch the train at Namur and give it to the Brussels cell. One of them catches the evening plane to London, plants it and rings Reuters to tell them where to find it. Of course there's a faint possibility that they won't believe it, but just in case we're going to put the Chairman's thumb print on the top copy, and that should clinch it.'

'But how will they know it's his thumb print? He hasn't been in gaol, has he?'

'As a matter of fact, he has. Didn't you know? It was during the war, when the Germans had occupied Denmark. He shot the wrong person or something. But never mind about that, I assure you it's all fixed. Shouldn't we go on about the departure arrangements? There may not be much time left.'

Anna hesitated. 'All right,' she said eventually, 'let's go on about the departure arrangements.'

At five o'clock Sister Agnes had finished her chores. She already had the nursery key, and sped up the back stairs to visit Piet.

'Darling, I'm so sorry I couldn't . . . Oh, goodness *me*.'

The nursery was large, but it was full of abandoned toys. Three rocking horses chased each other across the floor under the high gable window. A roundabout, six feet in diameter and bearing its ring of polychrome steeds, stood in the centre, flanked on one side by a pile of floppy animals heaped against the door of a toy sweetshop and on the other by a white tin bath on the dry bottom of which antique celluloid creatures lay higgledy-piggledy with toy yachts. Round and through and under the disarray a model railway line wound its way. Straddling it was a child's table of wicker work, covered with a cracked pink oilcloth on which traces of animal decorations could still be seen. A small round tray on top of this bore the remains of Piet's lunch. Behind it stood a large drop-sided cot, stuffed to the brim with a mixture of satin cushions and pirates' dressing-up clothes; and on top of the stuffing reclined Piet.

Sister Agnes laughed until she thought that she would have the hiccups. Piet clambered out of the cot, frowning, but eventually started to laugh too.

'Is this cot thing the *only* bed?'

'It is. There isn't even anywhere else to sit down except on a rocking horse, or in the bathroom. How could Anna expect us to be comfortable here?'

'Oh, dear, Piet, I'm sorry to be laughing so, but it's so funny, and you look just like a little boy. What *are* we going to do? I should have come up sooner, but I had so much to do and the others are being mean about the time off I've had. Listen, perhaps you'd better go back to the committee, then at least you can sleep in your own cubicle. Besides they're working hard on the ransom terms. Everything's changed, and this girl who broke in yesterday is really running things now. It's she and her boy friend who are in the bridal suite by the way – nothing but the best for the big brains, and as for poor old us . . .'

While she prattled Piet had been taking a proper grip of her. Now he silenced her with a kiss. It was a very long serious kiss, and when he let her go she was subdued and shaking.

'Listen, Agnes, I am not a little boy, I am a lot older than you, but I ask you to marry me, and I tell you one thing – that you stay here until you give me an answer.'

Sister Agnes gave a faint moan and steadied herself with a hand on the cot. 'What did you say that for? Now you've done it. Oh, Piet . . . If Agnes was real she'd say yes. But

. . . oh, wait and you'll see.'

She darted into the bathroom, closing behind her the door and thus projecting before Piet's desperate gaze a childish drawing, held up by pins which had been rusting in their place for twenty years, of Cinderella.

When the door opened again it was not Agnes who emerged, but a girl who seemed somehow smaller and thinner, a girl with black hair, short and straight, a girl with a peaky shiny face on which no trace of make-up was left. She wore a faded paisley dressing gown. As she advanced to within a pace of Piet, she stepped with defiance, but her eyes betrayed the fear in her heart.

Upon this apparition Piet looked first with open-mouthed astonishment; then with an expression of tender and humble love.

Thus they stood facing each other in silence among the forgotten toys of children who had long since grown up.

Anna joined the hunting party while they had their drinks before dinner, and listened charmingly to the tale of the day's activities. She was satisfied that they had noticed nothing unusual, and retreated in a mood of elation to her room for a light supper. Some bits of the committee's drafts were ready for her to read, and the last section, which Tertia had typed at top speed, was brought up while she was having her yoghourt. She read it with approval, but raised her eyebrows over one clause.

Marie was feeding yoghourt to Felix and talking about the same clause. 'Oh, it was a battle, chéri, I assure you. Some of them were so stubborn, I could have shaken them. But in the end they said it could go in, at least for Anna to consider. That nice Frenchman pointed out that she would have to decide anyway, which is true. I'd forgotten myself that she has the last word.'

Felix pondered. 'Well, that's all right. But why should she want to see the Maison du Peuple put up again?'

'I don't suppose she's ever heard of it. But I'll tell you a secret. She's going to take the Chairman's advice, and he's going to listen to me because he's afraid I'll tell him who she is. So . . . already I can imagine the tramload of stones travelling to the new site, the little monument to Horta which will be built outside, the . . .'

'Are you going to contribute your bit, I mean the piece you got the other day?'

'Of course. All the wicked people who have got bits will give them back. Now drink your coffee while I go off and bend the Chairman to my will. Back soon, but you can be impatient, it becomes you.'

Chapter 15

By noon on the next day everyone except Piet had had a final say on the drafts.

It was Luis, the meek Portuguese, who had caused the greatest stir by his intervention. In a short and dignified statement, he designated acts of violence and terrorism as constituting one of the worst features of the human environment and proposed that prizes be offered to those who could devise new means of any kind, technical or political, of quenching these activities. He added that in his view kidnapping should be identified as one of the activities to be quenched.

Brasfort, delighted by the irony, supported him at once. So did the Turk, seizing with pleasure on one item which would please Ankara. Lute, however, expressed serious doubt.

'I would not seek to define the environment too narrowly, but surely we are straying into a different category of activity if we adopt Luis' suggestion. We should be inviting endless discussions, such as are familiar to us at NATO, about how to define violence and terrorism. And, to be practical, can we really expect Anna to accept a provision which implies condemnation of her own action?'

Grannery wrinkled his brow, as was his habit when thinking hard. 'I don't know that it would be so difficult to define these things. The ordinary man would know what was meant. And he would like the idea. I guess there would be arguments, like David says, but they could be resolved if public feeling was strong enough. The real difficulty would be over including kidnapping. But I have a hunch that our Chairman might be able to draft that bit so that it would be acceptable to Anna. As I read her, she's not in favour of kidnapping, except just this once.'

The Chairman pondered. 'Supposing that we referred to "indefensible acts of kidnapping",' he suggested. 'That could be read two ways. It could mean that all kidnapping was indefensible; or it could be taken as drawing a distinction between most such acts, which are indefensible, and the rare, perhaps unique, such act which could be defended on Utilitarian principles.'

Luis said: 'I agree. And we can only do our best. Let us put this in and see what happens. My view is simple. A world in which rubbish is disposed of tidily but in which innocent people are murdered is not what we are trying to achieve.'

The Committee accepted this. Upstairs, Anna and Alexander the Great and Franz considered the point.

'I'm willing,' said Anna.

'I'm more than willing,' said Franz, 'and I think that the public will go for it. It is at the same time a very serious matter, and yet a humorous suggestion, given the source from which it comes.'

Anna nodded. 'There is another thing. I have not forgotten those Irish who caused so much trouble. This new idea might help to pacify Ireland, but I wonder whether we shouldn't have a separate prize for good ideas about Ireland – you see what I mean, focus attention on it as the worst trouble spot in Europe.'

'Is it?' asked Alexander.

'I think so,' said Franz. 'There is no other problem of quite the same complexity. A solution by the British is excluded, almost by definition. Yet who else is really trying to think of one? The whole question has to be regarded in a European context, indeed a transatlantic one. Of course, this is pure politics and goes beyond what we had planned, but the Irish tried to bring themselves into the act on Day One, didn't they? It would be a kind of poetic justice if the eventual result was a formula which brought peace to the island. But don't forget there *is* a prize already: let me see, how is it called? Ah, yes, the Ewart-Biggs Memorial Prize, named after the British Ambassador who was blown up in Dublin. It's not a very big one, but it's there, and it might seem a bit clumsy to establish a new prize, on a different scale, alongside it.'

Anna agreed. 'I too remember this, now that you mention it. The question is a delicate one. I think we should make the governments add something to this prize, not too much, but enough to be a real help – and the amount should go up annually, because of inflation, and as an extra incentive to work something out without indefinite delay.'

'A kind of double or quits?'

'Yes, something of the sort. Once we have a draft, it must be checked with the Committee. They may not like it, or they may want to broaden it – you know, vaguer provisions about minority groups and so on everywhere. But I want the finger put squarely on the Irish, I still haven't forgiven them for trying to supplant us . . .'

In fact, this afterthought slipped through the Committee quite easily, for they had now reached what they regarded as the interesting stage of considering the presentation of the document, and had become so absorbed in this that they had almost forgotten about its contents.

Brasfort had caused alarm by suggesting, some thought merely from force of habit, that the text should be handed out in French as well as English; but when the others pointed out that he would have to do the translation he shrugged and said that he supposed he could leave it to the French press. Lute had tactfully redrafted some passages which did not turn readily into French, and had also surreptitiously improved the English in a number of places. A few outstanding differences of opinion were indicated, in the traditional NATO committee fashion, by square brackets enclosing the disputed sentences.

Anna had the one and only copy, complete with marginal notes by Marie (on behalf of the Committee) and Franz (for the students). The winter sun shone through the window as she worked through it, taking the final decisions. At twenty past twelve she had finished, and pinned a note on top: 'Ready for final typing – Anna'. She rang the bell.

The document which she gave to Tertia began like this:–

RANSOM TERMS

Declaration of Impunity

The circumstances of the capture and confinement of the Senior Political Committee will be allowed to remain a pleasing mystery.

Should the identity of anyone concerned become known, no action will be taken against her (or him) by any of the NATO Governments or their agents.

Requirements

The fifteen NATO Governments will solemnly (but cheerfully) make the following undertakings and implement them jointly and severally as appropriate.

First, they will declare the institution of Atlantic prizes for work on the environment. The prizes thus established will include all those listed in Annex A, but may include others at the discretion of the Governments. The money to pay the prizes will be contributed by the Governments according to the cost-sharing formula for NATO Infrastructure which was in force in 1965 (that is to say, including France).

Second, they will build within three years a model town in accordance with the specifications given in Annex B. The town will be situated in one of the NATO countries, to be selected by lottery following whatever detailed procedure is agreed in the North Atlantic Council but weighted thus – USA, 10; France, Germany, Italy, UK, 5 each; Turkey, 4; Belgium, Canada, Denmark, Greece, the Netherlands, Norway, Portugal, 3 each; Iceland and Luxembourg, 1 each. The cost will be divided into two parts. One quarter will be paid by the country in which the town is built. The remaining three quarters will be shared out according to the above-mentioned infrastructure formula between all fifteen Governments. Exceptionally, the cost of re-erecting the Maison du Peuple (Annex B, Clause II) will be shared in its entirety between all the Governments except that of Belgium; the Government of Belgium will be responsible for transporting all parts of the building to the site and for providing the necessary technical advice on its re-erection.

Third, they will for a period of at least ten years, and more at their discretion, insert monthly full-page announcements in their major national newspapers (as defined in Annex C) which will in every instance contain information about what the government in question is doing in the field of environmental work, and practical advice to citizens on how, in their individual and family and professional activities, they may best contribute to this work.

Fourth, they will convey to the International Court of Justice at the Hague a copy of these terms, and will request the Court to be ready to give an opinion on any dispute or difficulty of a legal nature which may arise in the course of their discharge of these undertakings; and will treat such an opinion as binding.

Procedure
The agreement of the Governments to everything herein stipulated will be conditional on the return of the members of the Senior Political Committee, in good health (but without regard to colds and such minor ailments), to the NATO Headquarters at Evère, and will become absolute on their return. The return will take place at or soon after 1115 local time on the day following the announcement that the Governments agree, provided that such announcement is made before noon.

Tertia examined her large collection of headed notepapers and hesitated over a particularly thick sheet which bore the simple inscription 'The Vatican'.

'No,' said Franz, catching her at it. 'Absolutely not. No more mystification. Use that unwatermarked stuff.'

While she typed the first page he checked through Annex A. Marie read over his shoulder, skipping the preamble and looking only to see whether there had been any last minute decrease in the size of the prizes.

(A) *Ten prizes each of $200,000, to be awarded annually in December, for outstanding ideas or work in the fields of:*

air pollution
marine pollution
inland water pollution
noise abatement
population control
husbandry of natural resources

at least one prize to be awarded annually in each of the categories unless the Council find no contribution of sufficient merit, in which event the prize money will be carried over into the following year.

(B) *Two prizes each of $200,000, to be awarded annually in March for outstanding ideas on or the development of new techniques for the disposal or recycling of waste material.*

(C) *Prizes of $100,000, not to exceed five in any one year, for new ideas, inventions or techniques designed to diminish and ultimately quench the deplorable tendency to use violence, terrorism and indefensible acts of kidnapping to achieve political ends or to retard and impede the peaceful development of international and inter-community cooperation.*

(D) *The New Year's Day prize of $25,000 for the best popular book published in the previous year on environmental matters.*

(E) *A single prize of $25,000,000 in the field of aero engine design, to be awarded under the following conditions . . .*

Marie clapped her hands. 'Just as it should be. I was afraid that Anna would be mean about that one.'

'Well, it does seem like a fantastic amount, and so is the urban transport prize, although it is smaller.'

'Come on,' said Tertia, 'next page, please. I must get further on before lunch.'

'OK, here's Annex A. We'll go next door and check B. I'll get someone else to help Secunda at lunch time.'

Tertia's nimble fingers completed a rat-a-tat on her machine and she looked up as she swept the carriage-return across with an industrious whirr. 'Oh, good, maybe Ingrid would do it. But tell her that Piet's back – there's only one tray to send upstairs now.'

'And I'll take that,' said Marie, 'I'm the expert on my man's appetite.'

The Committee were glad to have Piet with them again. A closed community suffers in various ways; not least from the fact that one of the fundamental human pleasures, the communication of news, is largely denied to its members. Finding that Piet seemed to have little idea of what they had been doing, his colleagues competed with each other across the lunch table to bring him up to date.

'The most important prize is really the one for designing Nova Atlantis. I mean it's only a million dollars – or was it two million? – but imagine the competition for it, all the new ideas which are going to come out.'

'All we've done is to establish the framework. A hundred thousand inhabitants . . .'

'Half from the host country, half from the others, but five thousand places reserved for visiting students and research workers.'

''That's the point, the research is what matters. Just think, a complete ban on internal combustion engines . . .'

'Not even any smokers allowed near the place . . .'

Piet helped himself to Fegato alla Veneziana. His manner was amiable but dreamy. Benevolently he made an effort to show interest in the details.

'Good, good. But what are these hundred thousand people going to do? They will breathe the pure air and some of them will do research. But the others – how do they earn their living?'

Grannery waved a forefinger in the air. 'Industry, Piet, industry. A growth industry, too. Recycling. All linked in with the University, and experimental, but there are profits coming, you'll see.'

'And tourism,' added Lute. 'Of course it depends a bit where the town is, but people are going to flock there. This will be something really new, a new kind of community, on a different plane from anything we've seen so far. I mean, there are places called model towns in Britain and in France too, but they're just better versions of what we've got already . . .' He paused, and flashed a glance of enquiry at Brasfort. 'Don't you agree?'

'Entirely. One must not underestimate the importance of, for example, your Milton Keynes. The lessons learned there will be applied. But Nova Atlantis will be something more radical, a true point of departure. I envy the City Councillors who will direct the enterprise.'

'Who knows, my dear colleague, you may be one of them. Why not?'

'Perhaps because I am a bachelor, if for no other reason,' replied Brasfort lightly.

Chapter 16

The President's Adviser on the Environment lived in Georgetown, in a Federal house on O Street. He was fast asleep when the buzzer at his bedside began to beep, but he woke quickly, flipped the switch off in the hope that his wife would stay asleep, and padded through to his study. There he flipped another switch, said 'Yes?', and listened intently to the quiet New England voice speaking from the Operations Centre. After twenty seconds he said 'Right, hold it,' and pressed two buttons. One set the coffee percolating. The other would bring Hildegarde over from her Wesley Heights apartment in ten minutes.

'Go on,' he said, 'dictation speed.'

Before he had it all down he heard the clunk of a car door in the street and knew that Hildegarde would be letting herself in. He looked at his watch: twelve minutes past three. They would wake the President at seven. He supposed that there would be a National Security Council at eight. He would need two papers, one for the President to read over breakfast, maximum five hundred words, one for the Council, four or five times as long. The Secretary of the Treasury was the danger, but he didn't work nights, and the first set of sums was the one which the President would hoist in.

Hildegarde came in with the coffee tray. She looked very awake and smelled of pine.

'Hi. Sorry to bring you over at this hour. It's the ransom terms. I've just got them. State are doing a paper for the

President but they won't know what to say. I do, and I've got to say it fast.'

Hildegarde poured coffee into black stoneware mugs. 'Are they all right? I mean, is it yes or no?'

'Honey, so far as I'm concerned they're just fine, just as fine as could be . . . You know what they say over in Kentucky – if it's going your way, ride it . . .'

He was still laughing as he climbed into the old Sears Roebuck dentist's chair from which he liked to do his dictation.

'Tilt me right back, honey. Let's go.'

'I remember the fuss about this Maison du Peuple,' said the Belgian Foreign Minister. 'Mostly foreigners if I remember rightly. There wasn't much feeling here; it wasn't a political issue.'

'No, not at all,' responded his Chef de Cabinet. 'The Socialists might have used it, but after all the building belonged to the Co-op and it was the Co-op who wanted to pull it down. Their new building is much bigger. You can see how much bigger it is by just looking at the old buildings alongside. It really towers over them.'

'Personally I regard this as humiliating. Belgium has been singled out in an undesirable manner. None of the other countries is expected to re-erect a demolished building. Why should we? Anyway, could we? Have we still got the bits?'

'Sir, I agree most wholeheartedly. We must not be humiliated. On the other hand it seems that we do not have to put the building up again, but only to provide the pieces. The reconstruction will be an act of the allies. One might think of it as demonstrating a certain homage to Belgium which has sheltered the headquarters of the alliance in such a hospitable manner. As for the bits, we are certainly supposed to have them. There was some sort of pledge. But the Director of the Musée admits that there has not been a survey of the relics for some time. One is being conducted today.'

'This is curious. If we said we would keep them we should count them at least once a year. This is only normal, it is a matter of accounting. I do not wish to tell my colleagues that Belgium has failed to keep her word. But I like your idea of homage to Belgium. Here you have the Socialists and the Co-op, who are nothing but a manifestation of the left, and who destroyed a national monument, destroyed it with complete contempt for the, what shall I say? – inarticulate opposition of the little farmers, the small artisans . . . Yes, I see it; and now that we faithful guardians of the disassembled stones stand by the pledge which we inherited, our friends step forward, honouring our hospitable capital with the offer of a site which will at last do justice to the genius of Horta, this same Horta who . . . Hmm, there I go making a speech again. I still think it's all very vexing. But let's find out quickly whether the bits are there, I can't decide how to handle this until I know.'

In Bonn the American Ambassador was correcting a draft telegram to the State Department.

'. . . Emboff who visited Auswartiges Amt this morning found officials taking ransom terms seriously. I will see Fonmin at lunch and will cable again afterwards.

'Meanwhile you know that government majority stands at three, including potential splinter group led by Müller.

Speaking in Westphalia last week Müller highlighted environment issues, made favourable reference to motives of kidnapper. His associate Groenhof is professional architect, has authored book on Bauhaus. If these two hold key to government's survival, their influence on ransom decision likely prove decisive, and they expected press acceptance.'

The Ambassador wrinkled his brow at the last sentence and held his pencil over it in threatening fashion for a few seconds. But he let it go. The meaning was clear, at least to people who were used to reading this kind of thing. And the Chancellor was ready to pay a high price for survival into the New Year.

Beta heard the news from the Secretary-General himself. He telephoned at half past eight, just as Millicent was leaving for school, and waited patiently while she was despatched.

'Have you heard the ransom terms? No? Well, we have them, and they've been given on the radio, although they missed today's papers. Listen, I want to talk to you about them, but first you must read them and next you must talk to the other wives. I'll send the car round in a few minutes with the complete text. Can you get busy on the telephone as soon as you've read it? No, it's quite long, I couldn't read it all to you . . . Good or bad? Well, that's what I want to ask you . . . Well if you want a purely personal reaction . . .'

'Yes, of course that's what I want. What else would I ask you for? Goodness, you do sound official this morning. Please tell me what you think.'

The Secretary-General saw two Permanent Representatives advancing into his room, brandishing papers. They had a restless dissatisfied air, which had clearly been enough to bring them unannounced past his official staff. If only his personal secretary had not chosen this time to be on leave . . . The Secretary-General narrowed his nostrils and spoke softly into the telephone, swinging casually round in his chair so that he was looking away from the visitors. 'My personal view is that they're good,' he said, 'and what's more my personal wish is that you will think so too, and the other wives. Can you come and see me at noon, and report? You may have to wait a bit because of . . . No, I'll tell you what, come at one and we'll slip out together for lunch. There's a place I know in the country where they only serve trout and the other people are all fishermen. . . . Yes, of course I can if I say so. I really want to talk to you about all this, and it's impossible here. In fact I'm in a state of siege at this moment. See you at one then. Just get into the back of my car at the main door and I'll join you.'

He turned to his visitors. 'Gentlemen, I'm so glad to see you. I have felt the need to consult members of the Council.' He nodded sagely as the two Permanent Representatives explained why the terms were preposterous, tactfully established that they had not yet received any instructions and ushered them out. There was silence, unexpected and welcome. He sat and thought, tracing ahead through the day which had barely begun the path through which his official duties would take him. Alongside it he mentally sketched out a programme of unofficial activities.

The Ministerie van Buitenlandse Zaken in the Hague was in a state of real siege. The students of Amsterdam and Leiden had risen in the morning like flocks of migratory birds and swarmed on the capital. The Plein was full of them, so full that tourists could no longer get into the Mauritshuis, and members of parliament had to use the far gate to gain access to the Binnenhof. The students carried placards inscribed 'Yes to Everything', 'Tell Her We Will', and, most frequent of all, 'I am a candidate for the model city'. Those nearest the door of the Ministry kept shouting that they had come to be put on the list of Dutchmen who would have places in the model city.

A spokesman appeared at a window on the first floor and spoke vehemently through a megaphone. No decision had been taken about the ransom terms. No one knew whether the model city would be built. No list was being made of candidates. Would everyone please go away?

'Start a list, start a list,' chanted the students.

The KRO television commentator failed to explain to his audience exactly what the students were demanding. The impression spread that they were queueing for houses in a new model city in the Netherlands, perhaps one which was already under construction. Office and factory workers began to join in during the lunch break. During the afternoon more poured in from Rotterdam. At 4 p.m. emergency registration centres were set up in the Ministry, in the Ridderzaal and along the middle of the Lange Voorhout. Police with loudspeakers directed the crowds into queues. Officials worked at top speed taking down names and addresses into morocco-bound ledgers which had been found in the basement of the Ministry. The officials in the Lange Voorhout had to wear overcoats and gloves until the police set up braziers behind them. All the Hagenaar hurdy-gurdies converged on the scene, men began to sell hot chestnuts and rush torches as dusk fell, and the scene became poignantly beautiful. This was what was shown on Eurovision at

6.30 p.m. The commentator estimated that there were already 120,000 applicants to live in the model city. He added that the Dutch generally believed that they were first in the queue and that this would be taken into account when places were distributed between the nations.

The implications of all this were readily grasped in other NATO capitals.

The agency ticker tapes in the NATO Press Office chattered away in a protracted frenzy. Absolutely non-stop, thought Hermione Batt, who tended them, absolutely non-stop. She smiled, remembering the sign 'NON-STOP' in the shops at Split last summer. It only meant that they didn't close for the afternoon. Those funny Yugoslavs. That nice Yugoslav . . . Heavens, the UP one has got quite out of hand, it must be eight feet long at least.

She ripped off the UP tape. The machine, undeterred, went doggedly on building up the next eight feet while she scissored and edited the last batch. There was an interesting story from Belgrade, and she pieced together the three instalments with particular care, then flipped the result over for xeroxing and distribution. Weird, she thought, really weird. Last year I wasn't even supposed to let on that I worked here, not to any Yugoslavs anyway, though I couldn't help telling Nic, I mean that was different, and now here's a bunch of them clamouring for Yugoslavia to join NATO. Well, I must say a few Yugoslavs in this building would liven things up a bit . . .

She crossed over to the machine and read the next piece as it was jerked to and fro in front of her.

BELGRADE LEAD STORY PART FOUR
Armoured units of the Federal Army stood by while the student rally took place, but there were no incidents. Leaflets distributed in Serbo-Croat emphasised that Yugoslav membership of the North Atlantic Alliance would be confined to non-military matters, on the French model, and that negotiations should also be opened for associate membership of the Warsaw Pact on the same basis.
No immediate comment available from Federal Secretariat for Foreign Affairs or from diplomatic observers.
No immediate comment available
No immediate comment available
Sorry, end lead story.

LISBON
This morning's student demonstration was dispersed by the police but meetings are continuing inside the University. Fifteen students and two policemen have been hospitalised. A government spokesman said that he did not know purpose of demonstration. Government would need no urging to take all necessary steps to secure release of NATO Committee. Government deplored violence . . .

Demonstrations everywhere, thought Hermione. But not here. Why not a tiny demo in the lunch break? The girls in the pool would be game for it. 'International Staff welcome Yugoslavia to NATO.' There were plenty of cameramen about . . .

'Don't go down the lane,' said the Secretary-General to the driver, 'we'll walk and you can come back in an hour.'

He and Beta walked down the stony lane and across the empty car park to the tiny restaurant. There were two big square fishing ponds, and three fishermen. The restaurant was empty and they took seats by the window so that they could watch the fishermen. They had two trout each, and Beta wondered where they came from. The immobile attitude of the fishermen suggested that catches on the necessary scale were rarely made in the ponds.

'I hadn't realised that there were only five of you left in Brussels. But you say that you can collect the other two quickly?'

'Oh, yes, but it depends on the time of day. Some of them have children at school.'

The Secretary-General made a neat incision along the lateral line of his second trout and parted the flesh impeccably.

'It is remarkable, is it not,' he said slowly, 'that the Council have shown no desire to take an initiative to receive the wives? It might seem logical for them to hear their views, the views which you express so eloquently to me. Yet one has the impression that the initiative will have to come from elsewhere.'

'I don't think it's strange at all. I'm sure it's the last thing they would think of. Having *wives* appear in the Council Chamber and *speak*? Oh, no. You weren't really expecting them to invite us, were you?'

The Secretary-General poured a little more Muscadet into Beta's glass. 'No, I wasn't,' he said, 'But I had been wondering what my duty would be if the wives arrived, say at three o'clock this afternoon, and asked for an audience. I think that I would feel bound to recommend receiving them, although our debate will then be at a critical point, and their intervention might influence the outcome.'

They both looked at the fishermen for a few minutes. Then Beta burst out laughing. 'You know, if that was a suggestion, it was very naughty. It's lucky for you that we wives always act on our own initiative. We're very emotional and impulsive, I'm afraid. Excuse while I make a phone call –just one, but it will breed some others.'

David would have a fit, she thought as she went to the telephone.

On the way back in the car she looked out of the window at the military airport and said, 'You know, I wasn't joking when I said we were emotional. I suppose I seem quite calm to you, but I'm not really.'

'I know.'

'I sometimes wonder whether it's good to bottle things up. Take Maria, for example – she's the Greek wife, I'm sure you know her – she often weeps, but I think it's good for her. She needs an audience, although of course it's hard on them, especially if they don't know her and don't realise that she'll be smiling again a few minutes later.'

'And especially if they are men, I should think. I do know Maria, but not very well. I have noticed that she is beautiful and has beautiful clothes.'

'Yes, how I envy her. She always looks exquisite – just ready to be photographed.'

'Talking of photographs, we have been having a difficult time at NATO controlling the photographers. Perhaps you noticed that they have been kept away from the front entrance? Most of them are usually penned up in the shopping hall, hoping that some interesting people will choose to go out that way. But it does not often happen.'

'Doesn't it? The poor things. Still, they may be in luck one of these days.'

They exchanged glances of the purest innocence.

◇◇◇

In the Elysée a hand reached across the Empire desk and stubbed out a cigarette in the blue onyx ashtray which served as a reminder of the visit of an African President, long since assassinated and otherwise forgotten.

The same hand picked up a platinum Bic and wrote on the paper of the finest quality:

'The proposals are harmless. Their true cost is small.

'In a sense they offer a modest vindication of the decision of President de G. to withdraw France from the military side of NATO.

'These factors permit agreement.

'But the French people have not been stirred by the abduction. There is room for manoeuvre.

'If the agreement of France is to be given, it must be given in an individual manner. No one will take it for granted, least of all the Americans.'

The voice belonging to the hand said, 'Ten out of ten. It is very clear, your analysis.

A door opened and closed. The footsteps were almost muffled by the thick carpet. A feminine hand unfolded the late edition of *Paris Soir* on the desk.

A quarter of the front page was occupied by a photograph of a beautiful woman, her face twisted in an agony of grief, her legs evidently giving way under her as three other women anxiously supported her collapsing but still supremely elegant figure. The headline said 'The kidnapping "widows" received by the NATO Council. One of them collapses on departure.'

The Bic hovered over the photograph, ran down the text of the story below, and marked certain passages. Then it went back to the finest quality notepaper and amended one sentence so that it now read 'But the French people have not *yet* been stirred . . .'

The PM looked up and down the Cabinet table with deceptive affability. As a boy he had, incongruously, spent a summer near Sydney, at a beach called Dee Why, where he had learned to surf expertly and had had an almost disastrous non-affair with a freckled and powerful Australian girl called Betty. Reflecting in later life on this episode, which was difficult to assimilate neatly into the surging pattern of his rise to power, he concluded that it had been necessary for him to learn to surf so that he would always be adept at catching the crest of the wave. Distrustful of long-range planning, he looked only for a comfortable ride during the next short spell of time. It was with this purpose that he would tread water and eye the incoming rollers, careful never to anticipate the decision which could only be made in a second as the shape and speed of the water-wall were assessed.

He knew now that this was a roller on which he must ride. But several of his colleagues saw the matter differently.

The Chancellor was careful to avoid outright dissent. 'We may well have to pay this woman's price in the end. And of course it won't be a disaster. Apart from anything else I'm inclined to agree with the Minister for the Environment that there could be a net return on the investment, or should I say . . .' He tilted his domed and shining Balliol forehead towards the ceiling to emphasise the care with which he chose his words. '. . . or should I say might be? I think that is the way to put it. But the prizes strike me, and I believe many people, as excessive for the purpose. Quite simply, they are too large. A thirsty man will do much for a gallon of water. One need not offer him ten gallons. And if one's reservoir is not overfull . . .'

The Defence Secretary, who was irritated to find NATO, which he so often described as the bedrock of western defence, acquiring a new and to him irrelevant and distracting image, agreed. 'Let's not *rush* at this,' he said. He was well-known for taking everything at the rush. 'Let's not *rush*. After all the terms were only known this morning, and whatever the NATO Council is up to this afternoon they can't have an instructed discussion for another day at least, and that's bound to go on for several days; don't you agree, Foreign Secretary?'

'Ye-es, I think that's fair. We've had two telegrams from Lavenham this afternoon. No one has definite instructions yet. I should think that quite a few will have them by tomorrow, but it would be a miracle if they all agreed on the first round. Yes, I think we must expect the discussion to run into next week. It's lucky that we aren't working against a threat to execute the hostages tomorrow or anything like that.'

'Exactly, that's the other thing I wanted to say. There isn't a shred of evidence, not a shred, that these men are in any danger, and so far as I can see that would be the only reason for *rushing*.'

A junior from the Cabinet Office slipped into the room with a bundle of newspapers, and whispered in the ear of the Secretary of the Cabinet. A note was written and passed to the PM.

'Foreign Secretary, there seems to be something in the evening papers which Brussels haven't reported yet. D'you mind if we draw on unofficial sources?'

'Good heavens, no, the press often beat us to it.'

The evening papers were already being passed round. The London editors had not chosen the same photograph as their Paris counterparts. They had picked without hesitation a shot of Beta, Beta on her knees in profile with one arm outstretched to take the weight of her swooning Greek companion, whose bent and shapely legs closed the picture gracefully on the left. Beta was wearing some kind of hooded cape. The hood had fallen back. She looked, in a way, like a nun or a Red Cross worker. The set of her chin reflected British sangfroid, the upward cast of her eyes solicitude and something close to but short of despair. It was a very good photograph.

The PM eyed his copy dispassionately, and casually absorbed the accompanying text. 'While Whitehall dithers an Englishwoman has taken the lead in reacting to the mysterious kidnapper's demands. 38-year old Beta Lute, wife of Britain's captive diplomat, quietly demanded an audience this afternoon of the all-male NATO Council and voiced the views of the waiting wives. A blanket of security covers what she said, but it is known already that she voiced a powerful plea for an end to the agony of waiting and told the stony-faced Council "You ought to be doing more for the environment anyway. These are good ideas. Adopt them now." '

I knew she was a winner, thought the PM, this settles it. Aloud he said, 'This is rather extraordinary, and a bit irregular, don't you think, Foreign Secretary? But I was just going to say that I agree very much with what the Chancellor and the Defence Secretary have been saying. I think they're quite right. Still, there's one other point which deserves a little consideration, and that's the human aspect. We know – anyway we're fairly sure – that there's no danger for the prisoners. But we can't expect their wives and families to be so calm. This photograph speaks for itself. And this is what will impress the ordinary people of Britain.' He paused. 'I would say,' he added diffidently, confident that every one of his colleagues would be thinking now of next week's by-election.

The Defence Secretary's chin stuck out a fraction more than usual, like that of a boxer waiting for the knock-out punch. The PM delivered it.

'If we decide now, we'll be the first. That will make an impact on the others, and I suppose in party terms here at home too . . .' His expression was a careful blend of international statesman and party leader. 'But if we wait, even till tomorrow, I have reason to think that the President will have spoken first, and that he will have spoken our lines.'

Chapter 17

By dusk on Wednesday Anna had listened to fifteen broadcasts. The North Atlantic Council had been in session all morning, and again throughout the afternoon. When there was no sign of an adjournment at 6 p.m. the commentators began to predict confidently that a decision would come that evening. None of them seemed to expect a straight yes, but none predicted a straight no. The attitudes struck by the Italian, French and Belgian Governments were taken to rule out the former, while a flat rejection could not be squared with the public statements already made in London, Washington and Bonn. So the predictions were for a compromise offer. Smaller prizes were likely to be acceptable to the French; and everyone thought that Belgium would agree in the end, if the massive search being conducted in the grounds of the Congo Museum revealed that a respectable proportion of the pieces of the Maison du Peuple were still there. The Italians were unlikely to stand out alone.

Anna had not thought of the possibility that she would have to consider a counter-offer. She found it a disturbing idea, and sent a message to the Chairman that she would welcome his company for half an hour before dinner, under the usual conditions.

This was the Chairman's fourth visit. A kind of routine had been developed. As soon as the door closed on Jacopo, Anna tossed the Chairman a green velvet mask from behind her screen. Once he had put it on she came out and guided him to the sofa. There they sat, side by side.

'I'm worried. Suppose they don't say yes or no, but offer something smaller? Shall I tell you what I plan to do if they say no? I'll just let you go. And I think I'd do the same if they said anything but yes. But it might seem silly if they only altered the terms slightly. I suppose really that we could accept some little changes. But it would spoil the effect if we had to bargain, and anyway I couldn't keep things going here much longer . . .'

'What, are you going to have no exotic menus left?'

Anna laughed. 'We still have a few. It's not that. The trouble is that the atmosphere has built up. It's now or never. The students couldn't be expected to go on, it would be such an anti-climax. And some of them have to leave next week anyway. It really is rather nerve-wracking.'

The Chairman located and pressed her hand. 'Don't worry so much. Marie has been telling me a bit about the news, and I can guess what's going on in Brussels. I think that the French have been willing to agree all along, but once they saw what was being said in Washington and London they decided that they might as well make the others buy their agreement. I talked to Brasfort and he thinks the same, although he doesn't put it quite like that.'

'Yes, but that still leaves the Belgians. I knew that bit about the Maison du Peuple would cause trouble.'

'Oh, that's manageable, you'll see. If I was in Brussels I'd have worked out something by now, and the Secretary-General is twice as good as I am at that sort of thing.'

'You sound as though you're looking forward to going back to work – normal work, I mean.'

'Yes . . . with some regrets.'

They were silent for a few moments.

'And you really think that we may have won?'

'Yes.'

'Good,' said Anna in a small voice.

The Chairman thought to himself that the master-plotter seemed to need a lot of reassurance this evening. The mask irked him.

'Anna.'

'Yes.'

'You remember what you said to us when we arrived? There was something about a tragedy, perhaps in your family. Is that what made you do all this?'

Ann rose from the sofa like a bird from cover. 'Yes, but you must not ask me about it. It is too painful. I thought that I could make up for what happened by . . . by all this, but it is not possible, that is what I did not understand while I was busy with the plans. Now I can see. What we are making people do is good, I am happy about it, but there is no connection, there can never be a connection, we can build a paradise and there will still be no connection – nothing, nothing, nothing, can put right a wrong . . .'

The Chairman was sitting bolt upright. 'Yes, it can. I have atoned for something, and I know. The dead cannot be brought back to life, but atonement is possible, it must be possible.'

She saw that his cheeks, between beard and mask, were flushed.

'Perhaps. I'm sorry. I didn't mean to talk like that. I'm nervous. I . . .'

Suddenly, Anna decided to tell him.

He knew well enough what she meant when she spoke of a mining village not far from La Louvière. He had been in that region, had seen the slagheaps and smelt the foul air. He could imagine the impact of it all on a twenty-one year old girl and her twin brother when, still stunned by their father's death, they had discovered that this had been the infrastructure on which much of the family wealth had been based, that this ravaged landscape had been the unseen condition of their carefree childhood.

'Of course Papa had never really known, I'm sure of that. He only mentioned the place to us once – that's to say, he mentioned it to Robert, but I was there too. I remember his saying that he had never been there. It had all been arranged by bankers in Brussels long ago, and Papa was not interested, except in taking the money and using it to improve his estates here, which he loved.

'But we went, Robert and I, and we stood there by a black stream, looking at the derelict houses where the miners had lived and thinking that we, our family, had been responsible. We felt so impotent. The land was dead and most of the people had gone. That damage could never be undone. But Robert thought that if we could do something important, something quite big he used to say, we would somehow pay for what had happened. We had many talks about this, and with Jean-Louis too . . .'

Anna broke off as the buzzer sounded. It was followed by a booming voice. Alexander the Great always spoke too close to the microphone, perhaps because he was short-sighted. 'Anna . . . Anna. The BBC news is coming soon, in four minutes. Do not forget to listen. Should your visitor be taken away now?'

Leaning over the apparatus, Anna swiftly replied, 'Thank you, I won't forget. The Chairman will stay a little longer.'

Switching it off, she continued talking to the Chairman, much faster now.

'Jean-Louis was my fiancé. I was engaged to be married, you see. He was a friend of Robert, a little older, a student of town planning. He had so many good ideas. Sometimes I wished that I was at the university, with the two of them. Robert was going to be a doctor. But Jean-Louis always said that I was better than they were at getting things done, and that studying should be left to less practical people. He was not always serious in what he said, but he was very sincere, and I was happy that he saw this role for me – the woman of action, soon to be married to the man of knowledge.'

The Chairman noticed her use of the past tense and drew the correct inference, but found himself asking, 'And where are they now, Robert and Jean-Louis?'

'Dead. Both dead. They were killed together in an accident.'

Anna remembered the picnic, the care with which they had chosen a spot near the river bank, the way Jean-Louis had helped her unpack the food while Robert wandered away to see whether the river was still well stocked with fish.

The river had no fish. They could all see why when they walked along the bank afterwards. Jean-Louis filled their empty wine bottle with water from it and they looked at its colour and consistency in dismay. In the next field a farm machine started up noisily and unpleasant fumes drifted over towards them.

Jean-Louis said, 'I've had enough. Let's go back now.'

They gathered up the picnic paraphernalia and set off back towards the road, where the Land Rover was parked on the verge. Anna fell behind, picking a private bunch of meadow flowers for Jean-Louis, and was fifty metres away when they reached the road. The crash came almost at once.

'You would not believe what happened. A huge lorry full of birds went out of control on the bend and skidded over sideways on top of them. They were killed at once, and so were the men in the lorry, two Englishmen. The lorry had a big sign saying "South Durham Pigeon Racing Association". I couldn't understand it. All over the ground were cages, mostly broken – and many of the birds were dead on the road, like Robert and Jean-Louis.'

It had needed only a glance to see that Robert and Jean-Louis were dead, but Anna, panting from her run, had looked long before she turned away and began, mechanically, to open some of the cages strewn around her and to release the birds. The birds all flew off in the same direction, towards the North Sea and South Durham. Evidently they knew what they had to do.

So had Anna known, when the shock passed through her system and she was herself again.

'I find it strange, talking to you about these things. They are what is important to me, but I have not spoken about them to others for years. You must understand that I am the last, the very last, of my family. Sometimes I think that I have become a little . . . obsessed. But at least you can see now why I talk of wrongs which cannot be put right, and what I am trying to do and for whom, even if it seems crazy to you.'

The Chairman was silent. He did not know what to say. He was shaken in his mind by the bizarre scene which Anna had described.

Anna, seated again beside him, was grateful for his silence, but did not allow it to last so long as to embarrass him.

'If we win, I'll soon forget all these doubts. When I'm busy and things are going well I never have them. It's only the waiting which . . . oh, I forgot, the news!'

Anna crossed quickly to the radio and switched it on. She was just sitting down again as the voice said, '. . . agreed late this afternoon to a programme which corresponds in all essentials to the ransom terms. Speaking to the press at NATO Headquarters . . .'

'Oh, oh, oh . . .' Anna had landed closer to the Chairman than she meant, and her thigh pressed against his as she turned to look with shining eyes at the green velvet mask. His arms encircled her, and the rest of the news bulletin was lost as she returned his breathless, ambiguous hug. She pushed gently away for a second, then went limp as she succumbed completely to the unfamiliar sensations of a man's strong arms around her and a beard against her soft cheek.

The buzzer sounded several times before Anna answered it.

'Anna, have you heard? We've won. Come on down and celebrate.'

'Yes, yes, I'm so happy, I feel quite overcome . . . Listen, the Chairman is with me and you must have him taken down again. In a few minutes, you understand? I'll buzz when I'm, when he's ready.'

Before Anna buzzed she asked the Chairman something very solemnly. 'Suppose we meet again, some time, and you guess that it's me, what will you do?'

'What would you like me to do?'

Anna reflected. 'Well, you could ask me to lunch. But you would never never make any reference to all this. It would be starting again.'

'I think I could do it. I mean, of course I could ask you to lunch. I was just thinking about the rest. But . . . yes, you're right.'

Down in the Control Room Anna was greeted with cheers. Françoise poured a glass of champagne for her.

'Thank you, thank you, it is marvellous news – I didn't dare believe that they would just say yes.'

Alexander the Great laughed.'Well, it wasn't quite a pure yes, but I suppose it's near enough to count.'

Anna was obviously bewildered.

'Didn't you hear the full announcement?'

'I thought . . . but no, I must have missed something.'

'Ah. Well, they agree. But . . .'

'But, but, but,' interposed Franz. 'There are three buts.'

'Yes, the first is that there can be no question of overriding the laws in the NATO countries – that's what they say – so the bit about impunity is not accepted, although they add that in practice they don't expect any difficulty.'

'And the prizes are to be expressed in French francs, not in dollars. Can you guess who insisted on that?'

'Is that all? It does not seem very important.'

'No, there is the third but. The Belgians insisted that some other country should go through the Maison du Peuple penance with them, so in the end Britain offered to do it with the arch from Euston Station. Rather a strange combination, but that's how it worked out.'

Anna was pleased. 'Then there is something more to tell Mr Lute. I remember this arch. It will make a fine entrance to Nova Atlantis. This is really an improvement.'

Franz beamed. 'It certainly is. Now we must arrange a celebration for the Committee. Is it to be tomorrow night, when we drug them, or tonight?'

'Tonight, tonight,' cried Tertia, 'while they still have their beards. Can't we have a ball?'

'No, no, said Franz, 'not tonight, not if it's to be a ball. There's still business to be done. We'll have to brief them, and let it all sink in. If they're dancing they won't pay attention. Perhaps we could have a little dance tomorrow, if Tertia insists, and they can pass out one by one while they waltz – it will be unforgettable.'

'Franz is right,' said Anna, 'anyway about not having it tonight.' She hesitated. 'I could not attend a dance myself. And this Marie will have gone. So there would be six of you, hardly enough even if you dance with two men each. But we must plan that tomorrow. It's dinner-time, and I must finish preparing my broadcast. By the way, they know already – I told the Chairman to tell them.'

'I wonder whether he missed the same bits that you missed,' said Alexander the Great thoughtfully. 'I mean, we must see that Brasfort hears about the prizes being in francs, he will find that very amusing.'

'I'm sure he couldn't make that bit out if I couldn't,' said Anna calmly. 'Now, dinner. But first I must talk to Sister Agnes for a moment, upstairs.'

'Where have you been?'

'In the kitchen, of course; do you think I will leave you for two days without making sure that you are fed? It was also necessary for me to terrify the little girl who will bring your tray to you. After a night by yourself you could be stirred by a pretty face smiling over a bowl of Eshkeneh Shirazi, could you not?'

'Is tomorrow Middle Eastern day, then? I must say I could squeeze a dainty hand which offered me some Ful Medames. Have you ever eaten it for breakfast, in the desert, before a morning's dig? I . . .'

'Certainly not, and they are much more refined here. The main dish will be Tehran Zeresk.'

'What, with barberries?'

'I have seen the barberries with my own eyes, and the girl Ingrid seems to have some connection with the Shah's banquetmaster. She is highly competent. I am almost tempted to stay.'

'I wish you would. What does this girl look like, the one who's going to bring all these goodies?'

'You will never know, thanks to my precautions. She will be heavily masked and cloaked and trembling at the memory of what I said to her. But have you no messages for Mononk?'

Marie's departure was for the purpose of telling Mononk what had happened. They had realised that even his Ardennais aptitude for keeping silent might be strained if many more days elapsed without news of them.

Felix pondered. 'Well, tell him that I'll look forward to another drop of old Anderson's brew when I come back for the bicycle. I hope he doesn't mind keeping it for ten days – you'll have to explain that we couldn't leave it here. And tell him I think he was very clever to send us straight here.' Felix looked round the bridal suite. 'And that we've been very comfortable.'

'Right. Well behave yourself. I'll set off north early tomorrow, and I ought to be home by seven. I'll go straight to old Coppenfrons and make sure that the bicycles are really ready. I hope the plan works, I'll be watching on TV, if the boulanger has mended his set . . . See you Friday afternoon. Goodbye.'

The door closed on Marie. Felix switched off the light, crossed to the window and drew back the heavy brocaded curtain. One of the camionettes, with the two bicycles already stowed inside, was waiting by the kitchen door. Shafts of light waving up and down showed that a car was coming round the side of the hill. As it approached, the shafts swept briefly over the camionette; then the Volvo swung round into the visitors' car park. Two huntsmen got out and went into the chateau. All was silent again. Three of her long strides were enough to take Marie from the kitchen door to the camionette. The headlamps were switched on, and it was driven quietly away down the drive. Felix wondered what James Minor looked like, and what he would make of Marie. She was planning to spend the twenty minute drive questioning him about Sussex University, which she mistakenly supposed to be the principal centre for studies of Kipling.

Felix shrugged and put the lights on again. He started to revise the detailed plan for the return to Evère. The bridal room seemed very quiet.

'Who else knows about this?'

'No one,' said Sister Agnes. 'I don't want to tell anyone. I feel very sensitive. They're a good lot, but you know how it is. They'd make jokes, wouldn't they?'

Sister Agnes did not look sensitive, thought Anna. She looked sensuous, and dreamy; a kitten who had tasted cream and was looking forward to lots more. The thought both displeased and pleased Anna.

'But they will know, later. If one has broken rules, others will be tempted.'

Sister Agnes shook her head, so that the auburn curls jiggled on the white collar of her uniform. 'Oh, no, what makes you think that? I keep myself to myself, but I know the others well enough. They haven't any interest in the Committee, really, they won't give them another thought once they've gone. Why should they? It's not as though they're madly attractive, except for Piet, and perhaps one or two others like the Chairman . . . but then you're the authority on him, aren't you?'

A man would have seen no change in the expression on Anna's face, but Sister Agnes saw it. That was a shrewd one, she thought, really unkind, stop it Agnes.

'Besides, it'll all be very quiet, no publicity or anything, we're quite firm about that. And hardly anyone here knows who I am or remembers what I really look like. Don't forget, Sister Agnes says goodbye to the world tomorrow, there'll be no trace of her, will there?'

Except for private performances, she thought. If Ingrid thinks she's going to get the wig and clothes back she's got another think coming. But you *have* upset her, do something.

On her knees, she spoke imploringly to Anna. 'Oh, do let us have your blessing. I'd be so sad if you were cross, I'd cry. But this is our chance to be happy, we must take it. If only you knew how I long for your happiness too, for you to have what you want . . . Oh, Anna, *please*.'

Anna was easily moved. 'All right,' she said at length. 'I hope you will be very happy. Of course I wish this, it is just that I was worried . . . Really, I worry too much, and you mustn't mind me.'

She kissed Agnes on the forehead.

'That's all settled, then. Now I must talk to Franz and Alex. Of course I won't say anything to them.'

'. . . I hope that that is clear, about your beards. You are quite at liberty to keep them, but those who wish will be shaved before lunch tomorrow.

'Your valuables and the clothes which you were wearing when you arrived are being placed in lockers at one of the stations in Brussels. The keys will be delivered to the Chairman as soon as he is back at NATO, and there will be time for you to collect the things without incurring fines.

'I will speak to you again tomorrow, and thank you for your cooperation. Meanwhile you can think about all the arrangements which I have explained, and if you have any questions you can put them at clinic tomorrow morning. Goodnight.'

Franz pressed a button, and they listened for reactions. They could hear murmurs of comment, and a little laughter. It sounded as thought the Committee were quite ready to be drugged once more, and to be set on racing bicycles.

'It is fascinating,' said Alexander the Great, 'to see how they have changed. Even I am surprised. The abnormal has become the normal for them. I fear that they will have difficulty in adjusting to the routine in Brussels again.'

Anna listened to him with her usual kindly attention, but disagreed. 'I think that they want to go home. They will do what they are told, but only in order to be free again, to return to their old lives. I am sure that they do not really wish to ride on bicycles.' She laughed.

'Oh, I wouldn't be so sure. They've had some practice already. We thought that we'd better try the older ones out, especially the German, and they certainly seemed to enjoy riding up and down the hall. No, I think Alex is right, they've changed a lot in one week.'

'Perhaps.' Anna poured three cups of tea. 'And what of you, have you changed?'

Franz and Alexander the Great looked at each other in surprise.

'No, why?' Franz seemed almost upset by the suggestion.

'I am not aware of a change in myself, although others may perceive some. But I look at you, Anna, and ask myself whether you have not changed.' Alexander the Great directed his most Socratic gaze at her.

Anna sipped her tea. 'Yes, I hav[illegible] am astonished now by what I planned. I could never [illegible] such a thing again. It is not a question of courage, I still have that, but . . . this sounds strange, when you have helped me so much . . . I came to feel lonely and uncertain once it was all happening. Anyway, now I am pleased.' She added more briskly, 'I am very pleased. Let me give you some more tea.'

Chapter 18

The Camion Vert chugged round the bend in the tunnel and up into the open air again by the Cinquantenaire.

'It's lucky you're not going towards NATO,' said the driver.

Tim, sitting beside him, started nervously, and fingered his false goatee beard. 'Yes, yes, I heard something on the radio. But we'll be clear of that on the Liège road.'

The Head of Administration had decided that he should personally welcome the Foreign Ministers as they arrived at the front entrance. It was the Deputy Head who looked after the other arrangements. He wished that he had more moveable barriers; it was hard enough at ordinary Ministerial meetings to keep the press out of the confidential areas, but on this occasion there were ten times as many pressmen, and they were not all the quiet foreign affairs specialists who usually came. On the contrary, there was a team from *Paris Match* who looked like a commando group. The Deputy Head sighed and consulted his memorandum again. 'Traffic on the boulevard to be permitted, with the police enforcing a no-stopping rule.' Well, the police were no doubt doing that. 'Main gates to be open.' Yes, no problem, the difficulty would have been to close them with the police buzzing in and out like hornets from their nest. 'Wooden ramps to be in place on the steps at each flank door.' Yes they were there all right, the same ones which were used when supplies were wheeled in and out of the building. 'All doors in the corridor connecting the flank entrances to be pulled back, all obstructions removed, ditto for the doors to the Council lobby and Chamber, all human traffic in the corridors and lobbies to cease at 1105.' That was going to be the problem, stopping the human traffic. Still, the press didn't know about these instructions, they all seemed to expect the Committee to return through the front door, so perhaps the corridor could be kept clear after all. 1045. Twenty minutes to go.

'You're sure it's here you want to unload?'

'Yes, right here, into that space between the trees.'

The driver manoeuvred his vehicle in the lay-by until its rear projected over the grass verge into a small clearing. He opened the corrugated steel doors and began to lift the machines out.

'Publicity, is it?' he asked, eyeing his customer's large Michelin lapel badge.

'Yes, sort of. You'll read about it tomorrow.'

The driver hefted one of the bicycles in his left hand. 'Lovely, lovely machines, they are, aren't they? It was only last night we saw Eddy Merckx on television. D'you know him?'

'No, no. I mean, yes, a little. Come on, down with the last pair – good, here's your money and a bit extra. Now please remember what I said, keep your engine running but wait right here for a few minutes until I say "go", then go. OK?'

The driver laughed, pretending not to count his lavish tip. 'OK.'

1050. Five minutes to spare. Tim stepped back into the clearing, checked that the bicycles were all disentangled from each other, laid out six thermos flasks of coffee, a bottle of brandy, sixteen paper cups and sixteen croissants, then took station beside a tree-trunk, peering intently down the road. At 1055 the first of the two Peugeot camionettes came into sight, on the near side, heading for Brussels. Tim called 'go'. The Camion Vert pulled out and was several hundred metres down the road into Brussels when the first camionette nosed into the place which it had just left, closely followed by the other.

'Come along, Beta,' said Sir Ambrose, 'you shall walk down with the Secretary of State and me, but I think they're going to put you wives in an enclosure in the lobby. Ah, there's the Private Secretary . . . is the Secretary of State ready? We ought to go down. It's two minutes past eleven.'

'You're sure you can manage?' called James Minor from the driver's seat. Tim was busy taking off his beard.

'Yes, yes,' said the Chairman, 'the coffee was all we needed.' He had already bicycled round the clearing once. The German, about whom they had all been worrying, had taken to the saddle like a veteran. Only the Luxemburger had trouble, but the Belgian had lowered his saddle for him and he now seemed confident. 'Leave us to it. Thank you for all your kindness, you and the others, but hurry off now, you should be well down the road when we come out.'

The camionettes departed. In the back of the second one James Major put his beard in his pocket and opened the box of alternative number plates.

The Chairman wheeled his machine out into the lay-by, waited until the committee members had formed up behind him and then wobbled out on to the road. 1104, and only half a kilometre to the turning which connected with the airport road. There were three small boys at the turning, and they cheered as the cyclists straggled past, giving the older committee members strength to tackle the slight upward slope.

Felix showed his pass, slipped into the Council Chamber, and took his seat in the back row. 'Just got back from leave in time,' he whispered to the Defence Counsellor, who was looking at him and at his sports clothes with surprise.

The Secretary-General tapped his gavel on a block of wood and called the Council to order. 'Gentlemen, we have only one item on our agenda, or should I say two? Do I understand that you all approve C(M) 129 (FINAL), the paper which defines certain decisive steps which the allied governments have agreed to take in their battle to improve the environment? I may remind you that, as the paper makes clear, these steps are being taken of our own free will and not under duress.' The Secretary-General smiled. 'However the opportunity has been taken to clear up an incident which has distressed us all, and, as you know, the implementation of these measures is linked with the return of the members of the Senior Political Committee, which we are assured is imminent . . . Thank you. I propose to give a press conference shortly after our colleagues return, and I suggest for your consideration that they should be spared any contact with the press until they have been reunited with their families, who have places of honour outside in the lobby;

and until they have received instructions from you. Now, gentlemen, we must wait . . .'

'This is Henry Adams reporting from the roof of the NATO Headquarters. We have a fine view of the main gates, directly in front of us, and the question which everyone is asking, at nine minutes past eleven, is whether the mysterious kidnapper will keep her word and return the Committee members. As you can see the gates are clear, and traffic is moving normally along the highway to the airport, but the Belgian police are lining the route thickly, almost touching each other as far as the eye can see. We're just coming up to ten past and except for the police there's no sign of anything unusual. What? Oh, yes, George, you're right, there comes a team of racing cyclists – cycling is the national sport in Belgium and there's no more common sight than this, they get up a great speed do these cyclists . . . well they certainly can go fast, but this team seems to be taking it easy, perhaps they want to get a view as they go past, I can see the police waving them on, let's see, how many of them are there, eight nine ten . . . about sixteen I would say wouldn't you, George? *Sixteen* . . . and look at them, they're sweeping in through the gates, it must be, it's the Committee, why in heaven's name have they come back like this? . . . There they go, they've pedalled round to the side through the car park, we can't see them any more. Listen, listen to that cheering, they must be in the building, they're *underneath* us, great Scott, George, they must be riding right into the Council Chamber.'

The Chairman had slowed down as they approached the gates, so that the others could bunch behind him, and they had kept close together as they swept through the car parks and up to the side entrance; but from there on it had to be single file, up the ramp and along the grey linoleum of the corridor. By the time the Chairman wheeled left on to the gold carpet of the lobby they were strung out in a long ragged line.

Pedalling hard, the Chairman burst into the Council Chamber, round behind the back row of chairs, scraping the wall once, and came to a halt behind the Secretary-General. Brasfort penetrated into the Chamber too, and so did the Turk and the Icelander; but Portentoso stopped in the doorway, arrested by the shrill cry of his wife, and dismounted to pound across the lobby and embrace her. Lute braked hard behind him and fell off his machine sideways, almost at the feet of Beta, who cried wildly, 'I didn't know you could cycle, I never knew.' Within and without the Chamber chaos spread. Felix gazed round with an expression of astonishment as keen as those all round him; but inwardly he was calm and satisfied. This was how it was supposed to be, and this was how it was. He plucked at Sir Ambrose's sleeve. 'David must be out in the lobby. Shall I fetch him in to the Secretary of State or shall we go out and look for him?'

Sir Ambrose eyed the discarded bicycles and embracing figures which blocked the path to the door. 'I think we'd better sit tight for a moment, don't you agree, Secretary of State?'

The Secretary of State tapped his forefinger on the green leather in front of him and watched impassively as the Icelander mounted the Council table, towering above his Foreign Minister, and clasped his hands above his head in sign of triumph, wildly chanting something in Icelandic which at once set all three members of the Icelandic Delegation singing. Lute and Grannery came battling though the door, with other black and gold-jerseyed figures behind them, like a football team, waving and cheering. A slow smile appeared on the Secretary of State's face.

'Is that our man?' he asked.

'Yes, the little one coming this way.'

The Secretary of State stood up and raised his arm. 'For he's a jolly good fellow . . .' he began, and the UK Delegation sang lustily with him.

The *Paris Match* team, up on the flat roof, were uneasily aware that they were missing the action. They shambled rapidly to and fro, like disturbed simians, between the plastic ventilation domes, ears cocked to find the loudest source of noise below.

The loudest noise seemed to be coming from below the biggest dome, which was right in the centre of the building. The three biggest *Paris Match* men looked at each other, nodded, and took it by the lip with their long thick arms. Grunting, they heaved it off its base and uncovered the Council Chamber to the sky. Like paratroopers they dropped one by one through the aperture, landing in the circular space enclosed by the Council table twenty feet below, and at once started photographing the scene all round them.

The other roof-top press feared to make the jump, but clustered round the edge of the hole. One of them lowered a microphone down into the Chamber, where it hung bobbing over the UK Delegation and permitted listeners to the Dutch Radio to hear the Secretary of State inviting Lute to Downing Street for dinner.

'With Mrs Lute – the PM was very firm about that. We'll take off after tea, when things have been sorted out here. Do you feel up to it? We'll put you up of course . . .'

Beta had wriggled through the crowd and was standing behind David, holding his hand, an expression of affection which he normally discouraged. 'Oh yes,' she said, 'that would be lovely. But I'll have to change, and what about Millicent, she gets back from school at half past four. I thought she'd better go today – I didn't want to bring her here – but she's dying to see her father again. Anyway darling you'll want to see her before you go rushing off to Downing Street, won't you?'

The Secretary of State hesitated, but remembered the PM's parting words. He wanted the Lutes for dinner. Specifically he wanted to be seen welcoming the Lutes in the doorway of No. 10. Tonight was the only night which would do. 'No problem,' he said, 'she must come too, if she can miss school tomorrow morning. Ambrose, can you lay all this on? I'd better ring Downing Street before lunch, and I'd like to say it's all fixed.'

Above the hubbub the Secretary-General's voice could just be heard adjourning the meeting.

Epilogue

'It makes a change,' said the Secretary-General, 'and I've been enjoying it. Anyway it gave me an excuse to have all those models of missiles and things moved out of the lobby. Did you notice?'

The Chairman had indeed noticed. Back from two weeks' holiday, which the Council, mindful of their own desire to be away at Christmas-time, had decreed for him and the whole Committee, he had threaded his way to the Secretary-General's door through a sort of mini-exhibition of environmental projects, dominated by a large maquette of the reconstructed Maison du Peuple, wryly presented by the Belgian Government.

'Yes, I did. But tell me, how real is the change? I haven't had time to look at the Council records yet, but what the Spanish papers said about the debate last week made me wonder. To agree in just one day on the lottery! I was expecting to find that the argument had hardly begun . . .'

'It was a remarkable phenomenon,' said the Secretary-General. 'But the fact is that everything has speeded up. It has to, really. There's so much new work, and all the old things still to be done. But I suppose we only had to read our Parkinson to see what would happen. Work expands to fill the time available. Therefore NATO, or any other organisation for that matter, will always go on discussing something until there has to be a decision. But the time available is a fixed quantity. So if you expand the work you have a quicker tempo, and it spreads right through the building. I hear that even the Budget Committees have speeded up.'

'Fantastic. If the tortoises are running the hares too will be affected. I must see how the SPC take it. But I haven't discovered yet whether they're all back.'

The Secretary-General's personal secretary brought in a tray of coffee.

'Thank you.' Both men returned her smile. 'Or would you rather have slivovic? This Romanian observer – a very odd business, but they seem quite genuine about it, he's a town planning expert – has given me a case . . . No? Well, I can use it up at the Christmas party, but I have a feeling that he's going to give me another case for Christmas, and if the Russians really do send someone there'll be vodka to dispose of as well . . . My dear, you are hovering as though it is necessary to interrupt us.'

'I was wondering whether you'd like to have the note about the SPC.' The secretary glanced at the Chairman for a moment. 'There are so many changes.'

'I was just going to tell the Chairman. He can pick up a copy when we've finished . . . Yes, you will find that your flock looks rather different now. Let me see, first of all you must be ready to congratulate Sir David Lute, KCMG, and you must conceal the secret which I will tell you, that the honour was really intended for Lady Lute – oh, yes, there can be no doubt of that, it was she who . . . what shall I say? . . . who influenced some of the principal actors in our melodrama.' The Secretary-General paused, and added, 'Such as the British Prime Minister.'

'But David is back?'

'Indeed yes, I understand that Lady Lute insisted on staying until the end of the school year. But then I suppose he will have one of the big Embassies. Like Brasfort, now on his way to Rome, where he will find Portentoso already promoted to a high position in the Ministry. Grannery, of course, goes to the White House; no successor chosen yet. The Belgian has been put in charge of the Maison du Peuple operation, a rather spiteful appointment I think, as so many pieces are still missing. Incidentally, you must tell me some time how that item was put in, it seems so strange, like something imposed from outside on a pattern which is otherwise consistent . . .'

The Chairman watched the yellow curtains stir in the light winter breeze. The noise of a jumbo sinking downwards towards Zaventem delayed his reply.

'I agree, it was strange. But tell me, what about the Dutchman? Is he still going to Tunis?'

'He is, but not alone. Captivity must have done something to him. He is engaged to be married. Imagine, it will be in the presence of the Queen, she commanded it, and at the Nieuwekerk in Haarlem. There must be an invitation waiting for you.'

The Chairman recalled the two paintings by Saenredam, of which he very slightly preferred the one in Budapest, of the interior of the Nieuwekerk. Now he would have to break his rule, perhaps rather a silly one after all, against visiting any of the churches which Saenredam had painted.

He said no more to the Secretary-General about Piet. But it was Piet of whom he was thinking when he took his leave.

'Don't forget to pick up the note from Mademoiselle Clairvault. It will be impeccable. You know, my worst problem during the kidnapping was that she had gone for her leave; and knowing, as I and a few others do, her true and highly aristocratic identity, I did not dare recall her.'

'Someone told me that you had a Countess in your office, incognito, but I never realised it was Mademoiselle Clairvault. I have heard that she is most efficient.'

The Secretary-General laughed lightly. 'I sometimes think,' he said, 'that she accomplishes more than all the rest of us together.' He spoke with fractionally more emphasis than the Chairman would have expected. 'Be sure, now, to visit her as you leave.' He had repeated himself, which he did not often do.

The note which Mademoiselle Clairvault had ready was concise and informative. It contained details which the Secretary-General had not mentioned. But the entry for Piet was a brief one.

'I'm so surprised to hear about the Dutchman marrying. Is this all we know? Perhaps the press cuttings people have something more – I must ask.'

'Oh, they have sent us everything already. I have a little dossier. There is a lot more information, especially about how they met. You know, he went on this package tour to Finland, and she had chosen it too, and they sat next to each other in the aeroplane, and – well, it seems to have been a case of love at first sight.'

She sat down at her desk and reached for a folder of press clippings. 'Elsevier even has a photograph of the University Library in Helsinki, where he proposed to her – such a strange place to choose, don't you think?'

The Chairman was suddenly alert. 'It is one of Engel's most attractive buildings.'

'I agree. It is. But there are others nearby, equally beautiful, in which speech is permitted.'

'Perhaps his fiancée is a librarian? There must be some explanation.'

'The newspaper reports say nothing to suggest that either of them has worked in a library.'

The Chairman considered the precise formulation of this statement, while Mademoiselle Clairvault looked back at the clippings.

'We have one item in English, from Newcastle, but everything else is from the Dutch press. Do you read Dutch?'

She turned her head as she spoke, and then he knew. He had seen that head turn thus once before.

After a hesitation which was barely perceptible, he replied, 'No, only a little.' He made a small gesture with his right hand. 'But if you have studied the material I could perhaps ask you to tell me all about it. I wonder . . . would you be free to lunch with me one day?'

'Thank you,' she said. Her voice was cool, but she had lowered her eyes, and made an unnecessary affair of closing the dossier. 'I happen to be free today.'